KING OF
SHADOWS

BOOKS BY KATHRYN ANN KINGSLEY

For a full list, visit www.kathrynkingsley.com

KATHRYN ANN
KINGSLEY

KING OF
SHADOWS

SECOND SKY

Published by Second Sky in 2024

An imprint of Storyfire Ltd.
Carmelite House
50 Victoria Embankment
London EC4Y 0DZ
United Kingdom

www.secondskybooks.com

ISBN: 978-1-83618-289-4
eBook ISBN: 978-1-83618-288-7

ONE

"Hello, my dear."

Aon.

"How wonderful to finally meet you, Lydia."

There was no way around it—he looked like a nightmare come to life. His expensive, eccentric suit made him look all at once as though he didn't belong against the twisted and warped woods, and yet like there was nowhere else he should be.

Lydia tried her best not to cry. Tried not to scream or turn and run the other direction. Her bleeding knee felt like it was on fire, and the rest of her wasn't in much better condition. Aon stood before her, twenty feet away, the moonlight reflecting off his featureless black metal mask. He had not moved and seemed content to let her decide what she wanted to do.

She ran through her options in her head. She could try to turn and run. She could cry or scream. She could fall to her knees and beg. None of them felt right, so everything locked up. There was nothing she could do to stop whatever Aon wanted to do to her. She had nothing. No hope, no power, no knowledge she could bargain with. She'd done her level best trying to escape, and this is what happened. This was the end of the proverbial, and literal, road for her.

But there was one thing she could cling to in desperation.

One thing that she had left.

Defiance.

Lydia raised her head, straightened her shoulders, and did her best to look brave. Not because she felt brave, but because there wasn't anything else left to do except stare down her inevitable—and outlandish—death.

Aon chuckled and began to walk toward her. He closed the distance in slow, long, easy strides, seemingly in no hurry. Each step was a dare. Each step was meant to test her nerves.

She wavered. But she kept her ground.

One of his hands moved to tuck across his lower back as he approached. He was giving her the chance to balk and run from him. He was seeing her bet and raising it, pointedly challenging her.

Good God, he was terrifying. Far more so now that he was real and not a ghost in Lydia's dreams. Lydia knew her imagination was probably falling short of what that man was likely about to do to her. But man, it was *trying.*

When Aon finally got within arm's reach, he extended his gauntleted hand to touch her face, the sharp claws glinting in the moonlight.

Lydia flinched away from his touch, but by some miracle, she managed to stand her ground.

Letting out a quiet *hmm,* he curled his fingers in toward his palm and brushed the backs of the metal fingers down her cheek.

In the absence of adrenaline, she was shaking in the cold truth of her failure and the chill night air. The touch of metal on her cheek didn't help matters.

She ran through her options again. Sink to her knees and cry. Turn and run. Plead for mercy. Bargain with him for her freedom. Try to fight him. Faint was now solidly high up on that list.

Each one, she scratched off in order again. Not her style, wouldn't make it ten feet, pointless, pointless, hilariously pointless, and maybe, in that order. With no other option but accepting her fate, she resigned herself to whatever he was going to do.

"Tell me, what was it I have just witnessed play out upon these lovely features of yours?" His voice was low and soft but no less dangerous than before. When she shot him a confused look, he tilted his head back. He spoke again, and this time his voice was a rumble that made her stomach twist. "Indulge me..."

Great. He wanted to play with his food. Why was she not surprised? She stammered twice before getting a word out edgewise, but the monster in front of her seemed content to wait. She stopped, took a breath, and tried again. "Crying won't help. Begging won't work. I can't run, and struggling will do more harm than good. I... I've lost. The only thing left to do is die with pride. I guess."

"Mmh, beautiful." Aon stepped in closer. The talons of his gauntleted hand stroked through her hair slowly, brushing her blonde waves away from her face and tucking the strands behind her ear. She pulled in a breath and held it. Even if he wasn't hurting her *yet*, she had already seen firsthand how abrupt his moods could be. "Then you are no fool, my clever child, to see the truth so easily. Good. That will make this far more interesting."

"If you're going to kill me, please do it already." That was all she could ask of him. *Just please, don't let it linger.*

Metal fingers curled under her chin and broke her gaze from where she had fixated on his black-on-black striped tie. "Oh, my dear. Kill you? Why ever would I do that?" He sounded legitimately surprised.

Was he kidding? "I mean, last time... you..."

"Ah. Yes." He shifted his weight from one foot to the other, his masked face turning away for a moment as if in thought. "I think perhaps I have given you the wrong impression. What I did was merely to teach you a lesson. Hopefully, I will not have cause to demonstrate another."

He turned his face back toward her as he pressed the point of the thumb of his clawed hand against the line of her lower lip. He stepped in closer, just a few inches away. "No, beautiful darling, you are the first unusual thing to happen in this forsaken world in a long, long time. I have no desire to kill you. Far from it."

Before she could really spend any time thinking about that, her world suddenly felt unsteady. The ground tipped and swerved. She grasped Aon's arms in a desperate attempt to hold herself upright. "I don't—"

He let out a curious sound at her movement, and then realizing she was about to fall, wrapped his arm around her waist, pressing her to him. "Well, now, all you had to do was ask," he teased.

"I... uh. I don't feel so good." The world was spinning. She must have hit her head when she fell from the horse, and her fear and adrenaline had only lasted so long. Fainting was now solidly at the top of her options.

"My poor little thing," he murmured. "It is quite all right. You are injured. Do not fight it. I will take care of you."

"Edu's going to kill me." She was barely able to get the words out. Her head was reeling. Shutting her eyes, she felt the soft fabric of his suit against her as he pulled her closer to him.

"Oh?" The smell of books was there again, like an old library.

"To keep me away," the world spun dangerously, "from you, Edu..." Lydia couldn't hold on to consciousness anymore.

Her grasp on it was slipping, just as her hands were falling from clinging onto his coat.

His metal-clad face was close to her ear, and she heard his words—quiet, dangerous, and a threat even as it was meant to be comforting. "He will not harm you. With me, you will be safe. I promise."

* * *

Edu's drake landed with a hard thud on the dirt road. The bolt of lightning had not been a terribly subtle way to announce where he might find the girl. Or the foe he had suspected had arrived. He landed in time to watch her head roll to the side as she collapsed against a figure in black that he unfortunately knew quite well.

Aon leaned down and scooped up her legs with one arm and held her behind the shoulders in the other, carrying her like he might a bride.

Instantly, Edu wished nothing more than to pound Aon's face into the packed ground. The thought that the other man would seek to instantly claim such possession of *his* prisoner was beyond infuriating.

"Ah. Hello, Edu. I was wondering when you might arrive." Aon's tone was idle and dismissive as if what had transpired was no matter at all. "Wonderful evening, don't you think?"

Edu dismounted his drake and stormed toward the other man, his fists clenched.

"Oh, pull the reins, you great buffoon. You are king no longer. I see you have forgotten!" Aon's voice raised from casual and idle annoyance to sharp snarl of anger with no warning.

Edu shook his head, pointed at the girl, then crooked his finger back at himself. He did not have his empath Ylena there to help him. But he had enough history with the bastard in front of him—he knew Aon would follow his meaning without trouble.

He was not disappointed.

The King of Shadows barked a laugh. "Give her to *you?* Are you mad? You would murder this poor thing to spite me, no less. When have you become so callous? The years have been cold to you. Weren't you always the sympathetic, forgiving one? To cradle a butterfly in your hands, for fear it might die without your care? She must terrify you greatly to end her life without due cause." He tsked. "For shame, old *friend.* For shame."

Edu growled angrily, but the warlock paid him no heed.

Aon cast a glance down at the girl whose head was tucked into his chest, resting against the black fabric of his suit. Blonde hair trailed around her face in stark contrast to the tones of the man's clothing. "I must see to it that Lydia is attended. She is injured, and as she has been cast away from the Ancients..." Aon obviously enjoyed digging the seriousness of her rejection from the pool into Edu like a knife to the ribs, "she is fragile."

With that, the warlock disappeared. Merely blinked out of existence as if he had never been there at all. He took Lydia with him without even a swirl of power or a crack of thunder left in his wake.

Edu let out a wordless howl of anger and slammed his fist deep into a tree next to him in his impotent rage, splintering the bark. In the hollow emptiness left behind by his temper, he lowered his head and admitted his folly to himself in the silence of the woods.

He should have killed the girl when he had the chance.

He was too late.

Now, it may be too late for them all.

TWO

Someone's hand pressed a cold cloth against Lydia's forehead. It felt *fantastic*. It was the only thing about her that felt good at all. Every other part of her was aching. Not enough to call it pain, but enough to be incredibly uncomfortable.

When she managed to open her eyes, she looked up into a begrudgingly familiar face. Maverick, with his purple mask and flat expression that was both unimpressed and deeply annoyed.

"We have to stop meeting like this," she muttered at him.

Maverick merely smirked faintly in response and shook his head, removing the cloth from her forehead. "I fear if you attempt more flights of fancy like you did last night, we will meet like this quite frequently."

His tone of voice was a scolding parent telling her she really shouldn't have climbed that tree, and it was her own damn fault for falling out. Falling out of a tree would have felt better than what had happened to her—crashing off a rearing horse and all. It seemed Maverick would never miss a chance to lecture her.

"I don't think I'm trying that one again." She grunted in soreness as she shifted to sit up. "Can't promise I won't try something equally stupid, though."

Maverick chuckled. "I admit, I am disappointed you did not Fall into my own House," he said as he worked at cleaning a scratch on her upper arm. "I think we would 'get along,' as you more modern children like to say."

Everything ached yet was suspiciously dull and kind of numb. Drugs, she figured. She was grateful. "I think I owe you a big thank you. Both for this time and last time. Sorry I was freaking out too much to really express it the last time."

"Send me a card."

She laughed, even though it hurt. His deadpan delivery made it even better. In the world of what she had suffered recently, she honestly would still pick being thrown from the horse if she had to do one over again. She felt funny, with the painkillers running through her, but at least she didn't feel like she had been through a literal wringer like she had after the incident at the Ceremony of the Fall. "Am I gonna live, doc?"

"You have some scrapes and bruises. You fainted due to exertion and stress, I believe. Otherwise, yes, clearly your prognosis is optimistic."

Lydia snickered again.

He shot her a look. "I was not joking this time."

"I know, but you're still funny."

"You must inform my wife of such news. She will be ecstatic."

That time, she settled for a smile. Maverick was "good people," she decided. Finally feeling aware enough of what was going on, she took stock of where she was. It wasn't a cot or a jail cell. This was comfortable and... cushy. Extremely cushy.

She was lying in a large, expensive-looking bed. Black fabric was draped up over the posts at all four ends. The wood was carved to look like twisting vines that wound around each other with no pattern or reason. Whatever kind of wood they were made from seemed pure white in contrast with the deep black patterned arcs of fabric. It was the kind of stuff she'd see in expensive magazines showcasing European villas owned by the super-rich and eccentric. Nothing she ever expected to see in person. "Where are we?"

Maverick paused before answering. "Aon's estate. You are in his care now." His expression went quickly from flatly unimpressed to... dark. His visible yellow eye narrowed. "I counsel you to be careful."

She suspected she knew. But she had to ask. "Why?"

"You believe the Priest is ancient in his nigh two thousand years? He is nothing in comparison to Edu and Aon. Those creatures cannot even recall how old they are. Consider what that duration of life does to the psyche. One man survives his age with indulgence, the other with madness." He grimaced. "I needn't tell you which is worse."

Maverick stood slowly from her bedside and moved to walk out of the room. His hand settled on the doorknob. "Mind your words around Aon, I beg you." He opened the door and left her with his parting words. "Or the next time, I may not be able to find the means to heal you."

The door clicked behind him.

Letting out a long sigh, she decided to get up since lying there wasn't going to do her any good. Even if it was extremely luxurious. The comforter was a stark black with gold damask patterns, and the sheets underneath were, predictably, black.

Aon could stick with a motif, she'd give him that.

Bracing herself, she got out of bed. Instantly, she tilted and caught her balance on the nightstand. Her second attempt was more successful. "Damn, Maverick, that's some good shit." She chuckled under her breath.

The room was pointlessly large for a bedroom—*he's fancy, so is his house*—and there was another door out into what looked like a bathroom from her quick glance. A large mirror sat in a strange and ornate frame up against one wall. It was like Art Nouveau had done some acid and hung out with H.R.

Giger. It was twisted and warped, asymmetrical, morbid and strange. On one side of the mirror was the image of a face, caught in a silent scream and overgrown in the vines as if it had been overtaken by the roots of a tree.

The vines punctured through the face's eyes, forever depicting its moment of death and torture.

"I am *so* fucked."

Putting her imminent demise at the hands of a madman aside, she approached the mirror to take stock of herself. Bruises, scrapes, a bandage on her knee. But shockingly, nothing terrible.

The more she looked around, the more figures and strange displays of death and violence she found hidden in the art or the wallpaper. Nothing she could do about his taste. Focus. One thing at a time. Maybe the bathroom had a shower.

God, a shower sounded amazing.

She went to investigate. There was a large copper bathtub, looking like something from the days when servants were forced to carry water up by hand. Judging by the pipes and knobs, this one had been updated for modern use. It would do.

She sat on the edge of the tub and twisted the knobs. Water poured out, and she smiled, honestly loving the idea of soaking in some hot water and cleaning herself off. Carefully, she went about stripping off the torn and tattered gray dress. She undid the bandage on her knee and set it aside to reuse after she was done. Turning off the water, she climbed in.

Oh, it felt like heaven.

She went about cleaning herself, finding soap and a cloth, and even something she could hope acted as shampoo. The simple, familiar action was more comforting to her than anything else had managed to be so far.

She was worried about Nick. She even worried about Kaori and Gary, even if she had only briefly met them. Most of all, she found herself fretting about Evie. The first three were alive at least. The last one... who knew. Edu might have killed her the moment he had found her, by cutting her soulmark from her face and murdering her for keeps.

Nothing she could do about that right now. She'd ask Aon later. Maybe he wasn't so bad. Maybe everybody's warnings were just because they were jealous.

But she clung to the hope that she *hadn't* just fallen from the grasp of one tyrant into another in a weird, parallel world filled with monsters and creatures who seemed hell-bent on killing her.

The ridiculousness of the situation made her laugh. Her laughing made her cry, and she let herself sob it out for a moment, as the steam from the water poured up over her face. Lydia just let it all go. Let everything she had been holding in, rush out. When she was done, she honestly felt better. It was amazing how cathartic that could be when all was said and done.

Ducking her head under the water, she rinsed off her hair.

When she came up, she felt a presence at her side. Through her closed eyes, she could tell something was blotting out the light next to her, looming inches away from her.

"Making ourselves at home?"

"Fuck!" Her eyes flew open, and she thrashed, swinging at the shadow next to her and scrambling away from it all at once. But no one was there. She had merely managed to splash water all over the wall and the floor.

Frozen solid, she felt her heart pounding in her ears. There was nobody in the room. But she had felt someone and had heard Aon's voice in her ear. She knew it. There was no making that up.

Maybe she was just loopy from the drugs.

No. She knew better.

Narrowing her eyes, she gritted her teeth. *"Pervert!"* She wasn't even sure if he could hear her. She wasn't even sure if she cared. But there was a shelter in her anger, and she took it.

Remember, they think about things differently here.

Either way, the comfort of the hot water was gone. She stood and wrapped a towel around herself and dropped another one on the floor to mop up what she had spilled, more out of the desire not to step in the puddle than really giving a crap what happened to the man's home.

Exiting the bathroom, she pulled up short a few steps into the bedroom. Clothing had been arranged carefully on the black comforter. So someone *had* snuck in. Growling, she bit back her frustration.

So far, Aon was scary and creepy. But he hadn't done anything actually wrong yet.

He hadn't touched her or hurt her except in her dreams. He hadn't threatened her life like Edu.

She tried to take that for what it was worth.

Given everything that had happened so far, creeping on her and scaring her wasn't the worst thing he could be doing by far. Stepping up to the bed, she looked down at his clothing selection for her.

Part of her expected leather straps and a collar and little else. Honestly, she really wouldn't have been surprised. Instead, she found a long black skirt, underwear, a corset, and a dark gray and black striped blouse with short sleeves and a simple set of buttons down the front. Socks and a pair of boots sat on the floor next to the bed.

Repeating her mantra of the moment, she reminded herself again it *really* could be worse. Besides, Aon might not have anything else to give her. A clean set of clothes was a favor.

With a wavering breath, she glanced nervously around the room for any sign of someone looming in the shadows. It appeared she was alone, although all bets were currently off on that being true. Dropping the towel onto the bed, she went about changing. Aon had seen fit to give her modern underwear and not some massive flouncy pair of underpants. For his benefit or hers, she'd rather not know.

It took her far longer than she'd care to admit to figure out how the hell to put on a corset. It had clasps on the front, laces on the back. Okay, great. Still easier said than done. She must have fiddled with it for fifteen minutes before she figured out how to hook her thumbs into the loops where the laces doubled back on themselves and tighten it row by row that way.

Somewhere, a dead Victorian woman was shaking her head in shame.

Tightening it up enough for it to stay on, but not so tight it was uncomfortable, she decided it was the best she was going to be able to do on her own. Pulling on her skirt, she bent over to get her socks and grunted as she did.

All right. Respect paid to those dead Victorians who had to wear this shit all the time.

Bending over in a corset *sucked*.

Finally, she managed to put on the socks and the boots and made a mental note to put the shoes on *first* next time.

Standing, she slung the blouse over the corset and buttoned it. She was sure she was still half-dressed by traditional standards.

When she was done, she went to stand in front of the mirror to give herself a once-over. It looked like she was going to go to a Tim Burton-themed costume ball, but it wasn't bad. The corset made her waist look small. Breathing wasn't an issue, as she hadn't cranked the corset tight like she was sure she was supposed to.

She ran her hands through her damp hair. Well... now what? She could either sit and wait or she could see if the door was locked. Running hadn't done her any good last time. To be truthful, she wasn't up to trying it again right now, being half-drugged and semi-concussed, after all. But nobody had expressly told her to stay put.

Curiosity got the better of her, and she figured if the order was to stay in this room, the door would be locked. She walked to the door and hovered her hand over the knob. Debated turning it. Debated stepping out into that world and into Aon's estate.

Lydia shrieked as the door opened.

THREE

Lydia shrieked as the door opened on its own.

The person on the other side seemed just as startled, let out a matching shriek, and jumped backward.

A man dressed in all black, with short hair and no mask, was looking at her wide-eyed with a hand pressed to his chest. Black writing was etched onto his chin underneath his lower lip, looking almost like a soul patch goatee. That was funny—a soulmark soul patch.

"Shit!" The man lowered his hand from his chest. "You scared me!"

"*I* scared *you*?" She narrowed an eye at him. "Buddy."

"I wasn't expecting you to be standing there." Clearly realizing how silly it was to be fighting with her, the trapped mortal, he tugged on his shirt to straighten it and tried to regain his dignity. "Master Aon requests your presence."

She sighed and rubbed a hand over her face. Where the hell else was she going to go? What was she going to do, sit in the room and pout? At least she had a clean pair of clothes and had a nice hot bath. She felt more like herself than she had in a long time.

Besides, avoiding this was pointless. Aon could come to her easily enough. This had to happen. Throwing her hands up, she gave in. "All right."

"Oh, thank the Ancients." The man let out a breath in relief. "This way." He began leading her down the hallway.

She followed him and tried not to gape at the building around her. Louis XIV would blush. The ceilings were enormously high, arching up into the darkness. Black and patterned wallpaper was heavily accentuated by silver, gold, and painted wood carvings.

Mirrors were placed opposite each other, so as she passed, she saw the illusion of herself reflected a hundred times, each smaller and farther away. It was eerie. It was spooky. It made her feel like she was in a dream or like reality was just slightly out of phase.

She suspected that was very much the point.

Seeing the look on her face, the man in front of her smiled. "You get used to it."

"Yeah, sure."

That made him chuckle, and he shrugged. "I've only been here twenty-two years. I came in the last alignment before this one. It's not so bad." He stuck his hand out to her. "Name's Fabian."

It was nice to meet someone who didn't seem entirely displaced from the modern world. Lydia put her hand in his and smiled back. "Lydia."

"I know." Fabian grinned. "I've heard all the whispering between the staff. Can't help myself."

Lydia sighed, not enjoying the idea of being the butt of gossip. But there wasn't anything she could do about it, and she honestly didn't really blame them. She was news. Big news, if all the fuss was anything to go by.

They hadn't gone far before they approached a large white

door with mirrored inlay. Fabian went for the handle, then froze. There was shouting from the other side. Someone was hollering at someone else, and that person sounded *hideously* angry.

A quieter female voice was trying to intercede, but it was pointless. There was the crash of shattering glass. Lydia and Fabian both jumped back at the sound.

There was a pause from the other side. "*And just bring Lydia in already, Fabian!*"

Fabian reached out to grab the knob, looked to her, muttered "I'm so sorry," and opened the door. He stood aside to let her pass and apparently had no intention of following her in. His job was over.

She didn't blame him.

Even if she felt like she was walking into her own execution.

She had no idea how right she was until she saw Edu standing in the center of the room. Her steps hitched, and she froze. Edu had turned to watch her as she entered, and whatever the hulking mass was thinking, she couldn't tell from his body language. Standing at his side was the woman in the red dress.

She snatched a candlestick from a nearby table and held it like a weapon in front of her. Like it'd do any good. But it was worth a shot.

"He will not hurt you. And you can put that down. He is in my home now, after all."

Finally breaking her wide-eyed look of horror from Edu, she traced the source of the voice. It was only then that she realized she was standing in a massive library. It was two stories tall, the upper mezzanine being a thin walkway whose only purpose was to access more of the bookshelves that covered all the walls, floor to ceiling. It even had rolling ladders to climb up to the higher, harder to reach sections. It looked like a Baroque painting if you had melted it a little at the edges.

Old Edison bulbs, with their large filaments, cast amber glows against the woodwork from twisted, vine-like sconces on the walls. The ceiling was muraled, but with what, she couldn't tell. Her focus was demanded elsewhere.

A massive fireplace took up the far wall. The fire was casting flickering shadows across the floor. The light glinted off a wood table that dominated the center of the room, easily twenty feet long and eight feet wide. It was covered in books and papers and collections of instruments she couldn't name.

Standing by the firelight was a silhouette, cut sharply against the fire at his back.

Aon.

He was unmistakable. He lifted his hand and beckoned her closer.

She stayed frozen to the spot. She didn't want to obey him, and she didn't want to make him angry. Angrier. Whatever.

At least he seemed more patient than Edu. He held his gloved hand out, palm up, fingers outstretched. "Come, my dear. Please." His tone was softer, gentler. He was clearly *trying* to be a little less terrifying.

She had to give credit where credit was due.

One foot in front of the other, she made her way around the table to stand ten feet away from Aon. Her free hand fidgeted in her dress, since she had no pockets to shove it into, which was her usual proxy for hiding.

"Did you enjoy your bath?" Aon asked, his voice both pleasant and mischievous.

Oh, you dick. Lydia narrowed her eyes at him. Aon had just admitted it was him in the bathroom with her. "I did." She refused to give him anything more than that.

"Good. I am glad. Thank you for attending me without complaint. It is impressive what a little simple hospitality can do. Isn't it, Edu?" Aon pointedly turned back toward the giant warrior.

Edu growled low in his throat, his hands tightening into fists.

Ignoring the King of Flames' obvious anger, Aon turned back to address her. "Our mutual friend has given me some disturbing news. Edu refuses to return to his century of slumber, as was the agreement to which we both swore an oath so long ago. What do you think of this?"

"You're asking me?" She laughed once, astonished and confused. "I don't even get what's happening here."

"Then allow me to explain." Aon seemed excited to have the chance to expound on a subject. "I will keep this brief, so excuse me for omitting details I will supply to you in short order when we are alone."

Lydia idly wondered if Aon could keep anything brief. He didn't seem the type.

The warlock began his explanation with a wide gesture of his clawed hand as he leisurely walked toward her. "Long ago, there was a great and bloody war. Edu and I destroyed much of this world in our bids for dominance. When all was said and done, we had all paid a terrible price. It was decided that neither of us could remain in this world at the same time as the other if we were not to risk falling into the turmoil once more. Therefore—"

He reached out and took the candlestick from her hand. She hadn't even realized she was still holding it like a sword in front of her until he took it away.

He placed it on the table with a quiet *thunk* before continuing. "We arranged that we would trade places. He would reign as King of Under, and then I, in exchange, for a century each."

Aon paused, watching her. Or she assumed he was. It was hard to tell with the mask he wore.

She nodded, signaling that she was following along. As he had said, she found herself wondering after the details. What had the war been over? What was the price they all had paid?

How badly did you have to hate a guy to not be able to live in the same world together without starting a war? But Aon said to skip those for now, so she stayed silent.

"Edu has now decided that he will break this treaty. He will not return to his crypt. He intends to stay awake, to challenge me!" Aon slammed his fist into the back of a nearby chair, and the sudden action made Lydia jump. He had gone from zero to a hundred in a blink of an eye. "What say you to this?" Aon's voice was perfectly calm once more. The man's tone changed like quicksilver.

Right. He's nuts.

She paused. "Are... you... seriously asking my opinion?"

"Clearly, yes."

Lydia took a moment to think it over before responding. "I guess I'd ask why."

"Ah! Yes. Tell her why, Ylena!" Aon exclaimed and threw his hands up in frustration.

So that was her name. Ylena, the woman in red who seemed to speak for the mute King Edu, answered. "Master Edu wishes to remain awake until the mystery of your expulsion from the Pool of the Ancients is explained, or until he is allowed to take your life to prevent Aon from misusing your secrets."

"I don't have any secrets, and I'm not going to just walk over there and let you snap my neck!" Now she was tempted to throw the candlestick at Edu's head.

Ylena shook her head. "It is not your decision to make. If you are a tool of some unknown power, it will spell our ruin to have you at Aon's disposal." She sounded detached, but it seemed her words weren't her own. "Better you die now than be wielded later for his gain. It is best if you accept your fate before the true King of Under."

Lydia snorted. "No. *Fuck,* no."

"You admit you serve the warlock, then?" Ylena asked.

"First of all—" Lydia pointed at Edu. "I'm not a goddamn

tool. I'm at nobody's disposal, and I don't *serve* anybody. Second, *fuck* you, buddy, and that nightmare horse you fucking rode in on!" She stepped toward the massive man reflexively. She didn't care about being afraid anymore. "Your idiot puddle-gods decided to do this, not me. I don't have some secret super-power. I don't know jack shit about what's going on. But you know what? I don't serve either of you, whether you're kings or not! As far as I'm concerned, you're *both* assholes, and I just want to go home!"

Her rant deflated. Lydia looked up at the ceiling and shut her eyes and let out a long breath. Now she was going to die. Or lose a kidney at least.

The sound of muffled clapping startled her. Looking over to the warlock in the black mask, she blinked. Sure enough, he was the source of the noise, metal gauntlet on leather glove. It didn't seem sarcastic. Aon seemed... honestly pleased.

"I concur with her statements, Edu." Aon leaned on the back of the chair he had been standing beside. "She is but a mortal. No power dwells within her but clarity of observation granted by her lack of corruption. It is that trait that interests me. It is *that* power alone that I wish to wield. Her candor is refreshing in a world where all others offer only fear or platitudes. I seek to give her shelter as my guest, since the gate to Earth has now closed."

There went *that* idea.

It felt like a door had slammed shut on her last hope of escape, and Lydia winced.

Aon ran the tips of his clawed gauntlet over the twisted wooden vines of the frame of the chair. "Perhaps in the years to come, she will find a place here in this world. Perhaps she will come to think of it as home. Or, when Earth and Under realign, she may pass back into that world unhindered. Had I been awake when all this transpired," he paused and lifted his head up to look at Edu, his voice growing low, sharp, and dangerous, "I would have brought her back to Earth immediately."

Edu shifted, finally moving, and took two steps toward Aon, his fists clenched.

"He warns you not to speak such blatant lies," Ylena said.

Aon laughed, a cackle that would have made any movie villain proud. "It is no longer your responsibility to judge me for my worth, Edu. You are the trespasser here. Tell me, what will you give me in exchange for your continued awakened state, without pitching our world back into war?"

Edu's angry advance was cut short. He froze, although his shoulders were still hunched up toward his ears.

Ylena's voice was still as calm as it ever was. "He asks you to speak plainly, warlock."

"Shall I use smaller words, then?" Aon taunted. Edu merely growled angrily again. "Very well. You are in the wrong, my old *friend*. The elders will judge you as such. They will be forced to stand with me in a war against you, one you will surely lose. I remind you, I could wipe you from the face of this world without ever missing a moment's rest. What will you give me in exchange to allow you this incursion without consequence?"

Edu sighed heavily. There was a long stretch of silence. "He will no longer actively seek the girl's demise. He will allow her to remain here, in your... care." It was clear Ylena was carefully censoring whatever was coming out of Edu's mind. "If he can remain watchful."

"Very well. We may say to the Elders that we wish to work together to solve this mystery. Let there be peace on our time!" He slapped his hand on the back of the chair again, comically accentuating his incredibly sarcastic statement before biting out his next words in an angry hiss. "*Now get out of my house.*"

Edu glanced to her, the look lingering. Whatever he was trying to say or communicate was lost on her. He turned and exited the room, Ylena close behind. The door swung shut, and with the click, Aon turned his head to look at Lydia. He moved to close the distance between them.

She raised her hands as if to protect herself, staggering backward. "I'm sorry, I'm sorry!" Fear spiked her heartrate once more. Aon had been included in her angry rant as well. The last time she had mouthed off at Aon, it had not gone her way.

Chuckling low in his throat, he caught up with her quickly, his hands at her elbows, pulling her in toward him.

She squeaked and froze in terror.

"Be still, my sweet." He raised his clawed hand in front of her face and tapped the end of his sharp pointer finger on her chin. "And you are lying. You are not 'sorry.' You spoke those words in a moment of honesty."

Lydia stammered and broke off as Aon moved his finger to place it across her lips, shushing her.

"I am not angry. Your dubious choice of garish words and profanity was pointed betwixt us both. Your anger was rightful and served my needs quite nicely. I very much enjoyed watching you dress Edu down, even if perhaps I was included in your wrath."

She was trembling. She couldn't help it, not with him so close to her. *Oh Christ.*

"You are mortal. I will not harm you in the waking world, my dear. It would be far more permanent than what I would spin for you in a nightmare. Ergo, it would be far less entertaining. I meant my words when I vowed to you that you are safe here." Aon let his clawed finger trail slowly away from her lips, tracing up her jawline.

He continued. "And to address your earlier issuance?" He leaned toward her slightly, his voice lowering. The sound of it made her stomach drop like it was off the edge of a cliff. "Your claim that I am a 'pervert?' This, I will not deny. But if you think the depth of my depraved mind is limited to watching you bathe... you are *sincerely* mistaken."

Insinuation dripped from his words like wax. Still shaking, she pushed back away from him and felt her face go warm in a blush.

Aon seemed unoffended and merely shrugged as if to say, "suit yourself."

He turned from her, pulled out a chair at the large table, and sat down in it in front of a stack of papers and notes. "Forgive me if the choice of clothes does not suit you. The servants scavenged what they could find. Fabian can fetch you anything you like from the city tomorrow. His tastes are far more modern than mine," Aon said with a small chuckle at his own understatement. "Ah. Also, I have a proposition for you."

Please don't be sex, please don't be sex. "Oh?" Lydia asked warily.

"I suggest we spend our evenings here. I, in my research, and you to assist me. In exchange, I will answer any questions you may have in as full detail as I may have it. I expect you are desperate for information."

"What do you mean, assist you?"

"Nothing sordid or unpleasant, you needn't be so suspicious. Putting away my books, helping me sort and locate items, things of that nature. Utterly mundane, I promise." Aon was seemingly amused she assumed otherwise.

"And what do you get in exchange?"

"To observe our new mystery."

He was a madman who had tortured her in her dreams. But that was hardly the most traumatizing thing that had happened to her since this misadventure began.

The other option was sitting in her room, alone and confused. Answers sounded nice. "You aren't going to torture me?"

"Not unless you wish me to."

The man had a wicked sense of humor, and the look she shot him made him chuckle. For a long moment, she debated the intelligence of accepting his offer. But she didn't see any other way forward from here. "Sure. To the helping. Not the torture."

He snapped his fingers in mock disappointment. "Damn. But, I am glad you accepted my proposal. You are free to roam my home as you see fit. The gardens are yours as well, but go no farther. It is for your own protection, I assure you. Many creatures in this world hunger for the taste of human meat, and to them, you are no more interesting than as a rare delicacy."

He snapped his fingers again, remembering another detail. "Food! Right, yes. You are likely hungry, forgive me. I do not eat food with others, for obvious reasons." He gestured at his mask. "The kitchens are downstairs. Someone can assist you whenever you are in need."

He picked up a pen in his gloved, non-gauntleted right hand, and set about writing. He looked up at her after a long pause. "You may stay here with me if you like. I would ask you not to stare, though. It is a distraction."

This was the man who had attacked her in her dreams. A man with a hair trigger—and who was not a man at all, but a monster. A madman, by his own accounts. And now he was teasing her.

Why was she... almost disappointed the conversation was over? What was *wrong* with her? Why was she so curious about him? No. Staying here was a very bad idea. She turned for the door.

"Good night, Lydia," Aon called from behind her.

Her hand lingered on the doorknob. Whatever she was expecting from Aon the warlock, the madman, and the King of Shadows? It wasn't this. It left her unsure of her footing. It somehow would be simpler if he had just attacked her. Her mind was reeling, and she was exhausted, and that was at least a simple problem to solve.

Sleep was calling her name. "Can you stay out of my dreams tonight, please?"

"I will do my best to restrain myself, although I make no promises."

She tried not to laugh. She didn't want to encourage him. Yet she found herself smiling despite herself once more at his tone. It was time to go. Twisting the knob, she remembered her manners at the last moment. "Good night, Aon."

FOUR

Aon kept his word. For the first time in a long time, her sleep was undisturbed.

The next morning, Lydia woke up a little stiff from her fall off the horse but was surprisingly okay. A servant dropped off more *normal* clothes for her to wear, and she was happy to once again be donning a set of pants.

Despite the door being unlocked, she hesitated before setting out into Aon's estate to explore. It was strange to be such a free-range prisoner.

He could be torturing her. He could string her up in a tower and starve her, cut her open, or worse. She tried to keep her mind from wandering down the world of horrors he could do to her. Instead, he had given her a lavish room and everything she would need to be more than comfortable.

It wasn't that she wasn't grateful; it just made her *nervous.* Like at any point, some monster was going to leap out from the shadows and eat her face.

It was more probable than not, in a place like this.

But Aon had told her she could explore, and so she did. It was either that or sit in her room like a frightened lump. She had done that for a while, but after three hours of a very boring nothing, she'd given up.

The rest of Aon's home was anything but boring at least. The maddening hallways of twisted Baroque architecture often left her standing and gaping in awe at the rooms she found.

To make things even weirder, the place was filled with strange illusions. One of the hallways looked like it went on forever, only to shrink in size halfway down. Mirrors were arranged in such a way to make it seem like you were walking in circles. Her favorite room was one with mirrored floors that reflected an elaborate mural upon the ceiling. It depicted a night sky, filled with a dozen colorful moons and swirling stars.

Wait.

Under didn't have stars.

Weird. Maybe the people of Under crib artwork from Earth like they do their technology and... well, people.

She also met a few people in her wanderings, but most of them were uninterested in talking to her. Either they were going about their day, weren't terribly friendly, or seemed wary of her. The unmasked servants in particular—it seemed the title was taken literally—seemed not even to want to *look* at her.

Ironically enough, Lydia was the freak here.

When she had found the kitchens and decided to make herself a cheese sandwich, the people who were working there had almost fallen over themselves to both prepare her food and avoid looking directly at her at the same time.

No amount of fussing convinced them that they didn't need to be catering to her. All she needed was to be pointed in the right direction. She lost that fight real fast. Thanking them didn't seem to do much good either.

She felt lonely, wandering around Aon's home with nobody to talk to. His home was a walk-through exhibit of an insane mind. The morbid architecture and asymmetrical take on a very classic kind of building was as beautiful as it was unsettling. Each room looked like a different nightmare from the last.

It was long into the afternoon that she found a door she thought she might recognize. Many of the doors here were locked, but this one wasn't. Peeking inside, her curiosity was confirmed. It was Aon's library from the night before.

The lights were off, and there was no fire burning in the hearth. No one was home, it seemed. Lydia stepped in slowly and looked around the room for any sign of the warlock. Thankfully, it seemed like he was absent.

Taking the opportunity to walk along the long wooden table, she had her first chance to really take in the room now that she didn't feel in imminent danger. To say that it was grand would be to put it *mildly*. Every corner had detail. Every nook and cranny had some carving or painting.

There were four moons in the sky outside, and they gave off a bright glow through the windows in a strange mix of colors that cast bizarre, multi-toned shadows. The light reflected off the patterned wood floor, carefully inlaid with different patterns and what looked like silver.

The light was just bright enough to make out the artwork in the mural overhead.

It was the depiction of a great battle. Twisted bodies of monsters and men alike were so countless it was impossible at first to make out exactly who—or what—was fighting whom. She recognized two figures in the fray, Aon and Edu. Edu's massive sword was in mid-swing, a red dragon at his back. Aon had a strange, black fire around him, and an army of the rotted dead that were clearly at his command. Charming.

Warlock *and* necromancer. Not like she really figured there was much of a difference between the two in practice.

The rest were strangers.

A creature that looked like a werewolf who had decayed

away and left only a skull for a face, tattered fur hanging from exposed white ribs.

A woman whose dark blue hair was interrupted by a pair of long, elf-like ears with a dress in beautiful shades of sapphire, who floated above the fray, seemingly uninvolved.

Another man who, except for the white mask upon his face, could have been an angel in a church with his white wings and shining platinum hair.

And the last was a giant purple spider, venom dripping from pointed, deadly fangs.

There was a portion of the vast ceiling that had been chiseled out, exactly where a seventh person should have been standing.

Lydia let out a small "huh." She remembered the missing tapestry in Edu's home. Now, this.

"You're early."

Lydia screamed.

She whirled, her heart in her throat, and nearly fell over her own feet.

Aon had appeared behind her, and his words had been whispered into her ear. He was cackling at her fear, a sharp and dangerous sound.

"Don't do that!" She glared at him.

"Why? That was terribly fun to watch." His smile was apparent in his voice as he folded an arm behind his back.

"You're going to give me a goddamn heart attack, that's why." She took a step back from him, putting her hand to her chest. She took a deep breath and let it out, trying to calm down.

"Now, we can't have that." He lifted his hand and snapped his fingers. The lights in the room flicked on, and out of the corner of her eye, the fire rushed into a blaze. He wasn't wearing his black leather glove. Not surprisingly, he was pale. A black ink circle with strange etchings like something out of an occult book sat prominently on the back of his hand. "I expected you later in the evening."

She realized she was staring at him. "I wandered in here." Shrugging, she tried to play it off.

"Ah, for shame. I thought you missed me." Aon took a step toward her, trying to close the distance between them. Lydia made a matching step back. "You are still afraid of me." He was clearly still amused. He took a step forward, and she, another one away.

"Yeah. Of course, I am."

"You fear me in a way you do not fear the others, though. I see in you more disdain for Edu than fear. He could kill you just as easily as I could. Indeed, he has threatened your life, where I have not. What is different between us, save the obvious degrees of intelligence, which leads to this?" He took another slow step forward, and Lydia took one back.

It was a good point. It took Lydia a second to come up with a reason besides that the warlock was creepy. "You're sadistic. I don't think he is."

"A valid observation. Do you fear pain, then, but not death?" Aon moved forward, and she stepped back. He was slow and careful in his movements. It seemed he found her retreating from him enjoyable. He was a predator, like everything else in this world. "Well?"

Did she fear death? She never really thought about it. "To be clear, I don't *want* to die."

"Noted. But do you fear it?"

"Everyone dies. Uh..." Lydia paused. "Where I'm from, anyway."

He laughed. "Another fair point." When she retreated into the back of a chair, she let out a small squeak of surprise. He answered with another step in. He trapped her against the surface as he leaned his hands on either side of her, caging her in.

She went rigid, unable to escape without ducking under his arm. Her face warmed again, and she knew she was blushing. But why the hell was she blushing?

"I have seen in countless souls the difference between the desire to live and the fear of death. Oft one may be mistaken for the other. It is not until that one is stripped away that the other becomes clear in its distinction. In you, I see no fear. Why?" His voice was low, still sounding like a knife wrapped in velvet.

Panic and terror weren't sustainable emotions. They wore out and wound down over time. What was left in its wake was a strange kind of nervous anticipation. It confused the hell out of her, to say the least. It wasn't until he tilted his head forward just barely at her silence that she remembered he had asked a question.

"I work with death. All the time. I guess I'm... comfortable with the idea. I always have been." Her voice sounded a lot smaller than she'd like.

"What is it you do for a profession, then?"

"I'm a forensic autopsy technician." She found shelter in the normalcy of telling someone what it is she did for work, even if it was very much now in the past tense, she expected. "It means I—"

"I know. How wonderful! No wonder you stand so strong against the horrors you have witnessed. I am sure the ways you mortals have found to maim each other have only increased in imagination since when I last roamed Earth."

An odd compliment, but okay, she'd take it. "Which was when, exactly?"

"It was the year 1948 when last I was awake and our worlds aligned."

"Oh," was all she managed to find in response. There was a beat of silence. "Could you take a step back, please?"

"I think I'd rather not." His tone had a fiendish, if playful, air. "Unless you have a good reason. I will not accept the excuse of my poor manners this time, I will warn you."

"I—uh—" She didn't expect him to say no. He was challenging her, just as he did in the dream. "It's awkward?"

"You are dodging the truth of why you wish me to retreat. No. Try again."

"When you're this close, it makes me nervous."

"Nervous of what?"

"That you might do something."

"Better. Far more honest, if imprecise." He chuckled low. He was still wearing the metal gauntlet. She knew this, because he lifted it to put the tip of his pointer finger talon under her chin and tipped her head back. She had to go with the movement, or else he'd press it into her skin and cut her. She was afraid to even swallow in fear. "I think your definition of 'something' spans many categories, and I must admonish you for your weak political dodging of the subject. I will allow it, as I did not specify otherwise."

He changed the subject drastically, and his tone became light and casual, even as he had her almost up on her toes from the claw under her chin. "Did you have a nice day?"

She couldn't speak, and she expected he knew that.

Using the barest amount of pressure from his finger, he steered her away from the chair and began backing her up. "I enjoyed watching you. I must admit I made little progress on my other endeavors. Seeing you discover my world for the first time was far too tempting to ignore."

She squeaked again as he backed her up into the wall.

He stood in front of her, and only when he could block her escape with his nearness did he remove the claw from under her chin. He let his metal palm rest against the base of her throat, though he wasn't pressing down or squeezing. His claws were merely touching against the sides of her neck.

But the point was clear. Very clear.

He studied her for a moment. "Tell me, my dear, what do you think of my home?"

She stammered helplessly and pressed back against the wall, her palms against the painted surface. She didn't know what to say at first, through the pounding of her heart.

He seemed content to wait.

Finally, she swallowed the lump in her throat and managed to find something to say. "Beautiful. But terrifying." It was the truth.

"Go on."

"Like walking through a waking nightmare. Some of it I can't make sense of. It's just... dizzying in all the detail. It's, uh—"

"Insane?"

She paused. "Yeah." Wincing, she waited for him to stab her. "But beautiful."

But he lifted his bare hand and gently ran his fingertips along her cheek. She flinched reflexively, but that didn't stall or seem to offend him. His touch wasn't rough or calloused like Edu's, nor was he frail. His skin was warm, and he slipped his hand up to run his fingers through her hair slowly. He was... gentle. But the gesture was so intimate that it left her stunned.

She had made a passing attempt at making herself look somewhat human before going out and about into his home, and her hair had decided today it wanted to be curlier than usual. He seemed to be fascinated by that.

He wrapped a strand of her blonde hair around his finger, looping it idly, before letting it loose. "I am glad you think so." His hand returned to her cheek, this time resting his palm against her jaw and letting the pad of his thumb slide against her skin.

She turned her head away, but it didn't deter him. Her

pulse was racing, and she was sure he could feel it thudding underneath his hand.

There was the smell of old books and leather again, like a hundred-year-old library. It was heady, and the mix of his nearness and his touch had her face burning. Even as she had her teeth gritted together to keep from whimpering in fear, she couldn't help but blush.

"What do you want from me...?" She finally managed words, even if they were little more than a whisper.

The chuckle that left him was a low rumble. "Oh, my darling, what a foolish question."

"Why?"

"You will not like my answer."

Dread welled up in Lydia's stomach, and a terrible and strange kind of fear twisted in her as she wondered what he was going to do.

He hummed thoughtfully before continuing. "From you, I will have everything."

FIVE

Aon's answer was worse than what Lydia was expecting, even with his warning. She cringed.

He *tsked* at her reaction, and she felt him shift. His elbow pressed against the wall next to her head as he leaned in closer to her. His gauntleted hand slid up from her throat to cup her cheek and turn her head back to look at him. It was cold against her, a far cry from the warmth of his other hand a moment prior.

"You mistake me, my dear. I am not a violent simpleton like Edu. You have piqued my curiosity. My interest in you is not purely limited to those delights the flesh may offer. Although..." He trailed off teasingly. His voice was quiet as he lowered his head toward her ear. The long, dark tendrils of his hair brushed against her face.

She wouldn't touch that comment with a ten-foot pole, so she went around it. "I don't know why your Ancients rejected me, and—" she started, pleading with Aon to rethink why he found her interesting. She squeaked as he moved his head again, the masked surface hovering close to her cheek.

"While it is a charming mystery to solve, that is not why you intrigue me, my dear..."

She must be eight shades of crimson by this point.

He continued, "I do not yet know the measure of you. While we find out, know that I am no brute. I will not coerce or blackmail you to perform any deed you are not willing to do. If you come to my bed, it will be of your own free will."

"T—thanks." At least he wasn't going to demand anything like that from her.

"I will test your limits. I will tempt you and trick you. I will toy with you. I fear I do very much love to play games." His voice felt like a blade sinking into her soul. "But you may always refuse me. That is my promise to you. My *vow*."

Suddenly, it was like a light switch went off in his brain. He stepped back from her so quickly it was dizzying. That dark sexuality that had been pouring off him was gone in a flash. He barked a laugh, startling her again. "Shall we get to work, then?"

"Wh—uh...?"

Humming an idle tune, he turned from her and walked toward the far end of the table, leaving Lydia standing there like an idiot, leaning up against the wall and trembling. He pulled out a chair, sat, and began flipping through a book, sifting through notes as if trying to remember where he left off. "You may begin by returning those books at the end of the table to their proper homes on the shelves."

And just like that, it was as though she didn't exist. He lowered his head to his work and became engrossed in whatever he was poring over. Lydia stayed leaning up against the wall, feeling like a train had just whizzed by her at the station, leaving her gaping like a fool.

As the fear and adrenaline began to cool down and the twist in her stomach began to unwind, she remembered their conversation from the night prior. He had asked her to help him in his research in exchange for answering questions.

Letting out a long breath she hadn't realized she'd been holding, she debated her choices. She could walk out and go back to her room. She could pick up the books and start hurling them at his head. She could sink to the floor and cry. Or she could just... begin sorting books.

There wasn't anything to be angry about right now. Not really, when she considered the whole. Stalking her around the room was probably not a weird thing to do here. He hadn't hurt her. Hadn't threatened her. All he had done was invade her personal space. He hadn't *demanded* she work for him either—he had offered her a fair trade. Her help for his knowledge.

Lydia knew full well Aon could have her on her knees, licking his shoes—*or something else*—if he wanted it. As tough as she'd like to think she was, there was no doubt in her mind that if he pushed hard enough, she'd break. Anybody would. There was nothing shy about this man, and she was sure he had a long life of experience in hurting people.

It could be worse, she reminded herself. Less than two days ago, she was locked in a jail cell by a man who was still intent on killing her. This one was intense and hitting on her like a fuckin' champ, but asking her nicely to sort books in exchange for information. *Don't complain, idiot.*

Finally, she walked away from the wall and went to the stack of books down at the end of the table. She began to leaf through them and found that most of them weren't in English. French, Latin, German—oh, man, sorting the ones in Cyrillic and Hebrew was going to be a pain in the ass.

"How do you have your shelves arranged?" While she was afraid to interrupt him, she needed somewhere to start.

It didn't seem to bother him, as he responded with an even tone. "Alphabetical by author, then title."

Simple question, simple answer. So, she went to work. For the first hour, she only managed to replace two of the tomes as she tried to learn her way around the insanely tall and elaborate bookshelves. As she went, she leafed through the books in curiosity. Many were about magic. Ancient occult sciences, the history of the Earth, and so on. Many were topics or by authors she suspected weren't human.

Of course, they had their own literature and their own writing. Lydia had to stop thinking about Under as a phantom world. The people here had their own culture. These people had their own way of life. They probably had music, art, theatre, and were a society of their own.

It was confirmed when she came across *The History of Under* in ten volumes. She put down her stack of books and picked out the first of the volumes and opened it. It was in a mix of languages, shifting from English to every other option seemingly as needed.

"Nor'len, the author, while methodical, is terribly dry. I do not recommend his works unless you enjoy the telling of history as a kitchen appliance assembly manual." He hadn't moved from where he sat at the table or even lifted his head as he spoke to her.

She laughed quietly at his sardonic comment before shutting the book and replacing it on the shelf. "I can't read half of it, anyway. Why is it written like that? In all different languages?"

"We speak all languages of Earth that have ever been spoken, and many of our own. Some languages are better meant for certain usage over others. German makes for lousy poetry, believe me."

The quip made her smile despite herself. "I thought your language was all those... little squiggly marks?" She didn't know how to say it without sounding insulting.

"These 'squiggly marks,'" he repeated her term with an air of humor, "represent the language of the Ancients. No one, not even I, can read them. That knowledge has been long since lost. Yet they remain the source of our power. Only by blundering through their usage like wooden children's blocks may we find the combinations that bring our will to life."

The shapes were their source of magic. Huh. That explained the soulmarks and the marking on the back of his hand. "So, the more squiggles a person has, the more magic they can use? And the one on your face is unique to the person, but you can have others elsewhere?"

Laughing, he shook his head, clearly amused at her blithe treatment of what was likely a very sacred topic to them. The other option was he react with anger at her playful lack of respect, so she'd take him being amused any day. "Yes, my dear. Precisely. The weakest of us have a soulmark and no others. The powerful have many more."

"Edu has... a lot." She remembered the red markings that covered the man's body.

"He is a king. An idiot, but a king." He paused before asking with a dark, nearly threatening air, "How do you know this?"

She didn't think he was mad at her, but she couldn't be sure. "I was forced to attend his slaughterhouse tournament. Afterwards, I was dragged to his, well, afterparty. He asked me to sleep with him."

"And?" There was so much hatred in that one word, it made her turn to look down at him. He hadn't looked up, but he had stopped writing.

"I said no, Aon. Obviously." She fought the instinct to be offended. Sex wasn't taboo, here.

His shoulders loosened slightly. "Then how do you know how many marks the man possesses?"

She snickered. "His proposition was... um... full-frontal."

He sighed heavily and leaned forward to press his palm against the forehead of his mask. Even if he didn't know what the phrase meant, she was certain he was smart enough to guess. When he replied, he was clearly exasperated. "He dragged you, a terrified mortal girl, into one of his 'parties' and presented himself like the prime roast at the market?"

"Yeah. And when I refused him, he pointed out he was going to kill me in the morning, so I might as well enjoy my last night alive. He was shocked I still said no."

The warlock groaned. "No wonder you ran. As I said... he is a king, and an idiot."

Laughing despite herself, she was glad for his strange sympathy for what Edu had done. The conversation trailed off naturally, and she went back to her task. After another twenty minutes, she paused. Finally, she worked up the nerve to ask a potentially sensitive subject. "May I interrupt?"

"Yes, of course."

"Are my friends okay?"

"Their names were Greg, Kanori, and Rick, correct?"

That got her to laugh again. "Gary, Kaori, and Nick. But close." For a moment, she wondered if he'd butchered their names on purpose to be funny.

"Human names. They run together, forgive me. Nick has Fallen to the House of Moons with Kamira and her lot. He is fine. Adjusting, but fine. Kaori seems to have already adapted quite well to her new life with the warriors, with Edu in his house." There was a heavy insinuation there that she tried not to visualize. "And you saw how well Gary has come to accept his new world with Maverick and the rest of the scholars."

She paused before asking the question she dreaded to answer. "What about Evie?"

"She is alive. The doling out of her punishment has passed to me, now that I reign as king." He leaned back in his chair. "I will not take her life."

That was a small relief until she remembered Evie's words. *Edu kills; Aon tortures.* "Don't blame her for what happened. She only tried to escape because I did. She was helping me."

"It is still a deeply punishable crime, even before you count her original charge of attempted murder."

"Then split her fate with me. I won't have her suffering alone for my bad idea."

He spun his pen between his fingers deftly. "You would not survive even half of your little friend's sentence."

Shutting her eyes, she tried not to think about the specifics of that. "Please, I…" She trailed off, not even knowing what she was going to ask him. She had nothing to bargain with. Nothing to trade. Well. Nothing that wasn't illicit, anyway. And she wasn't quite at that point yet.

"I will take your request for mercy under advisement." There was a coldness in his voice. No, not coldness, just… matter-of-fact. The words of a king, speaking law. He had a world to uphold. She had never talked to anyone who even thought of themselves as owning that kind of power, let alone somebody who actually *had* it.

"Thanks," was all she could say to that.

Aon stilled the twirling of his pen and went back to his work without another word.

At least Nick was okay, even if she had no idea what he meant by "adjusting, but fine." She'd press him for more details later. She didn't want to push her luck.

After a little while longer of sorting books, she started to figure out the system. But that left her with one book in Hebrew and one in what might be Russian. Luckily, there was an empty slot in the shelf for the Hebrew one. Finding the Cyrillic section, she reasoned through a bunch by sorting by matching shapes. She used the existing order of the books— assuming it was right—to narrow down her options.

That left her with two choices. She stood there, staring at the two empty slots reasonably close together, and knew she had no idea which one went where. Lydia didn't want to ask.

She'd worked so hard to solve the puzzle up to this point, and it was her last book. Her pride was on the line.

Fifty-fifty shot. With a sigh, she picked up the book and went to slide it into the rightmost of the gaps.

"It's the other one."

"Damn it." She shouldn't laugh at his timing or that he'd watched her try to solve this problem for the past few minutes in silence without offering any help, but she cracked up, anyway. "Thanks." It was more sarcastic than not. She slipped the book into the other gap.

"Once you knew it was a guess, you could have simply asked." Was he chiding her for her stubbornness?

Whatever. She shrugged. He was right, so she let him have that one. "It was a puzzle. I like puzzles."

"Come here."

She froze.

Seeing her tense up, he sighed. "I will ask many things of you in the time to come that you will find frightening or undesirable. I request you take such simple presumptions of mine with temperance."

Not wanting to argue that his tactic of pointing out that he could be asking her to do worse wasn't a high selling point, Lydia walked up to him. Aon held his ungloved hand out to her, palm up.

She blinked at him, confused.

"Give me your hand, silly creature."

She narrowed her eyes. "Why?"

He leaned his head against the high back of the chair and let out another sigh. "You are impossible. I am not planning on snapping your fingers off." He said it with the air of a man dealing with a child who questioned the nature of their breakfast cereal.

"You sure?" Now she arched her eyebrow at him, finding a moment of humor.

"Mostly." He answered her jab with a riposte.

Talking to him shouldn't be so... easy. But there they were. With an exhale of her own, she reluctantly put her hand in his. She had no idea what he planned to do with it. But whatever populated her list of options, what he opted to do had not been among them.

Carefully, he pulled her closer to the edge of his chair. That didn't seem to be his only goal as he gently intertwined his fingers with hers. He played with her hand idly while he tapped a clawed finger on a piece of the parchment in front of him. "My work is an attempt to rekindle our understanding of those ancient glyphs. Excuse me, ancient *squiggles*."

He was speaking to her like a passionate tutor, even while his thumb was tracing a slow line against the side of her pointer finger, making it incredibly hard to focus on his words.

"I have broken it down into their simplest shapes—an alphabet, if you will—of over three thousand unique pieces. Each can be arranged with the others in any possible formation. That, coupled with the addition of geometric casework such as circles, squares, hexagons, and multi-sided shapes such as you see here, renders the combinations functionally limitless." He pointed at another sheet, which had elaborate ceremonial magic circles—concentric rings filled with archaic shapes—much like the one emblazoned on the back of the hand that was still gently caressing hers.

The symbols on the pages laid out on the table were remarkably like the ones she had seen mimicked in her favorite horror movies. "Is this the same magic like what people write about on Earth? Like Crowley?"

"Hm? Aleister? Strange man, but a clever one. Took a bit too much of a fancy to our libertine lifestyle, I'm afraid."

"You knew him?"

"I did. Indeed, Aleister and I met when he somehow managed to summon me. He became an acquaintance."

"He *summoned* you?"

"He believed he was channeling some fallen archangel. Needless to say, I was not what he was expecting." He chuckled.

She laughed with him. The warlock appearing out of a magic circle must have been a sight. "Weren't you pissed that he dragged you to Earth?"

"Think of it more like a request than a command. A ring of a phone. I answered the call out of curiosity. I was, how do you put it... bored."

"So... all this stuff seriously works? All those books about summoning demons and controlling people actually *do* something?"

"No, not always. More frequently that is not the case than the alternative. It may only be effective when our worlds are close, either passing by each other or falling into alignment. Sometimes, it lasts years. Otherwise, your world has not the fabric and resources to allow for the usage of such power."

"Huh." Many things made so much more sense now. All the myths and legends were real, if only sometimes.

He shifted her hand in his grasp again, this time to run the pad of his thumb along the underside of her fingers. It sent an unexpected shiver up her spine, followed by a warm rush, and she had to pull her hand from his. He let her without fuss, but his head turned from his work up to her, the metal surface glinting back the amber light of the fire.

She wished she could see his face. She suspected his expression would tell her a lot.

"What is wrong?" His tone was a lousy attempt at innocence. There was an air of mischief that told her that he knew exactly what was wrong.

Grateful she had a cardigan with pockets, she shoved her hands in them. It was a poor attempt at hiding, but it was all she had for options. "Why were you doing that?"

"Two reasons." He was so matter-of-fact. "First, simply

because I wished to do so. Second, your cheeks take on such a delightful color when I am near you, and I was testing the theory as to what in particular inspires such a reaction. Why did you recoil from me?"

"Because... I'm your prisoner. And..." She was once again faced with a bizarre question from him. What he was doing wasn't normal, fine. But in truth, she was terrified of what it had suddenly sparked in her.

She hadn't hated his touch.

Not at all.

And *that* was problematic.

He rose from the chair to face her, and she took half a step back to keep some distance between them. "I hope someday you come to see yourself as my guest. Your situation is unfortunate. I wish to make your time here as pleasant as possible." He sounded sincere.

"You tortured me in a dream," Lydia reminded him dutifully. Honestly, she was reminding them both.

"I was teaching you a lesson."

"By torturing me."

"It worked, did it not?" His voice held a thick layer of amusement.

"That's not the damn point."

"It is easy to forget you are not like us, that you are fragile and do not see violence so casually as we do. For those who cannot die, what I did was little more than an inconvenience."

She watched him curiously for a second. "Are you trying to apologize to me?"

"Perhaps." A slight lift of shoulders in a shrug.

"Then why don't you just say, 'I'm sorry for torturing you?'" She decided to see how far he'd let her go. "Or isn't that fancy enough?"

"I am what I am, my dear Lydia." He bowed low, folding his arm in front of him. He rose from the gesture slowly. "Should you come to predict or explain my behavior, you may write the most well-published treatise in all our world's ancient history."

Shaking her head, she walked away from him, needing some space. She made it a few paces and put her hand on the back of a chair and let her fingers run along the curved surface. "I know you could be doing worse things to me. Far worse. I do. I'm thankful you don't have me strung up from chains or being flayed alive. I'm thankful you haven't sent me to the chopping block. What you've done so far, giving me a room, clothes, food, freedom to walk around—thank you. I'm sorry I'm jumpy. I'm handling this as best as I know how."

There was a long pause, long enough she wondered if he was still there. She turned to look at him, and he hadn't moved. Finally, after another beat, he returned his attention to the papers on his desk and sat back down.

Silence hung in the air like a cloud. Did she say something wrong?

"Aon?"

"Hm?" He looked up and seemed surprised she was standing there. "Oh, hello again, Lydia. I did not hear you come back in. It is quite late. Did you get lost on the way back to your room?"

Wait, what?

Fear crept up her spine as she realized with a slowly encroaching horror that Aon wasn't playing with her. Whatever had just happened, he seemed to have jumped forward in time in his head as though hours had passed when it was only the span of a few seconds. He must have thought she had left, time had gone by, and she had walked back in.

Others had said Aon was insane, but she was starting to believe they might mean it very literally and not just as an insult.

"Y... yeah." She tried to think fast. "Sorry, this place is a funhouse with all the mirrors." Bringing up what had just happened seemed like a dangerous prospect. Either he'd get embarrassed or angry. Both options seemed like a bad idea.

"Of course! Go left from the door, and at the end of the hall, take a right. You will find your room halfway down the corridor." He picked up his pen to begin writing again.

"Thanks," she muttered.

"I hope you will return here tomorrow night. I hope I have not frightened you too terribly." His teasing was playful, perhaps not knowing how right he was.

"I will." She headed to the door. The realization of what she had witnessed was still settling on her.

"Delightful. Sleep well, darling."

"Yeah... you too." When she shut the door behind her, she put her head in her hands.

Why did she have the distinct feeling her life was going to get *very* complicated from here on out?

SIX

Lydia was suffering from a nightmare.

Aon knew this, quite simply, for he was the one who put it there.

She lay in bed, her blonde hair splayed like curls of light against black satin, her brows drawn in fitful slumber. He sat on the edge of her bed, a phantom come to plague her. He smiled behind his mask.

Earlier, she had come to his library and put books away. It had been hard for him to keep focus on his work, with such a distracting creature wandering about. She was a curious, unflinchingly inquisitive creature. She peppered him with questions, and he wondered if she had not been meant to Fall to the House of Words.

Indeed, he was glad she fell to none of the colors, if it meant they could play this delightful game that was quickly evolving between them. It was some of the most fun he could remember having in a very, *very* long time.

Not for the slightest of reasons being that she, despite her best interests and her best intentions, seemed... *drawn* to him.

How she blushed when he came near her. Her cheeks had

glowed like flame when he put his metal hand against her throat. Oh, her heartbeat had quickened in terror. But it had also grown in tempo for another reason that delighted him nearly as much—*desire.*

She *wanted* him.

The mortal young woman might simply not realize it yet.

How much fun it would be to teach her what dark pleasures loomed in the shadows, if he could convince her to follow him down those corridors. Truth be told, he was half ready to drag her.

No. She would make a better plaything that knelt willingly at his knees, not one whose legs had been broken.

The image of her between his legs sent an unexpected thrill up his spine. He rarely let others touch him. When his lust and boredom grew unmanageable, he slaked his interests on those who did only as he wished.

But her? This little mortal?

He wondered what those lips might feel like, wrapped around him. If she would fight him and struggle, or if she would obey his commands. He cared not either way. Both seemed delightful.

Sadly, tonight was not about his pleasure, or hers.

Tonight, was about *fear.*

If he were to manipulate her opinions of him, to change them to his liking, he first would need to know precisely what those opinions were. More aptly, he would need to know what it was that she feared he might do to her.

Subverting expectations was the key to keeping a captive unsteady. If he knew precisely what she was terrified he might do to her, he knew what actions to either withhold or to tread closer still.

He grinned, too eager for his own good, and leaned over her, resting his weight on his hand on the far side of her. With his other, he gently traced his bare fingertips through her hair. It was so soft. She was trapped in his spell and could not wake until he allowed it. He had no fear of waking her.

Aon trailed his hand lower, settling against her neck, and her skin was so very warm against his palm. He wanted to touch more of her. To let his palms wander her, to cup the breasts that were barely hidden behind her nightgown.

How I wish I could taste your skin.

His sudden desire caught him off guard.

What unusual things you bring out in me, my dear. His hand itched to glide lower, and instead he moved it from her altogether to avoid the temptation. *What unusual things, indeed.*

He shook his head. Tonight, he had come to sample her fear. Not to spend his lust on her sleeping form. The first time he touched her, she would be awake and aware. And either crying for mercy, begging for more—or if he had his way and his skill held true—both.

"What will it be, Lydia? Do you think I will tear you limb from limb? Torment you with needles, with saw and with claw? Beat you? Starve you? Perhaps carve you and eat you like a lamb?" He chuckled.

Hovering his palm over her head, he worked the magic that ran deep in him. It was the flex of muscle that was as natural to him as walking. The nightmare deepened, and she whimpered in fear, tossing her head.

He felt his desire surge, felt his arousal grow, answering her dismay with a fire that burned in his veins. She belonged to him. She was at his mercy. And she was afraid.

It was beautiful.

He pressed her further into the spell, and she arched her back, tempting him once again with her barely shrouded body. He let her terror grow to a fever pitch. His heartbeat thudded in his ears in time with her fear, if for a very different reason. Oh, by the Ancients, how he wanted her!

Patience, fool. Patience.

Like a chef, waiting for the masterpiece to be done and not daring to peek into the oven until the right time, he waited until her nightmare finished its rise. Until her fear peaked.

Placing his hand down upon her so his thumb pressed to the center of her forehead, he let himself slip inside of her dream. It was strange, to be inside another's mind and yet in the waking world, both at once. Most found it disorienting. He found it normal.

After all, he was insane.

He could not wait to see what torment she believed lay in wait for her in his home. "Let us see what kind of monster you think I am, hm?"

* * *

Another night and another nightmare.

This time, there was no running involved. Usually, dreams like this never really bothered Lydia. They were never scary, in the same way her favorite movies were no longer frightening to her. Honestly, she found them kind of entertaining. A free horror movie night.

But now the context had changed.

Now she knew what it was like to be caught by a monster.

She was strapped to a medical table. Her mind had conjured up that recent memory and somehow made it even darker and more twisted. A creature whose medical mask had been stitched directly to his face was busy dismembering her. He ripped away at flesh and sinew, digging into her organs and cutting them free.

In a way that only dreams would allow, she was not dying, just suffering. Only experiencing the fear. She was crying and begging for mercy, but the creature that was butchering her like a slab of meat didn't care. It didn't respond to her in the slightest as she writhed in agony.

"And here I am, insulted not to have been invited to the party." Like a dark snake slithering through grass, Aon's voice broke into her dream. "Forgive me for my intrusion, but even inside your mind I fear I do not like the prospect of *sharing*."

Someone grabbed her by the shoulder. The scene around her instantly shattered. But the terror still gripped her. She shot up, straight into someone's arms. Her heart was pounding too hard for her to care who it was. But the smell of old books and dust told her the answer soon enough.

After a long pause, Aon's arms wrapped around her, almost as if he were afraid to touch her.

It took her a long moment to process where she was and what was happening. She was still in bed, and not strapped to some horrifying medical table. It had just been a nightmare.

A stupid dream.

The warlock was sitting on the edge of the plush mattress. His bare hand was stroking her hair, and he was shushing her quietly. It was then that she realized she was clinging to him, her hands twisting the fabric of his coat. Finally, she let go of him and lifted her head from his shoulder. Confused, she shot him a quizzical look. "What happened?"

"You were crying out in your sleep. I came to ensure you were not in danger and found you mired within a dream from which I could not wake you." He combed his hand slowly through her hair.

She shivered at his touch and was entirely unsure as to why. As he reached to touch her again, she grew shy and shrank away from him. "Thanks."

"You are quite welcome."

"It's incredibly weird that you can be inside of my dreams, by the way."

"Perhaps I was not there. Perhaps you were merely

dreaming of me on your own. Your dark pursuer and savior all at once," he mused playfully.

"Really?"

"No."

She glared at him.

It earned her a chuckle. "I am quite jealous that you were dreaming of some other man dismantling you. I have not made an appropriate impression upon you, I see. I must try harder next time."

"Please, don't." She moved to shift away from him, to get out of the bed on the far side from him. His hand caught her wrist and pulled her back.

"I am merely teasing. You must learn to pardon me for the games I play." He took her hand in his un-gauntleted one, and Lydia could do nothing but sit there, confused, as he slipped her palm against the bare skin of his neck. It was warm under her touch. She could feel his pulse beneath her fingers. He let out a husky sigh and pressed his hand against hers, holding it there. "You make delightful prey, Lydia. How you blush when I come near, and yet you are so terrified of me. Both bring me great joy in equal measure. But I am not the butcher in your nightmare."

The moment seemed to hang in the air. It was poignant. Meaningful. But she didn't understand *why.* His skin beneath her hand... she felt pulled to him like a moth to a flame. "I don't understand what's happening. I don't get any of this. I just want to go home."

"I know. Do not fret." He slipped his hand from hers, before gently placing it atop her head.

As he did, she felt herself start to slip away into a warm kind of darkness. There was an odd tingling sensation.

"You are exhausted. Sleep."

She was suddenly so tired she couldn't keep her eyes open. "What're you..."

"Rest." The word was a command.

And she was helpless but to obey as a dreamless slumber came for her.

* * *

Chains rattled, the cacophony of steel mixing with the howls and screams of a monster. The transition of the Fallen into the House of Moons was always more difficult than the rest.

Lyon was standing against a tree, watching the creature in the clearing. It was an eerily lanky, spindly beast that would rise far past twelve feet if it could stand straight. Its limbs were long and skeletal. Its face was a distorted dog-like skull. To some, at first glance, it may look as though the corpse of a werewolf, left to rot in nature, had become warped and twisted. That it had decayed to leave this gaping, bony form in its wake, as some twice-cursed creature.

Instead, the truth was this was its intended form. It was suffering greatly, yanking against the collar that had been placed around its neck, but not from its shape. No, it was merely... upset.

Heavy iron chains ran from several loops to boulders around it in a ring, keeping it from moving more than a few inches in any direction.

The thing was clawing at itself in its agony, ripping welts and gashes that oozed dark blood in the quest to be free. It marked its throat and chest with the trenches of its vicious nails as it attempted to tear away its restraints. But the creature would not escape. This manner of work had been done many times before to every soul cursed to become as he—a shifter, one whose physical body was a fluid form.

An arm slipped around his waist, and he was broken from his thoughts at the familiar nearness. He had been sent to speak to the creature who suffered before him, and though that was now out of the question, the time here was certainly not wasted.

Lyon looked down at Kamira and smiled faintly at her. Speaking of a fluid form, it seemed she fancied to wear a tail tonight, as it wound around his right leg.

Many might have mistaken her horns as being part of her mask, but he knew better. He had, after all, seen her many times without the slab of carved wood she wore across her face. The horns that arched delicately back through her long strands of dark hair and beads were indeed her own. For now.

The Elder of Moons could command her shape at will. She could alter her body to share whatever features of their dark race she wished. Often, she chose to mix them about as she saw fit.

He would welcome her in any form she took. They were wed several centuries ago, after all. Physical affection and pleasure in this world may be free and commonplace, but love was revered above all. It was the rarest thing two of their doomed and eternal kind could find in each other.

"What troubles you, my Priest?" She nuzzled her head into his chest. She was taller than many, but still only reached his shoulder. Wrapping his arms around her, he held her and let his gaze wander back to the corrupted wolfman before them.

It was by his hand—quite literally—that the mortal boy had come to Under. The creature before him was what had become of Nicholas. But it was the young lady who had come here with him who darkened his thoughts. "I came on command of Edu to speak to Nicholas. To learn what he may know of the girl's unique condition."

"He knows nothing. I have already asked. He spouts clever obscenities and tells me where in my anatomy I could place various and sundry objects." She smirked, clearly having enjoyed the boy's spirit.

"I see I will not have the opportunity to speak with him, if he is not yet in command of his power."

"I have chained him not because he cannot control his form. The whelp has talent."

"Why, then?"

"He sought to march into Edu's keep and save his friend's life. Now he seeks to do the same with Aon. He wishes to *save* the strange one."

He sighed heavily. "Either action would merely amount to his death."

"I know this. And I have said this." His wife snickered. "And he has vividly told me how little he cares. He rightfully worries for her more now than when her life was forfeit under Edu's reign."

"I admit I worry for her as well."

"I would for anyone now kept in Aon's care." She began to toy with the edge of his white vest. The deep green markings that ran up her arm looked like stripes on some great beast of the wild. He would never tire of gazing at them.

"The warlock will not kill her. She is too interesting to him, I am sure." Though he could not keep the dismay from his voice.

"She is doomed all the same." She let out a small huff of a laugh in her throat.

He kissed the top of her head. Yes. His concerns were similar. "Aon has announced his traditional return gala. Will you attend?"

"Of course. It would be seen as an insult if I did not." Though it was clear she was disgruntled over the matter. "There is little I would like less than to be forced to watch him celebrate his return to the throne as if it were some *lauded* event."

"There are those who are loyal to him."

"Such as whom? That slug Otoi? The coward Maverick?

Feh! If you were still elder of your House, we would have him locked, four to two."

He sighed and bent his head to rest it atop hers. "First, I will remind you... Under is, sadly, not a democracy. He is our king."

"Second," his wife interjected, reciting his refrain he had repeated many times. This conversation was not their first time hashing through this debate. "You are an elder no longer." She paused. "Do you regret your choice yet, Priest?"

Two elders could not be joined as one. It was against all law, for the balance would be upset in the face of such nepotism. For her, he had given up not only his rank order, but also the mask he had been gifted as he rose from the Pool of the Ancients so long ago.

Never would he regret his choice.

He lifted his head to tuck the backs of his fingers gently under her chin and tilted her face to look up at him. Her green cat's eyes were sharp as she watched him, waiting for his response. He smiled faintly. She was indomitable. She was the untamable wild. "I made no sacrifice worth considering for what I received in return."

A sharp-nailed hand slipped up along toward the back of his neck and pulled him down to kiss her. He met her embrace and held her tighter against his body. "Stay by my side at Aon's rue ball." Her breath was hot against his tepid skin. It had been a long time since he had taken blood, and while he did not need it to survive, it did help to offset his cold body temperature. "You may keep me from murdering someone in my misery," she finished.

He smiled. "Well, when you phrase it in such an appealing way... how could I say no?"

SEVEN

When Lydia woke up, it took her a minute to remember what had happened the night prior and where the *hell* she was.

Aon had broken into her mind to wake her from a nightmare, and as far as she could tell, used magic to send her back to sleep once her terror was gone.

Jackass.

Part of her was offended that he was in the room while she was asleep. Part of her was grateful he woke her up. But mostly, she was confused. Why did he care? Why not just let her suffer?

As she sat up, she noticed there was a note on her nightstand. In careful, antiquated script, it read,

> *I have business to attend in the city today. You are free to roam my estate as you see fit. I will see you soon.*

It ended in a heavily flourished letter A as though she wouldn't have been able to figure out who left it.

There, beside it, was a black rose. It was beautiful—if horribly cliché. Although, if the warlock was as old as people said, maybe he was the source of the trope. It seemed a waste to leave it there, so after finding a glass in the bathroom, she filled it with water and put the rose back onto her nightstand. She honestly didn't know the last time she'd been given a flower.

Her thoughts dwelled on the rose as she got dressed. This time, she found a pair of black jeans and a black tank top waiting for her in her wardrobe. She pulled a—shocker—black sweater over it and sighed. He might let her wear what she wanted, but it seemed she was doomed to live in his color scheme.

It was clear Aon was flirting with her. But why? To what end? Amusement? Because physical affection wasn't a big deal here?

That was the topic she couldn't let go of as she wandered his home in circles for the rest of the day. Mostly because she was lost, partially because she had nothing better to do.

But the day came and went uneventfully, save for the fact that everyone seemed to be in a hustle. She ran into Fabian again and chatted with him for a few minutes, only to learn that Aon was throwing a gala in a few days, and everyone was in a fuss getting ready.

She had never really thought about how much work it must have been to put on parties for kings back in the day. The sheer number of people it took to pull it off was astonishing, so she did her best to stay out of the way.

Her dreams were quiet that night, and her fear of every shadow was starting to recede.

The next morning, after fetching some fruit and cheese from the kitchens—she was offered meat, but she remembered where it came from and said no—she decided to get out of the way of the hubbub of the approaching party and took her plate to go.

It was about halfway back to her room that she pulled up short.

"Come here."

It was a voice. She turned slowly and looked around, but there was nobody there. She was in the hallway alone.

"Hello?" For a long moment, there was no answer.

"Come here."

That time, Lydia realized the voice wasn't in the hallway, it was in her *head*. As it spoke, she felt like a hand was wrapping around her spine and clenching down. Like something had wormed its way into her being and was grabbing on.

She gasped, wavered, and realized the voice was not only inside her mind, but was also issuing a *command*.

It took eight steps down the hallway before Lydia realized she had started moving. The voice had *commanded,* so she had followed. She pulled to a haltering stop in fear, as she realized she had begun to obey automatically.

"Don't do that!" Her hands were shaking, and she had to hold the plate of food up against her side to keep it from rattling. "Just don't. Ask. All you have to do is ask."

There was a long pause.

"Please."

Shutting her eyes, she took a deep breath. There was no need to ask whose voice it was. There wasn't even really a need to ask where he was asking her to go. Now, once more in full control of her legs, she walked down the hallway, cussing silently to herself the entire way.

Slowly but surely, the winding and fantastical corridors of twisted, vine-like molding and black-on-black-on-black decor were beginning to become recognizable to her. Reaching the door to his library, she knocked.

"Come in," came the muffled response.

Pushing the door open, she stepped in and shut it behind her. It felt as though she was on the verge of tears. Aon had reached into her mind and commanded her to do something, and Lydia had done it.

She'd stopped herself—eventually—but how far could that

have gone before she could wrest control of her own body back from him?

The warlock was sitting at the far end of the table, a large brass and copper mechanism in front of him. Whatever it did, she had no idea. It was a twisting mess of tubing, braided cotton-covered electrical wires, and gears. He was fiddling with it and did not look up at her as she entered.

"Sit. Eat." He gestured with his ungloved hand. His other hand still wore the metal-clawed gauntlet, as usual.

Feeling her steps become stunted and unsure, she went to the far end of the table and put the food down.

"Not there. Here." He gestured to the seat next to him. After a pause, he added politely, "If you will. I prefer not to shout down the table."

Did she have a choice? Apparently, he could just fucking *command* her to do things. She picked up the plate and moved toward the head of the table. "Please... don't ever do that again."

"Why not?"

"It's terrifying. It feels... like being a puppet on strings."

He paused in his work, and his masked metal face glanced up at her briefly before looking back to his strange piece of equipment. It almost looked like some bizarre medical contraption. Something Frankenstein would have been proud of. "Frightening you was not my intention. Those in my house are accustomed to my summons. When one goes into the Pool of the Ancients and emerges in a typical fashion, knowledge of our ways is granted. It is easy to forget this is all quite foreign to you."

She put her plate down at the seat to his left, pulled the chair out, and sat. "You can control me?"

"No. It is not control, per se. I can only compel you or push you to do one thing or another. It is easy enough to fight. But to someone caught off guard, it must be terribly disconcerting. I assure you, scaring you was not my motivation."

"This time."

He chuckled at her cynicism. "Touché. Do forgive me."

The warlock was trying to apologize in his own way, and she didn't want to throw that back in his face. "Apology accepted. It's okay. I'll... get used to things eventually, I guess." She picked up a weird not-grape and popped it into her mouth. "Last time I got summoned to someone, it went differently, so I'm grateful for that. At least you aren't butt-ass naked and having an orgy."

Where she found the strength to joke, she didn't know. But it came to her like a tent against a winter storm, and she huddled inside it without question.

"Well, there go my afternoon plans." He sighed overdramatically.

It made her laugh, and she found herself smiling at his joke. For all his horrifying demeanor, there was an odd charm about him. She found herself watching him curiously.

Aon's only open eye hole in his mask was on his other side from her, and the left side nearest to her was perfectly smooth. It made her want to take her hand and wave it and see if he could see the movement, but she figured it probably wasn't a good idea to straight up taunt the demigod. "Doesn't only seeing out of one eye get to be a pain?"

"I can see out of both just fine. Our masks do not restrict our vision or breathing in any way."

"How the hell does that work?"

"Magic."

"Right. Magic. Magic's a thing now." She tried not to smack her own forehead at her idiotic question. Picking up a slice of cheese that looked like it was meant for a sandwich, she rolled it into a tube between her fingers, like she always used to do when she was a kid. Old habits. "Stupid question, sorry."

"No, it is not foolish. This is all much for you to attempt to understand in short order."

"So, if I had come out of the lake like everyone else, I'd just know everything about Under?" She took a bite from the cheese.

"More or less, yes."

"But Evie didn't seem to be okay with how things were."

"There is a stark difference between *comprehending* one's part in the fabric of this world and *accepting* it." He was a patient and dutiful teacher.

She looked down at her food thoughtfully. He was right. Knowledge and acceptance were two very different things. She went silent for a long time as he fiddled with the machine in front of him.

It looked as though he was attempting to feed a teensy, tiny thread through a series of equally small needle heads. The needles were arranged in a row, hovering over an empty spot in the piece of equipment, like a dozen sewing machine needles in a line, hanging over where you would put the fabric. But the gap between the points of the needle and the base was five or six inches at least. For every upright needle, there was one next to it at a nearly ninety-degree angle. It was to catch the thread and pull it back to the next one.

What would you need a dozen needles to sew, from six inches away? What went through this machine? And why were the needles hooked up to clear glass tubes like there was supposed to be liquid running through the needles like a tattoo gun?

Oh.

It was designed to tattoo someone in what looked like the worst way possible. Ink, combined with thread. Now the tilted angles of the other needles made sense. It was designed to thread the needle into the skin without needing to go all the way through the person.

Gross.

She decided not to ask why Aon needed something like this.

He was struggling and seemed to be unable to hold the needles still enough to get the thread through it. She watched him work as she munched on the food in front of her.

When he knocked one of the needles out from what was carefully balancing it in place, it fell to the table with a clatter. He growled furiously in his throat and slammed his metal hand down onto the table. She jumped in her seat at the outburst.

Letting out a disgruntled sigh, he leaned back into the chair. His bare hand resting up over his mask, he covered his eyes in frustration.

"Can I make a suggestion?" She was again not quite sure where she got the nerve. Perhaps she was simply past the point of fear affecting her sharp tongue.

"By all means," he said dryly.

"Maybe if you weren't wearing the claw, it'd be easier."

"Hm." He took his hand away from his face and looked at his clawed gauntlet, lifting it up and turning it over in front of him. "Yes! Interesting theory. Let us test it, shall we?" He began unbuckling the straps that held it on. He had such a suddenly malicious and heavily sarcastic air that it made her nervous.

She was really confused as to *why* he seemed suddenly snarky at her.

At least until the gauntlet landed with a heavy metal *thunk* on the table next to her. Aon had tossed it in front of her after detaching it from his arm.

Detaching it.

It wasn't hollow.

It wasn't a glove.

Lydia covered her mouth in shock with both hands. He held up his arm, which ended at the stump of a wrist. He had no hand! His gauntlet was not a piece of armor—it was a *prosthetic.*

"What a wonderful suggestion." He gestured his ungloved hand at his empty wrist. "So much better, don't you think?"

"Oh God! Oh God, I'm so sorry!" She wasn't upset with him; she was upset squarely at herself. How could she have been so brainless? "I'm so sorry. I didn't even think—I didn't realize, I thought—"

"You thought what, exactly?"

"That you just liked to wear it to scare people, not that— I'm so sorry! I'm such a bitch." She put her head in her hands.

He laughed as his anger at her seemed to dissipate. Picking up the gauntlet from the table from where he tossed it, he began affixing it back onto his wrist. When he had finished, he gave an experimental flex and point of each finger in turn. "You are half right. I could wear a simple hand, but I prefer the claws, yes. But it is merely an adaption to a wound dealt me by Edu long ago."

"I'm sorry."

"I believe you. But do not pity me. It was in return for my taking his tongue." He laughed again, this time a sinister sound, a remembrance of glee at another man's suffering. "I think I rather made out the better of us in the ordeal. I merely had to learn to write with my other hand."

Stunned and not sure what to do, she just looked down into her plate of food. She felt awful for assuming his gauntlet was purely decorative. But she was also horrified at the idea that he had cut out another man's tongue. "Why doesn't it just grow back? I mean, if people get eaten and die all the time?"

"The blade I used to remove Edu's tongue was cursed. In the treaty, I used the same dagger to remove my own hand. After many thousands of years, we have learned how to truly hurt each other, my darling." Picking up the fallen needle, he placed it back into the prongs that held it suspended.

She still felt incredibly guilty. "Do you want me to try?" She gestured at the machine. "I'm fairly dexterous, from my line of work." It was an odd thought that popped into her head, but an honest one, so she went with it.

He let out a small "huh" of surprise and looked at her with a slight tilt to his head. "Why... yes. I would appreciate that."

When she stood and moved to take his place, he didn't budge. She shot him a look. "I'm not going to sit on your lap to do it."

He let out a comically exaggerated shrug and a wistful sigh. "For shame. Very well." He rose from his chair and exited it with a flourishing bow to her as a gentleman might gesture to a carriage stairway. "My lady."

His antics made her smirk despite herself. He had a fiendish sense of humor, but the more she could see it for what it was, the less offensive it became. If she was going to be here with him for the rest of her life—however short that might be—she couldn't very well spend the whole time cowering in fear.

Sitting in the chair, she picked up the thread and put the end of it in her mouth, wetting it to get it to stick straight. She realized that was something he couldn't very well do, wearing a mask.

He was standing behind her, his hand on the back of the chair. "Weave it through each end, then the hole in the tip, then on to the next."

She leaned in to do it and was glad when it proved not to be too hard. She had to do hours of detailed work with corpses in her day, trying to remove flakes of metal from organs or bullets from inside tissue. It wasn't the work of a surgeon—her people couldn't die harder, after all—but it was still delicate work, mostly to protect the evidence, rather than the person.

All in all, it took her a few minutes, but she finished without too much frustration. She pulled a decent length of the thread out the other side and smiled, happy to have done something useful—even if it was threading needles—in this weird world in which she had found herself.

His hand settled on her shoulder and gave her a gentle squeeze. "Thank you."

It was a genuine sentiment. No mocking, no threats, no keenly dangerous flirtation. She looked up at him and smiled faintly in response. "You're welcome."

"Now, move."

And it was over just as fast. But she was still grinning as she stood from his chair, before repeating his mocking flourish from before right back at him.

He sat down and returned to tinkering, and so she went back to eating.

"There is a gala here tomorrow night."

"I've heard."

"I expect you to attend. Hopefully, without fuss."

"You could've just asked, you know." She rolled her eyes.

"In this, I regret you do not have a choice. The other Houses suspect I have killed or dismembered you. Or that I have removed your arms and legs and turned you into some manner of personal plaything." It sounded so casual coming from him, without any heed paid to the grotesqueness of his description. "To see you there in attendance, and not in chains, is a political boon."

"You're a king. What do you need to play politics for?"

"Ah, that it was so simple. All things flow smoother when the stream is unobstructed."

"I didn't figure you for a poet."

"Do not worry, I did not write that."

She looked away to hide her enjoyment of how weirdly witty the man was. It was easy to talk to him when he wasn't stringing her along by the end of a claw. "All right. I'll go."

"Good. Three of your friends will be in attendance."

Lydia didn't need to ask which three—Evie was still locked up somewhere. It was a keen reminder that he had her prisoner.

But the idea of seeing Nick made her smile. "You could have started with that."

"I wished to see if you would attend for my sake only."

Clever jackass.

"I've never been a party person, but I don't see any harm in going. As long as I'm not on the menu." That last part was still up for debate.

"Worry not, that will come later in the evening. As I said, I do not care much for sharing." His words were dark once more, and she looked away to hide her inevitable blush. But judging by his chuckle, it hadn't worked. "You make this game too easy."

"And you need to stop saying things you don't mean."

"Hm?" He looked up at her at that statement. "Clarify."

"Look, I get it. Sex isn't a big deal around here. You guys are a lot more casual about it. Good for you. *Viva la revolución*, I don't know. But I'm not used to people so... blatantly flirting with me, when they don't mean anything by it." It was a weird thing to try to explain.

"You think I make such comments in jest?"

"I don't know what to think. But what I don't think is that you..." She paused, not sure how to express it right. *You either aren't legitimately attracted to me, and you're just playing around. Or you are because it's no big deal to screw anything that moves. I'm nothing more than a blip on your radar.* She did her best to compress that into something less offensive. "I'm just a freak anomaly. That's the only reason I'm here."

"Interesting." He rose from his chair and moved toward her. When she went to stand, his hand on her shoulder pushed her back down to sitting. Grabbing the arms of the chair, the wood feet made a dramatic noise as he swiveled the chair ninety degrees to face him. He held on as he leaned toward her. "Very interesting indeed."

"What is?" She tried to sound firm, even if she suddenly felt very small and unsure of herself. He loomed over her like a nightmare in black, long silken tendrils of dark hair with the stray gray hair as the only accent against his black metal mask. It set her heart thumping in her chest again, and she leaned further into the cushioned back of the chair as he leaned in closer.

"If I did not find you worth my time, you would not be occupying so much of it. If I did not find you worth my attention," Aon purred, "you would not have it."

She felt her face go warm and cursed herself. He was right. It was easy to get her to blush. When she turned her head away, his clawed gauntlet lifted to turn her face back to him. He used the backs of his fingers, as he did not seem intent on threatening her with the points this time at least.

"I would have quite eagerly asked you to share my bed from the moment you arrived, but I knew you would refuse. It would have been unfair to you—perhaps thinking that your safety was tied to my pleasure. But know this, my dear. I am not one to take lovers frequently, as so many in this world do. I do not find many deserving of my affection." He lowered himself closer to her. "My interest in you may be many things, but you may rest assured that it is anything but *feigned*."

"I—" She stammered and swallowed the rock in her throat, losing her words in the fear and the intensity that came with Aon's nearness.

He curled his fingers and let the ends of his sharp nails graze against her cheek. She shivered, shifting in the chair, goosebumps rising.

He let out a deep, appreciative sound in his throat. "So responsive... I think you do not find my manner of flirtation as fearsome as you pretend."

She started to argue with him, but the words died in her throat.

With no small amount of horror, she came to a terrifying realization—

He was right.

Twisted up in her stomach like a pit of snakes were equal parts dread over what he was doing—at his claws, at his dark threats—and a terrible kind of excitement that matched it. He was a monster, chasing her in the darkness. Threatening to take her. And there was a real part of her that wanted it.

That wanted *him*.

It was enough to send her shoving the chair back away from him. He had to scramble to keep from toppling over as she shot out from under him unexpectedly.

Scrambling to put the chair between them, she shook her head. Her heart was racing, and she knew her eyes must be saucers. "I—No. No, I can't. I—I'm sorry."

"As you wish." He bowed low at the waist, and he took a step back from her. "And do not apologize. You may always refuse me, as I said."

Oh God. She needed to go back to her room. She needed to get away from him. She turned and headed quickly for the door, her mind reeling, her stomach still in a knot.

She had nearly shut the door behind her when he called after her.

"I will see you at the gala, darling."

EIGHT

All right, fine, Lydia had never seen a gala before, let alone one that looked like it was straight out of seventeenth-century France. Blame it on her for not knowing what to expect.

But holy *shit*, it was a lot more than she expected.

It was a ghoulish and unintentional masquerade ball. Everyone wore masks all the time, anyway, so to them, it was nothing out of the ordinary. For her, it was like something out of a surrealist film. Everyone was wearing their best attire in the colors of whatever House they belonged to. It looked like a twisting sea of gemstones, the way the colors glinted in the amber antique-style electric lights or overhead candles in their chandeliers.

Everyone was dressed to the nines. And that included her.

It hadn't been worth throwing a fit over when she woke up to find a dress on a hanger in her room. It was, of course, black lace.

It was off-the-shoulder, with long sleeves and a neckline that dipped down dangerously in the center. It clung in layers down to the floor and trailed behind her by a few inches. It was far more daring and far more garish than anything Lydia would ever willingly wear, but it was still far *less* revealing than a lot of what the other women had donned for the evening.

Lydia felt ridiculous and self-conscious. It didn't help that every time she passed a small group of people, they would go quiet and watch her as she went by.

Well, Aon had warned her. This was a political move on his part to show everyone she was okay. No bruises, no cuts, all limbs accounted for. Maybe she could down a few glasses of wine and find a dark corner to wedge herself and spend the night ignoring everyone and everything.

"Lydia!"

There went that idea.

But when she looked up, she smiled to see a familiar face, even if it was hidden under part of a mask. "Gary?" She laughed in disbelief as the man walked up and hugged her. He was wearing a deep purple suit and a matching tie with a black shirt underneath. He looked fantastic, and she said as much to him.

"Thank you." He did a twirl for her. The man was still so endearing. "A far cry away from the foolish professor, I must say. And you look phenomenal."

Smiling, she looked away sheepishly. "I feel ridiculous."

"Pah. Hardly. But more importantly, are you all right, my friend?" He picked up one of her hands in both of his. "Lord Maverick told me you were here, and I... well."

"Well, what?"

"I expected to see you in a far sorrier state. If you were here at all, we all expected you would be... on display."

The way he said it made her stomach turn. It had been completely possible that Aon could have chosen to string her up like a Christmas goose and lay her out on a table. "It's been fine, honestly. Aon is... super intense, but he hasn't hurt me." Now that she had to say it out loud, it sank in. He really hadn't.

"I have heard tell he is a sadist and a madman." Lowering his voice, he glanced around to see if anyone had come near them. "I have been worried sick over what he might be doing to you."

"I know he's both." She shrugged. "But he hasn't pointed that in my direction yet at least. Honestly, he's treating me better than Edu did."

"Edu isn't a liar. He's honest, in all things he does. Aon is not. He is duplicitous and manipulative. Please, be careful."

"I'm doing my best." Lydia tried to smile reassuringly. "For what it's worth."

Gary looked up as someone called him from across the room. He squeezed her hand tightly before letting it go. "I must go. But it was good to see you."

She was sad to say goodbye to Gary and watch him walk away. It was nice to have someone to talk to, at least for a moment. Now that he was gone, she was left to the staring crowd. With a sigh, she wandered into the ballroom.

It was enormous, large enough to fit throngs of people. It appeared well over a hundred guests were gathered around the edges alone. The ceiling arched high overhead in an awe-inspiring display of twisting and asymmetrical architecture. At the end of the room was a massive stained-glass window, stretching up fifty or sixty feet.

In the center of it was a seven-pointed star, angled down. At each point was a colored circle that seemed to glow from its own source of light. Red, black, blue, purple, white, and green. The seventh was... missing. Blocked out with a disk of metal. Again, a missing color.

She'd have to ask Aon about that, the next chance she had.

The music sounded like someone had put an opera singer, a chamber ensemble, and a heavy metal band onto the same tour bus and stranded them in the Arctic for a year. The singer bounced back and forth between classical opera and the sharp-edged tone of a rock star. An electric guitar was playing chords and progressions usually reserved for a Spanish guitarist.

It was eerie, it was strange, and it was morbid. Most importantly, like everything else here in Aon's estate, it was dramatic and theatrical. It was over-the-top and bizarre, and in the context of everything else, it seemed to all flow together.

And like the rest of his aesthetic, somehow, it worked.

Lydia could see Edu towering over the crowd by one wall, leaning against the decor. In his far more rustic getup that looked like it belonged to a Viking warlord, he looked very out of place.

A hand touched her arm, and Lydia nearly jumped a foot in the air. When she turned, she blinked. "K... Kaori?" Lydia hardly recognized the girl. She was wearing all red. Well, barely. The dress was little more than a series of straps over the top half, and a concession at something resembling a skirt on the bottom. She had a red mark emblazoned on her face, and she had a broad, bright smile right there alongside it.

"Hi! I wanted to just say hello. Now that I know how to." Kaori giggled.

Right. The people of Under could speak all languages.

"It's good to see you." Lydia was starting to get jealous of all these happy people who belonged. "You look good."

"I feel great." Kaori beamed. "This world is fantastic, isn't it?"

The girl wasn't afraid. In the few hours Lydia had known her, Kaori had spent all of it balled up in fear. Now she was bright-eyed and looked unafraid of anything. And judging by the faint bruises she saw on the girl's arms in the rough shape of hands, she'd found out how she liked to enjoy herself.

Lydia was happy for her, in a weird way. "Sure. More for you guys than me, I guess."

"Yeah." Kaori sighed before suddenly snapping her fingers. "Oh! I wanted to tell you that Nick wound up in the House of the shapeshifters. They aren't allowed indoors when the moons are full. He'll be outside."

Lydia's heart bloomed in hope. Nick!

"He's such a nice boy. I can't wait until Kamira lets him loose." Kaori flashed her a predatory grin. "Although, a leash suits him well."

Shoving those visuals in the back of her mind, she thanked Kaori and excused herself to head out to the gardens. It was nice to be outside. The cold touch of air on her face was a far cry from the heat of the crowds, and it was a very welcome change.

The twisting topiaries and hedge mazes of Aon's gardens were stunning. It was a well-maintained work of art that she could wander for days, finding strange statues and odd fountains. The plant life was both familiar and foreign, and she suspected a lot of it was deadly and poisonous.

She decided to take a look-don't-touch approach with just about everything here in Under. And that included the more human-looking denizens.

A pack of people gathered toward the center, so she made her way there. When she walked up, she saw a familiar figure leaning against a stone column that was placed as a decorative piece. He was wearing all white, which was only a shade lighter than his skin or his hair. Or the marble statues around him.

Lydia was surprisingly happy to see him. "Hey, Lyon." Only then did she realize he wasn't standing there alone. The other person blended in surprisingly well against the hedge wall behind her.

"How fare you, Ms. Lydia?" Lyon's placid expression shifted to a smile as she approached. He was standing next to a woman that Lydia recognized from the night of the Fall. She wore a long green loincloth and seemed to don a few more pieces of decorative chains than the last time. And she had a tail that swished around behind her like a cat. *Shapeshifters,* she reminded herself dutifully. *What did you think that meant?*

"I'm okay, I think. About as good as can be expected." She suddenly felt a little shy. The woman with the tail had piercing green eyes, slit like a cat's. It was intense, to say the least, the way the woman was watching her as if putting her under a microscope. As if just by glaring alone, she could unearth all of Lydia's secrets.

"Better than expected, I should say. You have all your limbs accounted for." The shapeshifter held out her hand to Lydia. "I am Kamira, Elder of the House of Moons."

The elder of the House Nick had Fallen into. Lydia reached out and shook the woman's hand. Her grip was strong, which wasn't a surprise. Lydia did her best to smile warmly. "A pleasure. I'm—"

"I know," the woman interrupted with a smirk. Kamira dropped her hand and returned to where she was leaning up against Lyon. The gesture was far too familiar to just be friendly. Huh. Well, good for him.

"I'm looking for Nick." She gestured to the crowd. "I was wondering where he was? I was told he was out here."

"He will be happy to see you. You are all he has spoken of. He wished to charge in to see you, but we generally aren't 'allowed' indoors, as if the warlocks could stop us." Kamira offered a nonchalant shrug. "But we are not fond of buildings, with or without such restrictions. Come." Kamira walked away, leading her and Lyon farther from the estate.

The gardens were decked out for the party just as lavishly as the interior. If there were a whole House not allowed inside, that would explain why. There was a small pack of people standing about the center of the garden maze. The plaza was dominated by a large fountain depicting monsters and demons, twisted about each other in a confusing and tangled mess. Some were the prey, some were the hunters, and some were both.

Perched atop the fountain was a creature with long, spindly limbs and wings. It had dish-like ears and a stunted muzzle. It was a giant, humanoid bat.

It wasn't the only strange monster in the courtyard either.

Another one looked like it may have been half panther. Another resembled a dog crossed with a lizard. "These are my people." Kamira flashed a sharp grin at Lydia's wide-eyed expression.

It was one thing to hear monsters like this existed; it was another thing to see them. There were people gathered about as well, drinking and laughing. Some had horns, or tails, or wings, and claws or canted legs like a beast. Some had several at once. As she stood there and watched, one of the massive creatures by the edges moved, and in mid-stride, changed its form to that of a human to grab a drink from a passing waiter.

"Lyd?"

Oh, thank God! Lydia threw herself into the arms of the person who raced toward her. She knew him on sight, even if he was wearing a weird collection of scraps of leather for clothing and had a wooden mask covering over a third of his face. "Nick!" She almost wept with joy.

Lyon tugged on Kamira's arm, and the two walked away, leaving Lydia and Nick alone.

"You're okay! You're okay. Oh, fuck, I've been so worried..." Nick was squeezing her tight and had his head buried into her shoulder. "I tried to come, but they chained me up, and they wouldn't listen—"

"It's all right, I understand. It's just so good to see you." She held him tight and tried to keep tears from escaping.

Finally, he let go of her to move back half a step, resting his hands on her shoulders. "Holy shit, Lyd. You look, um, you clean up okay." Nick laughed.

It was still Nick. Unable to simply compliment somebody. He, meanwhile, was bruised and scraped up. There was a red and purple ring around his neck from where something had been cinched there. "And you look like shit. What happened?"

"I'm learning. It's hard. But I'm getting there."

"I figured you'd wind up a servant." She reached up and

tapped her finger on the wooden mask on his face. From the looks of things, he had quite a few marks to cover.

He snorted and shrugged. "Yeah, well, I guess I'm worthwhile to somebody, finally. Lyd, I went into that pool, and suddenly everything made sense. Everything. I can't explain it. It's like... I finally know who I am. I finally know where I belong. And people here? They look at me, and for the first time in my entire goddamn life, I feel like I matter."

Gary had found purpose. Kaori had found freedom. Nick had found value. Lydia had found a living nightmare. She was proud of him, but for the second time that night, a little jealous. "I'm glad you're doing okay, man."

"I'm doing great. This place is pretty wild when you get used to it. Have you seen Kaori? Shit. Do you think I'm allowed to howl at women now?" He snickered, then quickly changed the subject, seeing the look on her face. "How're you? I heard about what happened between you and Edu, and now... you're here. I've heard Aon is a major asshole. But, I mean, you can't be doing too badly." He looked down at her and smirked cheekily.

She slapped her palm on his chest. "Asshole."

"Yeah. But seriously, how are you?" Nick insisted.

"I'm terrified. I'm afraid every second someone's going to tear my arms off."

He stepped in and hugged her again. "I've heard the warlock is nuts. Has he hurt you?"

"No." She had to admit it out loud again. Aon wasn't mistreating her. Not really. "He's just... a bit much. But this whole world is a bit much."

"Understatement of the year."

"You all belong here now." She wrapped her arms around him and let her head rest on his shoulder. "You've all found something here. I... I know I'm going to die. It's just a matter of when and what gets me first."

"I know." He was always such shit at comforting people. He wasn't ever one for platitudes or making people feel better. It was still the same guy. Still her best friend. Somehow, that broke her heart even worse.

"My lady," someone interrupted them. A servant dressed in all black bowed before her. "Master Aon wishes to speak with you."

"Speaking of." She sighed.

"See you soon." Nick shoved her shoulder in a familiar gesture, although he had to know neither of them could say that for sure.

She could only smile at him weakly as she walked away and followed the servant through the gardens and back inside Aon's grand estate. Up the flight of stairs, and they returned to the ballroom.

The King of Shadows stood by a small group of people dressed in white, blue, purple, and red, each listening to him speak with interest. He was wearing a black tuxedo that looked as though it dated from the turn of the century. His long black hair was tied to the back of his neck in a ponytail, although some strands escaped and fell along the sides of his black metal mask. It was impressive how imposing he could be, even in a situation like this.

As she approached, all eyes went to her. Holy hell, she hated that sensation.

Aon turned to her with an "ah!" and excused himself from speaking to the others. "My dear, you look absolutely... ravishing. Did you have a moment to meet with your friends?"

"I did. It meant a lot to get a chance to see them all." She forced herself to smile. "I don't know if you had anything to do with it, but if you did, thank you."

He bowed his head. "I thought perhaps it might give you some peace of mind."

The song had wound itself down to a close, and there was a

round of polite applause from both the dancers and the onlookers as the couples bowed to each other and moved from the floor.

He lifted his hand, palm up, interrupting her thoughts. He offered her his gloved hand, and not the clawed prosthetic. "I wondered if you might dance with me."

"I, uh—" She stammered uselessly. "I don't know how to dance at all. Like, literally, at all." The idea of dancing in front of everyone made her feel as though she were standing on the edge of a cliff. "I'm going to just embarrass you."

"It will not be a problem, I promise you." He sounded deeply amused. "Take my hand, and none will be the wiser."

People were watching the scene unfold with interest. She swallowed nervously. This was why she never signed up for drama class; she hated being on stage. One woman was leaning into another woman at her side, whispering.

"If a teapot starts singing, I'm out," she muttered. He wouldn't get the joke, but it didn't matter.

He was, once again, patiently waiting for her. The musicians were even watching them, wondering if their king would take to the dance floor.

She realized everyone—quite literally *everyone*—was holding on for her response.

"*Shit*," she bit through her teeth before putting her hand in his.

"It will be fine, my dear." He closed his fingers around her and gently led her out to the floor.

"Oh God." She tried not to be sick from nerves.

"A flattering nickname, I must say," he teased. "Tell me, is that what you will pick, were I to make you cry out in a moment of bliss?"

It was so blunt, so direct, that her face lit up like fire. "I'm not even going to respond to that. It was a cheap shot to see my face turn colors."

Chuckling, he took her to the center of the floor. "And it worked."

The other dancers filled in around them. At least they wouldn't be there by themselves.

When he curled his hand along her lower back, she placed her hand on his upper arm. Oh, hell, she was nervous. "What kind of dance is this going to be?"

"If you do not know how, does it matter?"

"Touché."

The music began. It was a classical chamber ensemble lead-in played by an electric guitar. It was a bizarre combination. It was met with chords from a harpsichord at the same time the singer began to sing in a language she didn't understand.

With that, they began to move. He was leading her, and she really had nothing to do with it.

She should be terrified. She should be locked solid. She should be a staggering mess, even if he knew what he was doing. Somehow, she stepped along with him in time to the arching and theatrical minor key combination of heavy metal and opera.

"Now, is this so bad?" He was teasing her again as they gracefully spun through the sea of twisting colors of the figures around them.

She felt as though all of this was some strange nightmare. "I guess not, but—" Her words were cut off as he twirled her in time with the music, and when she returned, their bodies were nearly touching as he pulled her in tighter.

Instead of going taut, instead of pressing away from him, her hand was now against the back of his shoulder. She hadn't put it there.

She hadn't been doing any of this.

It took her an embarrassingly long time to realize she wasn't in control of her actions or of her body and the way she was moving.

Aon was.

"You're doing this." Her eyes went wide. "You're controlling me again."

"Of course. Is this not how your people dance in your world?" The false innocence was thick in his words. "Every partner upon this dance floor has surrendered control to the other. One to the other, in equal, knowing, harmless, and temporary submission. It is how we dance in Under. Is this not better? More graceful?"

"Stop it."

"Is this not what dancing is at the core? Willful surrender to another?" He was terribly proud of himself; she could tell by his tone. "At least in *our* world, it must not always be the man who leads."

"Stop it," she ground out between her teeth.

"Oh? Which? The music or my control over you?"

"Either. Both."

"One would disappoint the other dancers, and the other would make you a fumbling mess. You could break this spell if you truly wished to do so. It is a parlor trick, nothing more. You are strong-willed. If you want to plant your feet and go no farther, do it."

She stayed silent and glared at him, even as they continued to dance.

"Go ahead, then, free yourself of my command and see the result." When she still didn't answer, Aon chuckled. "Of course, you do not wish to do so, for you would become a staggering embarrassment. I see how you hate being the center of attention. You would rather be my temporary puppet than be laughed at by the others."

She growled but couldn't deny it. The last thing she wanted now was to trip all over herself. Even if she could break herself of his control, she suddenly didn't want to. But it was his fault for putting her in this situation. "This isn't a game."

"Isn't it? This is a harmless dance. You are in control of your own mind. I have merely borrowed you for the duration of a song. There are fifty other people around us doing the same. Is that so offensive?"

"Yes. Yes, it is. This isn't okay. You know that, right?"

"I fear I do not." Strands of his long black hair brushed against her face. "You relinquished control the moment you took my hand."

"I didn't know this is how you people dance." She tried to keep her voice down as best she could. "That isn't my fault."

"Nor is it mine. If I am to be held liable for all you do not know, the magnitude of my crime would be beyond comprehension."

"Now you're insulting me? Great. You're not doing this for any other reason but to watch me squirm." She glared at him, even as they continued their bizarre dance.

"I am doing this for many reasons, my sweet. Do not presume so quickly to understand my motives." His quiet air of a threat rumbled in his chest, enough that she could feel it even more than she heard it. "You willingly approached me and took my hand, an act witnessed by all in attendance. You are unharmed. Unbruised. Unmaimed. Any concerns the others may have that you are my weeping, tormented prisoner are now suitably assuaged."

Her leg was suddenly around his, hooking onto Aon as he dipped her backward. He was doing it to taunt her, and it made anger and fear in equal parts tangle around in her stomach and vie for supremacy.

When he tilted her back up, her body was pressed flush against his. "Yet," he rumbled in his chest again, "I will admit I am deeply enjoying this for other reasons as well." The music had stopped, and he held her against him tightly. She could feel the warmth of his body through his tuxedo, and it made her hold her breath.

All at once, he released her.

She felt the ability to control her own body snap back over her like a light switch. Taking a step back, she curled her hands into fists.

That asshole!

She wanted to shout at him or to slap him, but that would likely only succeed in ensuring he cut off her hand.

"Careful..." He warned, seeing the look of wild-eyed anger etched on her face.

The desire to punch him didn't fade. "Don't come near me."

"Be wary. This was not an insult to your pride. This was merely a necessary political demonstration." He tilted his head back just barely—the words haughty and imperious—the words of a king.

His tone was what turned her red-hot anger into cold, seething hatred. Lydia let out a small, disingenuous laugh. So, that was how this was going to be. Fine. *Fine.*

Lydia stepped into him and lifted onto her toes to put her head close to his. He bowed his head in response, eager to hear what she was going to say. "Ever since I came here, I've heard about what kind of a monster you are. The liar, the sadist, the manipulator, the disgusting fiend. I wanted to take a moment to thank you... for proving them right."

She took a step back and turned from him without another glance. If she did, she'd lose control of her temper again. Keeping her steps even, she made sure she didn't storm out or make a scene. She was going to go back to her own room, lock the door—for what good it would do—and contemplate hanging herself from the bed's canopy with a sheet.

Passing a waiter, Lydia snagged the bottle of wine out of his startled hands. She didn't care at this point. She was strung halfway between anger and tears and needed to get away from it all. From the garish decor, the lavish party, the strange music, and from Aon. From all of them.

But mostly from Aon.

"Ms. Lydia, wait—" someone called after her.

She stopped walking but didn't turn around. She knew the voice already. "Leave me alone, Lyon. Please."

The sound of footsteps behind her slowed to a stop. "Tread carefully with Master Aon..."

"I don't care anymore!" Lydia whirled to glare at the Priest. "Everything in my life is gone. Everything. All I have left is myself, and he wants to prove he can take that away from me too. I don't care if he's angry. Let him kill me. Let him torture me. I thought—" She clenched her fist at her side as she choked up and felt tears threaten to fall again. No, she wanted to cry in privacy, not in front of the tall, pale statue of a man. *I thought I was just starting to catch my footing. I thought I was just starting to find a baseline. I thought he wasn't what people made him out to be.* "I was wrong."

Lyon shut his eyes and hung his head, and for all intents and purposes, he might have been a cemetery angel, weeping over the grave of some damned and forgotten soul. And chances were, to him, she was.

She resumed her retreat to her room and made it there without any other interruption. Shutting the door behind her, she threw the bolt and leaned her back against it.

Finally, then, she let herself release a cry of frustration and anger. She punched the wall, hard enough to jar her wrist and send a sting of pain up through her arm. That had been the point. It was wonderfully cathartic, and she let out a wavering sigh.

Walking into the room, she took a swig from the bottle of wine, then put it down on a table by the door. She wanted out of this stupid dress. She wanted to get trashed and sit on the floor and cry.

She made it about two steps before a hand twisted in her hair and yanked her head back hard.

"Ignorant child," a voice seethed next to her head. Aon. "You think to presume that you have suffered? That you know the depths of my cruelty because we *danced?* You become too bold. Let me correct your assumptions. Let me show you whose mercy you truly enjoy!" He laughed harshly, and the world shifted around under her feet.

It felt like that gateway from Earth to Under all over again. Everything ripped around her like physics itself had conceded in a fight. Her stomach lurched dangerously as the sense of movement came to a halt as quickly as it had begun.

He threw her to the ground, and she fell painfully, barely able to catch herself on her hands before she impacted it at full force. When she landed, it was not on a lavishly tapestried carpet, but rough stone. The air smelled damp and carried the tang of spilled blood. That and the mix of a scent like acid stung her nose.

"See now what you could suffer at my whim. Look upon my work with despair."

A hand in her hair yanked her back up to standing and threw her forward. She staggered blindly and caught herself on a table. It rocked with the impact. It took her a solid few seconds to truly understand what she was looking at.

Evie.

Oh God. Evie.

The girl was strapped to a table, a wooden gag shoved in her mouth and viciously held onto her head with tightly cinched leather straps. Her lips were chapped and broken and looked as though they had already been chewed past the point of bleeding. Her eyes were pale, glassy, and unseeing.

Her skin was a ghastly shade of pale blue. Lydia knew what a dead body looked like. But dead bodies didn't whimper like Evie was. Thick needles that looked more like they were meant for horses than humans were fed deep into her body, maybe a half dozen in total. The skin around the needles was purple and blue in harsh bruises where they dug into her arms, her legs, and one looked as though it fed directly into her heart. At the back end of each needle was a glass tube attached to a hose that trailed off to a machine next to the table.

The machine let out a *click* as it turned on with a timer. It whirred and came to life. There was a horrifying suction noise as Evie screamed into the gag and thrashed in pain. The glass tubes at the backs of the needles filled with blood. Or at least some blood. There should be more than that...

Unless it had already been taken.

Evie had been here for days, after all.

There was another whirring sound, and it took her a moment to realize Evie's left arm was trapped inside another machine. It was a series of needles at strange angles. It looked almost like a sewing machine and a tattoo gun had a deviant child. That machine, Lydia recognized.

It was the one she had helped Aon thread the previous night. At the back of the apparatus was a vial of purple liquid, and it was stitching black thread into her skin. The thread oozed with the same color of violet that was in the tube.

The machine was creating small marks. The same language of the Ancients. Stitching into her skin like the girl was a living quilt.

Aon's hand was in Lydia's hair again and yanked her head backward. He was at her back, keeping her pinned between him and the table on which Evie was strapped. "This is my work! This is why the others fear me. For I can take the marks from their flesh as I see fit. I have drained from her the pure and saturated source of her power she previously bore and am now attempting to stitch new ones back onto her."

"Why?" Lydia struggled, but Aon was too strong. He

wrenched her head painfully in response, and she let out a cry and stopped fighting before he snapped her neck.

"Such is the goal of my work. I seek to learn to bestow marks at my discretion. And your friend here... has become another part of my experiments." The metal of his mask touched her cheek as he pressed in tighter to her. "Do you see how she suffers? Isn't it quite beautiful?"

"Stop, please—"

"No! Not until you understand how much of a fool you are! She has lain here, like this, as part of my experiments since you decided to run from Edu. You live lavishly in my home, every need cared for and a guest at my ball. Yet you think yourself *mistreated*? Bah!" He threw her head forward, almost doubling her over the table, as he stormed away from her, growling in his throat. "It was a game, nothing more. What she suffers is far from the childish imposition I paid you."

Lydia made it about one pull on a leather strap to release Evie before she was suddenly on the ground, the wind nearly knocked out of her. Aon stood over her, his fists clenched, towering over her prone form. He was a terrifying thing from a nightmare, cast in stark shadows in the dim light. "Audacious creature..."

"Let her go," Lydia begged as she pulled herself back up to standing. "Please."

"No. Our work is not yet done." He pointed back at the machine with his metal-clawed hand. It glinted in the dim light. "You wound the thread that mutilates her. You have a hand in her suffering, same as I do."

Tears ran down from Lydia's eyes unchecked. She didn't care at this point. "Let me take her place."

He let out one loud burst of laughter and shook his head. "Worthless. You would die in an instant, and even if you did not, you have no power for me to wield."

The suction began again, and Evie screamed, muffled into the gag, the scream ending in a broken sob. With it, Aon turned his back on Lydia and moved to go back to the table as if to inspect his work.

Lydia stepped in between them, making him pull up his steps as she did. "Let her go, please..."

"No."

There was nothing she could do. And as loathe as she was to admit it, Aon was right. She'd lived as his guest for the past week. What he'd done in the dance hall was nothing compared to what he was doing to Evie. The dance had only been Aon toying with her for political gain. It was a game to him. This was not.

Something in her broke at that thought. Something in her just gave up. "I'll do whatever you want. Anything. Just, please, I can't let her stay like this..."

A clawed finger curled under her chin, lifting her face to meet his masked one. All the anger in his voice was gone, and instead there was a strange quiet intensity. "Anything, you say. Tell me, what do you have that I could want?"

"I don't know." The admission hurt as much as whatever had broken in her enough to say it.

He stepped into her, narrowing the distance between them, calling her bluff and testing her commitment to her words. She wavered but held her ground. "If I commanded you to undress, to give yourself to me, would you do it...?"

"Yes." Lydia meant it.

"You would *kneel* before me, to spare another's suffering?" he pondered. When Lydia tried to turn away, his clawed hand shifted to clasp her chin and pull her back to him. Firm, but not forceful. "How charmingly selfless." With a sudden shove from him, she wound up between him and the table once more. "And how utterly wasted."

"I won't let her stay like this."

"You have no say in the matter. You are powerless."

Yet again, Aon was right. There wasn't anything Lydia could do. If he locked her away, she could only claw at the doors until her hands bled. Still, how could she have any hope of freeing Evie? There was an odd sort of calm that came along with the realization of how utterly helpless she was.

"Then just kill me, please." She looked down at his shoes.

"Oh, do not be so *melodramatic*." He sighed and stepped into her. This time, Lydia didn't withdraw from him, and just shut her eyes as he slipped up to her. "You do not mean those words."

"Don't I?"

"I fear I am not allowed to take a life, by law. But shall I go fetch Edu, then? He will gladly take you up on your offer."

She cringed and, squeezing her eyes shut, lowered her head. Once more, he was right. Once more, he had her backed—literally and figuratively—into a corner.

"You do not wish to die." Sharp claws drifted down along the neckline of the dress, drifting along the swell of her bust and toward the center. They turned north to trace the edge of the necklace she wore, and it felt like knives were running over her skin.

His hand curled around the back of her neck, settling there, with his thumb at the side, pressing against her thudding heartbeat. "If I wished to kill you, I would have found the means. If I wished you to suffer, you would be. If I wanted to see you a broken, empty-eyed creature bent to my every whim... I could have it. I desire none of this."

She didn't open her eyes. She couldn't look at the nightmare before her. She just couldn't. "Then what do you want?"

She felt the touch of a metal mask against her cheek, and his mouth was close to her ear. "Can you concede that, while you feel dutifully insulted, you have not been truly wronged by me?" he whispered. "That my game was cruel, but that you are unharmed? That your insults were born of indignant anger and a sense of disrespect, not of honest hate?"

She nodded, unable to find the words in her throat which felt like she had swallowed a ball of cotton and it had become stuck there.

"Can you come to admit that you are my guest, and enjoy my protection, and that you are not my mistreated prisoner?"

She nodded weakly again.

"Perhaps... I should not have played so viciously with you in public. I was thinking only of how it would benefit me, and how delightful you would look when you realized what I had done."

"I want to go home."

"This is your home now, Lydia."

The truth of it drew a choked sound out of her. She desperately tried not to cry in front of Aon. But tears slipped down her cheeks regardless. She managed to keep the sobbing at bay at least.

He wrapped his arms around her slowly, pulling her into an embrace. It was a hug, and he ran his gloved hand up and down over her back. As if he was really trying to console her.

"The girl will be set free immediately." His words were a whisper into her ear again. "Pardoned of all crimes. She shall live on the outskirts, free of a House or a master. She shall have all this, but know that you *owe* me. You owe me a favor, and someday, I will call upon it." The machine clicked off, and she heard Evie weep, muffled and agonized.

There was a sensation of motion again as the world melted around her, and when they reformed, she would have fallen if it weren't for his arms still being wrapped around her. He had brought them back to her room.

He stepped away from her, and when he spoke, his voice

was no longer angry or intense but jovial and casual as if nothing had happened. "Good night, Lydia. I must attend to my guests. I will see you tomorrow, as per usual." He bowed, and with that, was gone in a blink.

Lydia sank to the carpet and cried.

NINE

Lyon dropped to one knee, bowing his head before the man on the giant wooden throne before him. Fires crackled and burned in metal cauldrons, casting the room in dramatic flickering light.

Even if Edu was no longer the reigning king, he was still royalty and Lyon's superior.

"Please rise, Lyon." Ylena's crimson lips upturned in a kind smile from where she stood beside the throne. "Lord Edu scolds you for such deference. You know it is not necessary."

Lyon stood, brushing some soot from his white pants. "Old habits, my lord."

The massive man in question was reclined on his carved wooden throne that depicted a valiant war—scores of dragons tangled about each other, roaring their eternal and silent battle cries.

Edu rubbed a hand along the underside of his chin, scratching the stubble of a beard that was just visible under the lip of his mask. "Lord Edu wonders after your opinion of last night's affairs."

An odd request. Lyon kept his quizzical response from

showing on his features. Keeping a placid expression was both his gift and his curse. But, perhaps the king's curiosity was due to the fact that Edu had never attended one of Aon's galas before. Edu had always been asleep in his crypt when it had historically been held. "I did not note anything out of the ordinary. Whispers and politics, perhaps, but little else."

"Have you ever known Aon to... dance?" The disgust was thick in Ylena's words, removed as it was from who had urged her to speak them.

Lyon could not help but furrow his brow. What, precisely, was Edu after? What was his goal? Aon's behavior with Lydia was strange, yes. But the warlock was a madman, and men of such natures were, by definition, unpredictable. Especially when given a rare bauble such as a mortal prisoner.

Edu certainly knew this. The warrior king knew the warlock better than anyone else, alive or dead. There was no question the King of Flames still heavily suspected the girl of being a part of some deep and dangerous plot that circled around Aon and likely still desired her death.

While Lyon did not wish the girl to die, he was sympathetic to the concern, nonetheless. "Why do you ask?"

"Please answer the question, Priest." Ylena's tone was strained.

Lyon had no doubt the king had not used such gentle language, judging by his body language. He knew the empath often worked to soften the man's behavior in translation.

"I have not seen him dance with a partner before at one of these events, no." Measuring his words carefully, Lyon continued after a pause. "He is toying with the girl. It is plain to see that she is caught on his strings. I believe, as well, he wished to demonstrate she was alive, unharmed, and under relatively little duress, considering the circumstances."

Edu looked off, debating Lyon's explanation of events.

"The girl Evelyn has been pardoned of crimes and released, has she not?" Ylena asked.

"Yes." Lyon was surprised at the swift change in subject matter. It meant something else was moving behind the scenes, and Lyon was not happy for his own unwitting part in it.

"Why?"

Lyon could only shake his head in an admission that he did not know. Why the girl had been freed in the midst of the event and shuttled off by Aon's servants, he could not say. He had a suspicion that Lydia might have had a hand in it—but for Aon to show mercy to a prisoner at the behest of another was... strange. And to Edu, it would be cause for war.

"Where is she now?" Ylena asked for her king.

Lyon shook his head again. "I do not know, my lord, forgive me."

"Master Edu wishes you to discover her location and report it back to him." The woman in crimson barely moved as she spoke. Her long, straight, black hair cut a sharp contrast to her flowing crimson dress and matching mask.

"What of Master Aon?" Lyon wondered if it was his fate to always be betwixt the King of Shadows and King of Flames in their games. "Such inquiries will raise his suspicion."

"Lord Edu cares not for Aon's suspicions, any more than he cares for anything else of the man." Anger cracked Ylena's voice briefly. Her response flared in time with the clench of one of Edu's fists. She managed to temper herself before continuing to speak, her voice turning calm once more. "He has no claim over the girl now that she is freed of her crimes. She belongs to Maverick's House, and her continued existence is a matter for the Elder of Words. Lord Edu is insistent that you do as he has asked."

"Yes, my king." Lyon folded a hand in front of his waist and bowed. It was clear Edu was dismissing him now, and he turned to walk from the room.

Was he now subject to the whim of two kings? Should he tell Aon what Edu had bidden he do? What manner of war would that bring? No, that was out of the question. Lyon's mood darkened accordingly as he realized the state he was now in. Were he still the elder of his House, this would not be the case, but he had given that up a long time ago.

Lyon was at the mercy of them *both* now.

Ancients preserve him.

* * *

What a bucket of misery.

Just the entire thing. The whole thing was a giant, rusty tub of depressing, and Lydia was wallowing in it.

She had taken up sitting in the thick windowsill of one of the large, arching windows in her room. It overlooked the gardens below, and she could see the hedge maze in its entirety from up here. The fountain in the middle was glinting in the light of the several moons that soared overhead.

It was, if the clock was to be believed, two in the afternoon. It was funny that Under used the same system to measure time as Earth, but as everyone here had once been a human, she supposed it made a little sense.

Lydia had been sitting there for hours. All damn day, actually. The windows had interior wooden pocket shutters, and when she leaned her head back against them where they folded away, they clicked against each other.

Her mind would not stop retracing the events of last night. Going over it all, again and again, rethinking every second, every word, every decision. Each time she went through it, she hoped she'd remember something new to help her resolve her turmoil. No luck.

It had been fantastic to see Nick. He was a... were-some-thing-or-other now. If his mask was any indication, he was relatively high up in the ranks. He had finally found somewhere people would see him as having value. It was a far cry from the life of an internet junkie and entry-level security guard. As weird as it was for her, she was happy for him. She was honestly glad he had finally found somewhere he fit in, even if it was as a were-whatever.

But it just... felt weird.

Like she was being left behind, somehow.

Because I am.

After hour six or seven, she had enough. She needed some fresh air. Needed to get out. Even if it was only to the hedge maze below, she didn't care. She threw on a thigh-length black coat she found in the wardrobe and struck out into the estate. She was beginning to know her way around, and it wasn't long before she stepped out into the chill air. It felt terrific, and she let out a sigh of relief as she headed down into the maze.

Maybe wandering in circles would help her clear her mind.

It reminded her of the Public Gardens in Boston, with rows of statues and carefully maintained plants, all meticulously arranged as if to be viewed from high above. It was funny that it mattered so much what the gardens looked like from higher than the average viewer would ever see it, and yet she could tell by the twisting walkways that it was a work of art. Winding and asymmetrical, as was everything else in Aon's home, but with a definite purpose.

Three moons glowed overhead, blue, white, and green. It painted everything in a teal hue that was beautiful, if eerie. The plants here clearly only needed the light of the moons to live and flourish. She'd never seen anything like the plants on display, and like everything in Under, they looked distinctly dangerous.

Look, don't touch.

The statues stood like cemetery angels, dotted in the darkness, catching the reflections of overhead moons, like lonely guardians caught in poses both stoic and horrific. She reached the colossal fountain she saw the night prior at the gala where the House of Moons had come to hang out. It was genuinely fascinating to her that all the famous monster myths had been born out of this place. Vampires, warlocks, werewolves, witches, who knew what else?

What other great monsters were inspired by the creatures of Under? Dragons? Sea monsters? Fairies?

Warlocks. Aon.

She winced at the memory of what had happened between them. He'd taken advantage of her—in as harmless a fashion as that man might be capable, but he'd done it, nonetheless—and she had lost her temper. Then she learned what a *real* temper looked like.

Oh God. Poor Evie.

She had been wandering the hedge maze for an hour now, maybe longer. She didn't really care. It wasn't like she had anything better to do. Like hell if she was going to wander into Aon's library at this point. There was no telling where they stood now after last night's altercation.

It was after another half hour of mulling over her own misery that she heard something rustle from behind her. Turning, there was nothing there. It was the first time since coming out here that she suddenly felt unsafe.

Maybe I should head back...

As if on cue, there was a growl at her back. Whirling around the second time, she saw the same result—nothing.

Yep. Time to go back inside.

Quickly, she headed around a corner to head back the way she came. Pulling up sharply, she could only stare. There was no path there. Just an alcove with a statue looming over her.

No. No, she had definitely come down this way. She *knew* it!

Another growl from the darkness, and she didn't have time

to debate the impossibility of her exit being blocked. Turning, she went the other direction from the demonic rumble, walking quickly while trying to hide her sudden fear. She wouldn't run. Whatever was there might be spurred on by that.

A right, a left, and another right, and she found herself right back where she started ten minutes before.

She gaped. The statue in front of her was unmistakable. It was a man with a spear through his chest, and he was clinging to it in both agony and joy. A half mask sat at his knees. This was the exact same statue from before.

The growl near her broke her out of her debate, and this time, she ran. Left, right, straight, left, straight, another right, and—

The same statue.

This isn't possible! But she was in a world of monsters. Of myths and magic. She was trapped in a hedge maze that reminded her more and more of something from the Red Queen's palace in *Alice in Wonderland.* Maybe—just *maybe*—her being lost wasn't her fault.

The maze itself might be to blame. It was moving. It was alive.

And it was being a dick.

This time, when she heard the creature snarling, she turned and caught sight of it. It blotted out one end of the maze. It looked like ink splattered onto the world, black tendrils writhing and stretching out toward her. Its shadow moved out of sync with its body as though they were two separate monsters. It was reaching across the ground as if the source of light that was casting the shadow was changing.

Instinctively, throwing caution to the wind, she screamed and ran. Tore away at full tilt, running for her life. The thing was going to do something awful, and she didn't need to know what. This time she went right, straight, left, straight... and came across the same statue.

Letting out a sob of hopelessness, she just kept running. Now the creature was nipping at her heels, chasing her through the maze. Each time she went to turn one way or the other, the nightmare creature was there, blocking her path. It had too many limbs. Its shadow was reaching ever closer to her, eldritch and horrible.

In an ill-timed move, she stepped on its shadow while attempting to flee from it.

It snapped around her ankle and tripped her, dragging her painfully to the ground.

She struggled and fought as it began pulling her across the cobblestone ground toward its shadowy mass, screaming for help. But she knew no one would answer.

The monster didn't even look as though it could possibly be grabbing her, merely that she was cast in its shadow.

Kicking and fighting as hard as she could, she managed to break free of the tendril that had caught her. Scrambling up to her feet, she ran once more, fleeing as fast and hard as she could.

For what little good it did.

She was in a dead end.

The hedgerow ended abruptly in front of her. Her heart sank into her stomach, and she let out a whimper of fear.

"Boo."

Whirling, she didn't even realize what she had done until she had kneed the person behind her squarely in the gut. The figure in all black let out a surprised and pained *unf* as her flight response turned into fight, if only for a moment. Cornered and terrified, she ran past the figure without even stopping to think about what had happened. Panic consumed her.

A sharp-edged laugh was at her back as she found the nearest corner and turned.

Stairs.

She hadn't been expecting stairs.

Her foot left the top row, and it wasn't until the ground

was rushing abruptly up toward her face that it even occurred to her that anything was wrong.

Something impacted her from behind as she tumbled toward the ground. The world was a blurry mess as she finally landed. But not on stone. Whatever she had fallen on was slightly softer.

And it groaned in pain.

Her cheek was pressed against warm fabric. Not cold stone. Not a ghastly shadow monster. Arms were wrapped around her.

Someone was chuckling, pained and amused at the same time. Looking up, finally, she saw where she was, and her cheeks instantly went warm.

Sprawled out face-down on Aon's chest.

He was on his back, lying on the ground, and she was on top of him. His masked metal face was raised slightly to look at her.

She had run full-tilt off a half flight of stairs, and he had caught her. The groan of pain had been from him, from taking the impact instead of her. "Something's—"

"I know."

"But—"

"Do you think I would let anything else hunt you? I've told you I do not like to share. Although..." He laid his head back down on the stones and grunted. "I believe I both won, and lost, this little game of ours."

"That was *you?*" She pushed herself up onto her elbows on his chest and went to roll off him. Instead, he grabbed her wrists in both of his hands and pulled her hands up over his head, which pulled her weight off her elbows, and she landed flat back against his chest. "Let go of me."

"In a moment." He bent his knees, and she went wide-eyed at what she felt underneath her as she was sprawled on his chest with her legs between his. "I am enjoying this."

Yes, it was suddenly very clear he was.

"I'm not!" she squeaked and felt her face light up like he had set it on fire. "Let me go, Aon!"

With a disappointed sigh, he released her hands. "I promised you could always refuse me. Very well."

She scrambled off him and got up to her feet.

He lay there for a moment as if mourning her absence before he, too, rose to his feet and brushed himself off, straightening his clothes. "I would ask for thanks for saving you from emptying the contents of your skull all over my garden maze, but you would likely point out that if I had not been chasing you, you would not have been in such a predicament, I suppose."

It took a lot of the bluster out of her argument when he made both halves of it for her. "Why were you chasing me?"

He began fixing his cufflinks. "You were far too tempting, wandering about my maze, lost in abject misery. I couldn't pass up such a wonderful game. And oh, how beautiful you were. So stunning. So terrified..."

"What were you going to do if you caught me?" She was afraid to know the answer but felt obligated to ask.

"Whatever your heart desired." The sudden change to his tone sent a shiver up her spine.

She turned to walk away, her stomach in knots and feeling far too confused to deal with this. When she rounded a corner, he was standing there directly in front of her again.

She drove her fist into his chest. "Stop doing that!"

When she went to punch him a second time, he caught her wrist and pulled her toward him. Before she could say or do anything else, she was back in his arms. "What is this? This is not your typical response. You are angry with me. Why?" He seemed honestly confused.

"You don't know?" She shoved against his chest, trying to

push away, but this time he wasn't having it and kept her caught tight.

"It is over your friend Evie. Over our dance last night." He sighed. "I had hoped we settled this."

She didn't know where her outburst came from. Maybe she had just had enough. She pulled back and slapped Aon flat across the metal mask. It hurt her far more than it hurt him, she was sure. Her hand stung as he rocked his head to the side with the impact. She forced herself out of his grasp and took two steps back from him. Now she was a dead woman; she knew it.

Well, if she was going to die, she might as well make it count.

"Settled *this?* Settled what, exactly?" Tears were stinging her eyes. "What part? That I'm here against my will in this goddamn world? That you're toying with me for your own sick enjoyment? Or that you were torturing my friend? What part have we settled? Remind me!" She was at her wits' end. Being chased through his maze as part of his sick *game* was the last straw.

He stood there silently, watching her. He didn't move as she ranted. Once she was done, he let the silence hang in the air for a long, tense moment before speaking. "Your friend Evie was a fugitive. A prisoner who had committed a crime. You may disagree with what our world may be, but it was my right to dole out her punishment as I saw fit. She would have been in my care for a few more weeks before she was set free to live her life. Edu would have ended her life instead. Would you have preferred that sentence?"

"You were torturing her!"

"It was that or permanent death. At least the torture she suffered served a purpose. She played an important part in my experiments. Which would you have chosen for her? A few weeks of agony, or the void? Tell me." His voice was even and low. Not upset, not passionate. It was as though he were trying to talk down a panicking deer.

Wiping her eyes, she tried to find an answer and found it missing. "I don't know."

"Answer me this, then. Would you rather be Edu's prisoner or mine? At worst, you would be dead. At best, he would demand your body at his every whim. Which would you prefer? That, or to be subject to my—admittedly—childish games?" He took a small step toward her. "I would not have hurt you..."

She froze as Aon took another step forward and reached down for her hand. She didn't know what to do except let him take it. And just like after her nightmare, he placed her palm against his neck. She felt his heartbeat once more, thudding underneath her touch. He cupped his palm to the back of her hand, keeping it there.

It was an attempt to humanize him. To make her realize he was more than just a demon in a mask. And though she hated it, it... kind of worked.

"As for your imprisonment upon this world. Yes. That, I cannot deny. If I could return you to Earth, believe me, I would. But that is outside my power to grant. I keep you here to keep you safe. Safe from those who *would* harm you."

"You were just hunting me." Her anger was failing. The warmth of his skin under her hand brought something very strange out of her that she didn't know what to do with.

"Yes, and I reveled in it. If I had caught you, and if you had even *begun* to surrender to me... I would have ravaged you. I would have taken you as mine. I would have shown you bliss as you have never known." His low voice set her cheeks on fire once more as he placed his clawed gauntlet upon her hip. "But you refused me. As is your right. As was my vow. But know I would hunt you through this maze once more in a heartbeat. For the joy of it. For the hope you might change your mind."

Everything was too confusing. It was all too much. He was

all at once compassionate and a monster, hunting her in the shadows and consoling her in the light.

A gentleman and a beast, who was asking permission to do terrible things to her.

In the same breath, she was terrified of him, hated him for what he had done to Evie, and yet she understood the logic behind his reasoning.

She... hated to admit that she would have chosen a few weeks of torture over permanent death for her friend.

Worst of all, the threat of what he wanted to do to her left her in knots. Her hand was still against his neck, and the feeling of it made her imagination run wild. Made her wonder what would happen if he *had* caught her. She shut her eyes and lowered her head, looking away from him, unable to face his metal mask.

"Are you changing your mind?" he teased.

That broke her out of her turmoil, and she glared up at him.

Perhaps that had been his point, as he laughed and released her. "Come, darling. Let me show you the way out." He held out his human hand to her.

As her heart lodged in her throat, she put her hand in his again.

TEN

This was a desolate place. It hovered on the edge of the encroaching void that was slowly consuming their dying world. Edu recognized the village through which he walked, his boots thudding heavily against the packed dirt of the street, adding the only noise to the oppressive silence that loomed about him.

No other creatures would come this close to the edge of existence. Edu could see it on the near horizon, that endless nothing that was shrinking their world ever smaller. This had once been a thriving village of creatures making their livelihoods, yet now it sat abandoned and empty. Empty, save for the terrified few who had nowhere else to go.

No creatures would choose to live here if they had any other choice. Ylena walked behind him, her footfalls too light to make any sound against the dirt and gravel. Only her presence in his mind was a clue that she was still near him. As they walked through the rows of empty and abandoned homes, he heard the shutters of one window quickly close. As if that would protect them from his arrival.

He was not concerned with these exiles and outcasts. He

cared not for their plight or their suffering. He was here to find one person in particular.

Reaching the house he was told to find, he walked up to the door. The Priest had done his duty, as he always would. Lyon was one of the few in this world Edu felt he could trust.

He could see firelight flickering through the slats of a door that had once been poorly constructed and was now steadily rotting away. In a rare show of manners, he lifted his hand and rapped his knuckles against the softened wood surface.

There was no answer from within. He knew the girl was here. He knocked again.

"Come in." The voice was tight and frightened. Of course. Even if she did not know who had come to see her, any visitor would be an unwelcome one.

He pushed the door open and stepped inside the dingy, dilapidated abode.

Evelyn sat by the fire, a blanket pulled tight around her. The young woman once had such a life about her, but now she had a pale, sallow tone, and her yellow eyes that were the mark of her House were wide and fearful. They had lost their flicker of mischief that he had seen before.

It would take a long time to heal from what Aon had done to her small frame. And some wounds were irreparable. The warlock had seen fit to drain her dry and remove the power from her body.

When those big eyes looked at him, her face twisted in terror, and she flew out of her chair. She collapsed against the wall, arms clutched to herself in utter panic.

"Be still, little one." Ylena's tone was gentle. "Master Edu has not come here to harm you."

"Please, please—" Evelyn sank to the floor, cowering in fear, arms moving to cover her head. "I can't—I don't—"

Fear was nearly palpable in the air. She could only beg him

to rethink whatever horrid violence she was convinced he was about to wreak upon her.

Ylena spoke for Edu once more. "If he had wished you dead or harmed, he would have done so already. He could not stomach your death when he reigned as king. You lingered as his prisoner for a reason. Do you think he would change his mind now that you are free?"

Edu took a slow step toward the cowering young woman when her hands lowered slightly from her face. She winced, but she did not flee. He approached like one would a deer, caught in the torchlight of a hunting party. When she did not bolt, and merely watched him with those wide, beautiful eyes, he sank down to crouch in front of her.

"Master Edu could not stand to see you punished for what would have been lauded in his own House," Ylena said, her voice even and measured, as it always was. "In his home, you would never have had cause to suffer. You could have risen above those whose weak souls were gifted such false power over you. You dallied as his prisoner, for he mourned for the task he would have been required to perform. Aon has been forbidden from granting anyone true death, ever again. For once, Master Edu is glad for the treaty. He is glad that you have been pardoned."

Evelyn was watching him, and although she still trembled, she lowered her arms to her lap. Her eyes were wavering on the edge of curiosity. Good. She was beginning to believe his words, and that he was not a threat.

The desire to speak for himself was a keen-edged knife at this moment, as he wanted to tell the girl how he would have taken her under his wing if he had been allowed. But her crimes demanded otherwise. The little redheaded spitfire was a charming creature he had marveled after for some time. He had already tasted her and often found himself wanting her company yet again. He wished to protect her. To keep her as his own.

"He wishes to offer you sanctuary within his home." As Ylena spoke, Edu held out his hand to the young girl. "Away from this bleak and dreary place."

"Why…?"

"He wishes to see what you can become, where the strength of your soul is all that matters."

"But… Maverick—"

"Will have little to say over the matter, he assures you."

Evelyn hesitated. Edu could see it in her expressive features, scattered as they were with those beautiful freckles against the pale background. How he wished the life restored to those empty features. Aon had no right to do what he had done to the girl.

Death was one thing. *Torture* was another.

Please, Evelyn, Edu begged the girl silently. Ylena thankfully did not convey his words to her this time.

Cautiously, Evelyn placed her hand in his. It was dwarfed by the size of his palm.

He took it carefully and stood, helping her rise. Her legs gave out, and he quickly moved to scoop her up into his arms. She was weak, exhausted, and broken, and had not likely eaten or been given any provisions by Aon upon her arrival.

Then he saw the thread stitched into her arm as she slumped against him, now barely conscious. The skin around the thread was bruised and swollen and wept fresh blood. It was in the recognizable, if indecipherable, shape of the symbols of the Ancients.

That cretin. That accursed bastard!

Edu tried not to tense for fear of scaring the girl. He merely held her in his arms and turned to signal Ylena that it was time to go. Before he vanished from this forsaken place, he vowed to all the gods of old, that for what he had done, one thing was certain.

Aon will pay.

* * *

Lyon had become accustomed to sleeping outdoors. He spent most of his nights at Kamira's side, and the woman would not sleep indoors unless she had no choice. After his duties as a priest of the Cathedral of the Ancients were concluded for the day, he would find his way into the deep woods, where Kamira and her pack would camp.

The shifters traveled in small groupings, each with their own internal pecking order and hunting rights. Kamira was, of course, the leader of hers. The other shifters in her pack had become nervous of late, and Lyon could hear them moving about nearby.

There was a new addition to the pack. A new pup—the boy, Nicholas. Lydia's friend from the mortal world. And such a thing tended to upset matters until a new order was established.

When Lyon arrived, the boy was sitting with his back up against a tree. He looked battered and bruised, likely having been involved in altercations to settle the matter. Judging by the number of marks in emerald greens that ran down his arms and bared chest, he was a formidable foe.

Shifters did not care for age; they cared only for strength. If Nicholas had challenged another and won, it was his right to stand above them.

Kamira was lounging on a rock on the other side of the clearing, stretched out, an arm underneath her head, dozing.

Lyon walked up to her and leaned down to kiss her. Kamira smiled before the kiss landed. Despite her sleeping appearance, she had sensed his approach like a great cat. Lyon was never able to successfully catch his wife unawares. Not in the fifteen hundred years they had been together.

"How fares the boy?" He smiled down at her.

"Just fine. Already, Nick has defended himself against another and declared them the new bottom of the barrel." Kamira opened her green eyes to look up at him. "He is a fine addition to my hunters. He dispatched Renar without much trouble, if much whining."

"I can hear you, you know," Nicholas complained from the other side of the clearing. "And that guy threatened to rip my dick off."

"And you did as you must to protect it." Kamira laughed.

"This sucks." Nicholas sighed.

"I do not understand why you use that word that way, Nick. I know what it means, but not how you use it." She turned his head to watch the boy.

"It means this blows," Nicholas grumbled.

"I know what it means to suck and blow." She flashed Nicholas a devious grin. "But again, you say it as if it is a bad thing."

Nicholas stood up and glared at her. "You can tell what it means!"

"Yes, boy, I get the gist. I am teasing you, is all." Kamira sat up and stretched. "You are wound too tight. Perhaps your friend Kaori should pay you another visit."

Nick walked off into the woods, throwing up his hands in frustration.

"The young ones are too much fun. They know all they must know of Under when they rise, but they adjust so differently. It is always so entertaining to watch." She flicked a braided strand of her hair over her shoulder.

"Be kinder to him, my love. He likely frets for his friend." He placed his hand on her shoulder.

"He also hates being beaten. He may have won the last

fight, but he lost the previous four." She pulled him down for a kiss, taking hold of his suit coat. When she broke the embrace, her words were quiet. "Our world is not kind. He is learning this."

"As is his friend."

"You should go to her. She will need a calmer presence. Take pity on a girl whose only company is Aon." She shifted to settle her legs on either side of his.

"I do not believe he means to harm her. But your point is taken. I will look after her as much as I can."

As much as Lyon suspected anyone could.

* * *

Lydia's dreams were quiet, for once. No nightmares, no Aon. The warlock had led her from his horrifying hedge maze and brought her to the door to her room and bowed to her, wishing her a good night. Sleep had sounded amazing.

When she woke up, she had the overwhelming need for a cup of coffee. Dressing, she went to fetch a mug and went out to stand on one of the balconies overlooking the hedge maze. Funny how innocent it looked from up here. Just a maze. Not a weird, living, magically-rearranging, evil hedge monster at the personal command of a madman.

Sipping the cup, she was glad they had something that tasted like coffee here. It wasn't the same, but it was close enough. Her thoughts were once more circling Aon and how she felt about him. The answer was... complicated. It was clear she found him more than a little attractive, and that his presence was as deeply alluring as it was incredibly alarming.

But he was a monster. *And you enjoy that,* she argued with herself. A creature that played games and hunted her. *Even as he's kind to me.* He tortured Evie. *Instead of killing her.* She was his prisoner. *So he can protect me.*

If only half her head would learn to shut up. She was starting not to care which side. She sighed and looked down at her cup and spun it between her fingers.

"Ms. Lydia."

"Sweet Jesus!" She whirled, startled out of her wits, nearly spilling her coffee off the edge of the balcony. Lyon was standing there, watching her with an apologetic smile.

"Forgive me, I did not mean to scare you." Lyon folded a hand in front of him in a slight bow.

"Oh, holy hell, God damn it all. You stupid people and your teleporting! You're going to kill somebody. Namely, me." She put a hand over her eyes.

"I did not teleport." Lyon was still smiling faintly. "I walked up."

"Well, then walk louder, or wear a bell or something." Letting out a faint laugh, she shook her head. It wasn't his fault. "It's fine. It's fine. I need to get used to it. Hi, nice to see you. What're you doing here?"

"There is a meeting today of all the heads of the Houses of Under. As Aon is a newly risen king, there are politics to discuss." Clearly, he dreaded the subject.

"Are you here with Kamira, or, uh..." She realized she didn't know what the creepy little guy was called, the one who ran Lyon's House. "Your boss?"

"Otoi." The smile on Lyon's face was offset by a sudden sadness in his eyes. "Neither. I am asked to attend by a matter of exception."

"Why? You're just that awesome?" She grinned.

"I was once the Elder of the House of Blood, not Otoi. The elder of the order of priests who dedicate themselves to the Ancients." It sounded like it was something he had become accustomed to saying.

"Oh... I'm sorry." Should she ask why? She hated this kind of moment. Like a coworker saying something about their mother being sick and not knowing if she should follow up a question. The answer might be anywhere between the sniffles and cancer, and either way, it was probably awkward.

"Be not so. I gave up my rule so Kamira and I might wed. Two heads of House are not allowed to be joined in such a way."

How sweet. She didn't figure this place for anything like that. "What's marriage like in a world like this? Where everybody just..." Trailing off, she realized she didn't know how to tactfully bring up the rampant and open sex. "I mean, why make it official?"

"I understand your confusion. It means we are recognized legally as one. Should something happen to one, the other may claim full recompense regardless of House. More importantly, no king or elder may wield our bond nor can they pit us against each other in warfare or for political gain, against severe recourse. It means our love is... untouchable by others." His expression returned to its usual seriousness.

"Huh." She looked off into the distance thoughtfully. Yes, that probably did come in handy. "And, let me guess, you're a secret romantic."

"I am. I will admit that Kamira protested. But I eventually wore her down."

What an oddly endearing man. "So, you're here because... they still want you around?"

"No one respects Otoi. Least of which, Master Aon. Keeping me in the shadows is a means of undermining him." The conversation lulled for a moment, and Lyon seemed very interested in turning the conversation away from himself. Suddenly, she realized he might be a little shy. "I am quite happy to see that you are... intact. I was anxious, after the events of the gala."

She cringed at the memory of what had happened that

night. "He didn't hurt me. He showed me things I wish he hadn't. But he didn't hurt me."

"Like what, if I may pry?"

"My friend Evie, from Edu's prison." She let out a breath. "He showed me what he was... doing to her."

"Ah... you are the reason she was set free. I loathe considering what you bargained away for such a thing."

"A 'favor.'" She added air quotes to add to her sarcasm.

Lyon was silent, and when she looked up at him, he was gazing off, a troubled line between his brows.

"What?" She blinked. "That bad, huh?"

"No, forgive me." He studiously smoothed his expression again. "It is simply unlike Aon to bargain with someone with, well, such limited impact. A favor from you is..." He trailed off as he realized he was going to insult her.

"Worthless." She finished for him. When he cringed, she waved her hand. "It's fine. It's true. A favor from me really *is* worthless. I have nothing to offer. I might be dead in a week when something here decides to eat me. Besides, I don't think a dumb favor was what he was after. He was trying to get me to accept I'm trapped here and there's nothing I can do about it."

"Did his plan succeed?"

She paused for a moment. "Yeah. It did."

"You speak as though you have admitted some great flaw. That you are weak in accepting your current conditions. It is not, for if you were to rail harder against the bars of your gilded cage, you would only injure yourself in your attempts. Nothing else would come of it. Better to conserve the parts of your soul that you can and accept things as they are."

It was a good point. Somehow, taking advice from a man who was nearly two thousand years old was an easy thing to do. He'd seen it all, she figured. Which lead her to her next question. "Lyon? I have... a strange question."

"Do not hesitate to ask me what you will. It is the least I could do to someone in your plight."

"You sure? It's awkward."

"There is little you could ask me that would be a surprise."

"Does Aon typically have girlfriends?"

"Excuse me?"

Right. Old. Very old. "Sweethearts. Paramours. Y'know, lovers."

"Ah." Lyon paused and looked off thoughtfully again. That line reappeared between his eyebrows.

So much for not being able to surprise him. Sipping her coffee, she was disappointed to find it was growing cold. "I can't tell if he's just flirty because everyone here likes to sleep with everyone else, or if he's... I don't know. It's a stupid thought. Forget I asked."

"I have not known Aon to show true romantic interest in another. He has taken a lover from time to time. Yet the interest has always been fleeting."

"Fleeting why?"

"Aon breeds a deep-seated feeling of disdain and disregard for all around him. Very few can keep his interest for long." Clearly, Lyon didn't think much about Aon's private life.

"Oh."

"He is reclusive, even to those in his own house. He rarely speaks to others, entertains guests more rarely, and confides in no one. Even his own second in command is often left guessing as to what his goals may be. To take a lover for longer than a night or two of physical pleasure is a strain for him, I imagine."

That was very different from her experiences with Aon. He seemed to seek her out, to enjoy her company, and to *want* to talk to her. If she said she wanted to spend the day at his side, she was confident the man would say yes without hesitation. But Lyon painted a picture of a man who locked himself away in his tower. Evie had done the same. Indeed, everyone she'd talked to so far told her of a very different man than the one she had met.

Lyon interrupted her thoughts. "When Aon finds a lover..." He paused again as if afraid to continue.

"Say it, please."

"I do not think it would be helpful."

She glared at him. "You started. You can't stop now."

He muttered something about always finding himself in these situations before finishing his thought. "When he is known to take a lover, I think it is a matter of conquest. Once the deed is done, I believe he grows bored and quickly discards them."

Ah.

That explained it.

She was Aon's new toy, the one who turned down Edu. He'd get his giggles, and that'd be that. Maybe it wouldn't be a bad thing. It'd make her life more comfortable if he was bored with her. It'd be less unpredictable at least.

Why did the thought of Aon becoming bored with her hurt so much?

I'm so fucking stupid. He's playing me. That's all! God, I'm such an idiot.

"Ms. Lydia, are you all right? I am sorry if I have upset you."

"No, it's fine. It explains everything. I'd rather not go into this ignorant of what's going on." But it still felt like a kick in the teeth.

"Has he been making attempts to... eh... secure your affections?"

She couldn't help but laugh. He was so bashful about it, it was adorable. "You mean, has he been trying to fuck me, Lyon?" The look on his face at her harsh use of language was worth it. It almost cheered her up. "Yes. He has."

"Please come to the library."

"Shit." She winced and put her hand to her head.

"He has summoned you?" Points where they were due, he guessed correctly.

"Yeah." She rolled her eyes. "At least he *asked* this time."

"Go, then. It is best not to keep the man waiting." He put his hand on her shoulder. "I am sorry for any undue strife he is bringing you. Please, let me know if there is anything I can do to help."

Putting her hand on his, she smiled. "Thanks, Lyon. That means a lot. Just knowing I have someone to talk to is wonderful."

The tall vampiric priest smiled back at her faintly before she heard Aon's voice in her head again.

"Now, please."

"Yes, okay, I'm coming!" Heading toward the door, she tried not to get irritated at the warlock. It wouldn't go well. "Bye, Lyon."

"Goodbye, Ms. Lydia."

It took a few more minutes for her to find his library in the winding corridors. She knocked on the door, and hearing a voice bid her inside, she opened it before realizing it hadn't been Aon's voice. Too late.

"Oh. Uh—" She was looking at a group of people standing around the room. Some she knew, some she didn't. Lyon had mentioned a meeting, and she had just walked right into it. "Sorry, I'll go."

"No, no, do come in, my dear," Aon called with no small air of amusement. He was seated at the head of the table, fingers steepled in front of his masked face.

"You must be joking," said the fat little man in white who reminded her of what would happen if the Michelin Man had an affair with a particularly ugly puffer fish. Otoi.

"Be quiet. She is a guest in my home and learning about our world. I see no harm in having her here. Does anyone else object?" It was clearly a challenge from the warlock.

No one else spoke up. Shyly, she shut the door behind her and edged into the room, trying to stay out of sight. She thought maybe she'd hide in the darkness of the massive library, where it might be safe.

"She is so adorably skittish." Kamira laughed, her tone unmistakably flirtatious.

"I have a sense of self-preservation." She kept her tone from being too biting. But she was getting tired of being the butt of everyone's jokes.

"Then you are wise beyond your years," the woman with pure white hair and the blue mask said. Her words carried like a stiff icy breeze in the room, and it killed the grin on Kamira's face. "I am glad to know you are well."

"You already knew, Ziza," Maverick said from across the table from the white-haired woman.

"I am making conversation."

"Well, stop." Maverick mustered a dry smirk. "It's unnerving, at best."

Around the table, she recognized only Maverick and Kamira. The woman in blue with the white hair and the matching white eyes—Ziza—she hadn't met except at the Pool of the Ancients. Same with the pug in white, Otoi. Green, black, white, blue, and purple were accounted for. Red was missing. Namely, the giant horny ox in the skull mask was notably absent.

Maverick beat her to the question. "Where is King Edu?"

"Busy, said his attendant." Aon provided a dismissive shrug. "It matters not. This meeting would have occurred without him, anyway, and he knows it."

"Then Oanr would have attended in his stead." Kamira leaned back in her chair and spun her glass of wine between her fingers. "We should not call the meeting without all Houses in attendance. Such is custom."

"Edu deigned not to attend. He is the one who dismissed

the custom," Aon argued back, "not I. Nor did he send a replacement, unless you wish his squire to sit in our conference?"

"Then we cancel," Kamira snapped. "Simple as that."

"What do you think, my dear?" Aon asked Lydia.

She froze like someone had swiveled a pair of moving spotlights onto her. And yet again, she didn't know her lines. "Wait —what?"

"I second her question," Kamira said with an incredulous huff. "What are you doing, asking her? She is not of Under."

"The perfect reason for her to adjudicate on our debate. She is unbiased," Aon replied.

"Unbiased? You are well aware that is a crock." Maverick tapped his finger on the table thoughtfully. "She has been under your influence for well over a week. That amount of time is all it takes—"

"To do what, precisely? Bend her to my will? I do believe Ms. Lydia would take offense to such insinuations. She is not my slave."

"Please. You mean to tell me you haven't mounted that mare and broken her in yet?" the little weasel in white said with a snort. "What kind of fools do you think we are?"

"It matters not what you may think." Aon laughed once dangerously. "I do not find the need, such as you, to force my partners into bed."

Otoi sneered at her. "At least once I get a partner in my bed, I can keep them. I'll tell you what. Since you don't want her, if you tell her to wrap that pretty little mouth of hers around my cock, I'll let her decide whether or not we hold this farce of a meeting."

That was it.

She'd had enough.

Fuck. All. Of. This.

Walking from the shadows to stand at the edge of the table,

she knew the look of rage on her face would have been clear enough to prove she wasn't about to take the slimy little cretin up on his offer. When she spoke, it was a thin hiss. "Aon? May I?"

He silently gestured for her to continue.

Every ounce of frustration and anger she had pent up in her since this stupidity all began came out in one swift moment. She picked up a metal tray off the table.

And decked Otoi across the face with it.

It made an amazingly cathartic *clang* as it nearly bent in half. She had struck the man with every ounce of fury she had stored up. She chucked the tray against the wall, where it fell with a loud clatter. She wasn't done yet. Grabbing the weasel by the collar and twisting it in her hand, she cut off his air.

Pointing in his face, she let all her rage flow. "Listen to me very clearly, you hideous, repulsive little piece of shit. Do not *ever* speak to me like that. Or I swear to God, I will take that mask off your face, fold it in half, and shove it so far up your ass they'll need to make an incision in your chest to get it back! Do you understand?" When Otoi didn't answer, Lydia slammed his head against the back of the chair. "I said, *do you understand?*"

"Y—yes, ma'am." Otoi held up his fat, overstuffed hands in a show of surrender.

She let go of him and wiped her hand on his napkin, more out of a show than anything else. It was about then her anger cooled enough to wonder if she was going to get in trouble for accosting the head of a House.

Aon was laughing. Loudly. He was slapping his gloved black hand against the table, and he wasn't the only one caught up in amusement. He wasn't the only one. Kamira was cackling in joy, clapping her hands at Lydia's efforts. Even Ziza, who looked like facial expressions might cause her pain, was smiling. But it didn't seem like it was out of enjoyment at Otoi's suffering, but some other kind of peace that Lydia couldn't name. Maverick was trying his best not to smile and was failing.

"You are not wrong, Aon. She is of her own mind. Very well!" Kamira said through her laugh. "Yes! Let someone with that kind of spine judge for us. Tell us, Ms. Lydia. The House of Flames is absent, by their own admission. But this is a meeting of all the Houses, as is required to be held after the reign of a new king begins. What should we do?"

Walking away from Otoi, she took a spot by an empty chair and leaned her arms on the back of it. It was so surreal to be asked this question when she felt she knew so little about Under. "So, first of all, I don't even know what you people talk about at these meetings. From what I can tell, Edu and Aon are opposing forces. If this is supposedly a meeting of all the Houses, it's silly to have it without someone from that House here. But Edu elected not to attend, which is weird. If it were me—and I'm really not saying it is—I guess I would wonder what Edu's so busy with that he couldn't be here. Or at least send somebody in his place."

"A question worth answering." Maverick leaned back into his chair.

Aon was silent, fingers steepled in front of his face again. What he was looking at, or what he was thinking, was impossible to guess with him wearing a full mask. "Continue."

"So... I suppose..." Why was he playing this game with her? "I'd cover the parts of the meeting that don't involve a vote... and everything else, I'd wait until Edu decides to show up."

"Well! Leave it to the mortal human to have the level head." Aon finally sat up in his chair. "We shall cover matters that are not a subject requiring a show of hands, and all others we shall defer until Edu's distraction has resolved itself, one way or another. Are we agreed?"

"Aye," said all—even Otoi, reluctantly.

"Thank you, my dear." Aon motioned for her to sit.

Without any idea of what else to do—which was how she went about her life in this place—she took a seat. Far away from the others, but at the table, nonetheless. The meeting went on, and it was just about as dry and uninteresting as a conversation about the politics of a bizarre and morbid parallel world could be.

Aon's posture clearly indicated his boredom. He was leaning heavily on one arm of his chair, and she wondered how to tell if a man wearing a full mask was paying attention. If it weren't for his periodic interjections, he might've been asleep.

The House of Flames passed the following laws during Aon's sleep. There were four attempts of murder, two successful murders, and ten disappearances. Maverick reported on his research. The forest shrank by so many square kilometers from the encroaching void, and the need for lumber had therefore increased.

What encroaching void? She would have to ask Aon about that later.

After what the clock said was just over three hours, the conversation finally ended. They had made a list of questions to be put to a vote in another meeting with everyone present. At the end, when everyone stood to leave, she stood as well and suddenly realized that was dumb, since she had nowhere to go. Did Aon expect her to leave? Or stay? She had no clue, and hoped the sense of being a fish out of water might go away someday. If she lived that long.

Everyone bade each other good night and left, with Kamira being the only one remaining. She walked up to her at the last moment and leaned in to speak softly to her. "Anyone who puts Otoi in his place... is a friend in my book. Do not let Aon crush your spirit. It is worth taking to your grave."

The wild woman kissed her on the cheek, and it was a slow, sensual gesture that made Lydia's face grow warm. The woman grinned against her skin, and when she withdrew, put a hand on Lydia's cheek. It was a profoundly sexual movement, and it made her flush harder. The shifter chuckled and tilted her head slightly to the side. "That blush. How beautiful. I am jealous of you, Aon. Are you sure we could not bargain an exchange for an evening?"

"Ms. Lydia makes her own decisions in these matters, and I fear Lyon is not my type."

Kamira cackled at Aon's joke, angling her head away from Lydia's to keep from laughing in her ear. She stepped back and grinned at Lydia fiendishly. "She does, does she? Very well. What say you, sweet one? Spend the night with me."

"I—uh—I don't, um, swing—um—swing that way. But, um... I'm flattered, thanks?" She cleared her throat.

"If you live long enough, everyone 'swings' every way. But, suit yourself. Do let me know if you change your mind." Kamira walked out of the room without another word.

Letting out a rush of air, she leaned back against the table once the door had clicked shut.

Aon laughed. "She can come on rather strong."

"Says the guy who comes on like a freight train. Nobody here is subtle." She put her hand to her face. "Christ."

"Touché, yet again, my dear." He stood and stretched, and she heard a crack from across the room as he bent his neck to one side and then the other. "I apologize for making you sit through such a dreadfully dull meeting, but watching you attempt to pay attention was all that kept me awake."

"I'm glad my stupidity amuses you."

"Not your stupidity. Your ignorance." He walked to stand by his fireplace, his back to her, clawed hand folded behind him, the other resting on the mantel.

Lydia didn't know what to do. She wondered if she should go for the door and leave, or... Damn her confusion. Damn this complicated mess. She wanted to go back to her room. Or go get food. Or stay here with Aon. She really found herself wanting to stay here with Aon. And that was stupid. Especially after what Lyon had said.

Damnit, I'm such an idiot! She put her head in her hand, resting her elbow on the back of the chair, and kept silently yelling names at herself.

"Are you feeling ill?"

His voice was suddenly so close to her, she nearly jumped out of her skin. One moment Aon had been standing by the fireplace, and the next he was at her side.

"I'm fine." She swallowed the rock in her throat.

When he lifted a hand to stroke back her hair and let the backs of his fingers linger against her cheek, she couldn't help but pull in a breath through her nose and felt her face grow warm. She swore again at herself and pulled back from him.

He let out a thoughtful noise, and pondered her for a moment before speaking. "I must say, your treatment of Otoi was hysterical. I think I am changing my opinion of your childish invectives. They have their uses."

"I couldn't take it anymore."

"Take what, precisely?"

"Being pushed around, being... I don't know. Stuck here, helpless. Powerless. The butt of everybody's jokes." She shook her head. "I'm trapped. I won't be insulted on top of it."

"Most in your predicament would be an inconsolable mess. You are doing admirably, given your situation. I had hoped to become your distraction, as you have quickly become mine. Yet I think I am only adding to your turmoil."

She blinked at his words and looked up at him, surprised. Okay, he wasn't *wrong*, but was it that obvious? She tried to play dumb while she scrambled for her thoughts. "What do you mean?"

Playing dumb was a bad decision. He stepped toward her quickly, and before she could react, he had her pinned up against the table. He leaned the length of his thigh against hers, keeping her trapped.

As she bent backward away from him, she had to press her hands against the smooth wood surface. He merely followed, and she quickly found herself caged in by his arms on either side of her.

Her face bloomed in warmth as she felt the press of him against her body. She swallowed thickly. It felt like she was on fire. His nearness—his touch—simply *did* things to her.

"This." His voice was low and husky, not helping matters. "Is what I mean." He lifted his flesh-and-blood hand to her chin and turned her face toward his masked one. "You want this. I know you do. I can see it, mixed with your fear. It is as intoxicating for you as it is for me, but you resist. Why?"

"It isn't right. This isn't okay—" She felt breathless even as she argued. "You're..."

"I am what? The dread warlock? The King of Shadows? The liar, the tormentor, the sadist? I have heard them all. What am I to you, my darling, that gives you such pause?" He pressed in closer and let out a low appreciative sound. Lydia could feel him—*all of him*—up against her, and her mouth went dry.

"I—" she stammered. Oh, how she wanted to give in to him, right here and now. Lyon's words echoed in her head with her own conflict, reinforcing her turmoil. "You're my captor. I'm a prisoner here."

"You would be a prisoner anywhere on Under. You are my guest here in my home. I do not keep you in a cage. I do not keep you lashed to the wall. Mmh, well... so far at least." He chuckled as her eyes went wide. "There, once more, I can see it. You fear me, and you *love* it. No small part of you wishes I would make good on my threats, am I wrong?"

Turning her head, she shut her eyes, unable to face him. "Please, Aon, I..."

As quickly as he had put her there against the table, he withdrew and took a few steps back from her to give her space. He bowed his head to her. "As you wish."

Pushing off the table and back to standing, she didn't know *what* she wished. Not anymore. Namely? Because he wasn't wrong. And that wasn't okay. She flinched and turned away from him, wanting to hide her face. She was entirely torn in half. Yet she felt like she had paid the man a steep rejection. Would he be mad, like Edu? "I'm sorry, I..."

"Never apologize to me, Lydia. You suffer the imposition, not I. I am not angry with you for this. Decide for yourself what it is you want. I am patient." He walked away from her to go back to the fire.

"I need some air." And out of the room. She headed toward the door.

"Do as you will. I am going nowhere." He chuckled at his private joke.

And neither, apparently, was she.

ELEVEN

Lydia barely slept.

She was too restless and too wound up to really turn off. Frustrated, she gave up around midnight and went to go find something stiff to drink. She usually wasn't one to resort to drinking to help put her out, but damn it if she didn't feel like she deserved some alcohol.

Unfortunately, the only place she knew she could find some was Aon's library. It was late, and while she wasn't sure of his schedule, she hoped he'd be absent. Not that she was avoiding him, per se, but he *was* the source of her sleeplessness.

His words ran through her mind, again and again. "You fear me, and you love it." He was right. She did. Both of those things were true at once.

Villains and monsters had always been more exciting to her, more interesting, and the more alluring characters in everything she read or watched. But to discover she was now attracted to one, in the way she was starting to admit she felt for Aon? That couldn't be healthy. Never mind the fact she was trapped in a nightmare world and entirely at his mercy.

Reaching the library, she took a breath and steeled herself

for what might happen. The ornate door opened silently. Sticking her head through the gap, she peeked inside.

The fire was still going, but it was low, filling the room with a comfortable smell of smoldering wood. The electric lights were off, and the moonlight was glinting on the railings and carved wood surfaces. Maybe Aon was asleep for the night. If he slept. She assumed he did, but she thought a lot of things that were probably very wrong.

Most importantly, she didn't see Aon. That didn't mean much. The room was full of shadows, and the man wore all black. That, along with his hair and his mask, made him an inverted version of trying to see a polar bear in a snowstorm.

Carefully closing the door behind her, she walked over to the bar by one wall and began mixing herself a drink. She had to sniff the decanters to try to figure out what was in each one. But, honestly, it was guess-and-check. All the food and drink she'd had so far in Under was a close-but-not-quite approximation of everything on Earth. They grew their own unique kind of food, so, therefore, they had their own unique type of alcohol.

Finally winding up with something that was close to a Manhattan, Lydia put the stoppers back in the various decanters.

"Cannot sleep?"

Squeaking, she quickly turned at the sound of Aon's voice. He was nowhere to be seen. Furrowing her brow, she said nothing.

"Neither can I." The voice came from near the fireplace, but she still couldn't see him. Picking up her glass, she walked down the length of the table and stopped as she finally spotted the warlock. He was lying on the floor. His legs were kicked up on the side of a high-backed chair, crossed at the ankles.

"Um…"

"Yes?"

"What're you doing?"

"Thinking."

"On the floor."

"Apparently."

She went silent at his matter-of-fact and entirely unhelpful explanation of why he was lying there. *He's insane, don't forget.* With a shake of her head, she decided to let that one, literally and figuratively, lie. "Want one?" She held up her drink. "Warning, I have no idea what I made." She took a sip. "It's not half bad, though."

He chuckled. "No, thank you. I fear I could not drink it in your presence, regardless." Aon tapped a metal claw against his mask with a series of metallic *tinks*.

"Right, sorry. I keep forgetting." She sipped the drink again. Yeah, it really wasn't that bad. "Do you eat and drink, though?"

"Yes, of course. Although I can go far, far longer without either than you can." He folded his hands over his stomach, lacing his fingers together. "What is keeping you awake?"

You. She kept that bit to herself. "Everything. How about you?"

He did not respond for a long moment. "My imagination." The way he said it, thick with innuendo, made her look away as her cheeks went warm. Her reaction turned his chuckle into a full laugh. "Come, join me." He patted the ground next to him, and she realized he meant it literally.

After a pause and a quick debate, she shrugged. Downing the rest of her drink, she didn't see the harm in it. He wasn't asking her to blow him, he was asking her to lie on the ground next to him. She sat on the floor a foot or two away and lay down, looking up at the ceiling overhead.

They lay there in silence for several minutes, looking up at the ceiling. The mural stretched overhead, depicting some great and horrible war. The painting looked ancient, but then again, everything here was. Lyon had claimed to be two thousand years old, give or take. She suddenly realized how little she knew about her "warden."

"How old are you, Aon?"

"I do not remember. I was ancient when the first history books were written, some five thousand years ago. So, however old I may be, it is much longer than that."

She laid there in stunned silence for a moment. "I don't even know how to wrap my head around that."

"Neither do I," he said with a small snicker.

"What do you mean?"

"You have witnessed it for yourself, I know you have. The others call me a madman and not entirely in the pejorative sense." His tone turned grim. "Think of what it means to be so very old. To have so many memories. I think perhaps sometimes I go to times and places that once were. I have too much in my mind to hold it all at once."

"What about Edu?"

"He is nearly as old as I am, though how I know this, I cannot say. Younger to Under by only perhaps a year or two. Whereas I perhaps think of too much, he solves the issue of his advanced years by thinking about nothing at all."

His cheap shot made her chuckle, and she let the conversation trail into silence as they looked up at the mural overhead, the one with the missing figure. "Can I ask what I'm afraid might be a touchy subject?"

"Why is there a missing House, in all the depictions where all are gathered? I know you have taken note." Aon pointed up a claw that glinted in the firelight at the chipped gap in the ceiling. "Always six where it seemed there was once seven. You are correct. Many are loathe to speak of it, and others might refuse to answer you."

"I'm sorry."

"Shush. I will tell you, my dear. Such was our accord. If you attend me here in my library, I will answer your questions, and you certainly have been quite patient with me." He lifted his clawed hand to gesture at the ceiling. "There you see depicted in all its glory, my greatest moment of sheer *idiocy.*" It sounded like she was in for one hell of a story, by his tone of voice.

He clenched his fist, and Lydia let out a small gasp of surprise as the painting suddenly came to life. She hadn't realized how faded the colors were. But before her eyes, it began to swirl and the empty spots filled with bright pigment, restoring itself to what it must have looked like. The painted sky was filled with stars, and so much more detail in the imagery came to life.

The figures began to move in animation, but most importantly, the missing section that had chipped away started to fill in. It repopulated—piece by piece—until the empty area was filled with the painting of a massive, scaled and feathery creature. Not quite a dragon, but not quite a snake. It was a stunning shade of turquoise. Its giant feathered wings stretched around it in a hundred shades of sea green. Its head had carvings of symbols upon it, etched straight to the bone of its visage and even on its dangerous, pointed fangs.

"The Great War. *My* Great War." He lowered his hand as the creatures on the ceiling fought in their slow animation. "For thousands of years, there were seven kings and queens of Under, and we ruled in relative peace. Edu, House of Flames. Ini, House of Fate. Vjo, House of Words. Rxa, House of Blood. Dtu, House of Moons. Aon, House of Shadows. And Qta, House of Dreams." Each time he spoke a name, the figure on the ceiling would move in response.

"We reigned over our vibrant world, each commanding our own Houses. For greater matters, it would be put to a vote. This sense of equality was offensive to me. I wished to rule it all. I wished to destroy the others and take my place as the rightful king of all Houses. Of all of Under."

He snarled, but the anger seemed pointed inward as much as it was outward.

As the mural animated, it seemed like all the others were fighting Aon in unison—but he was winning. From the ground around him rose skeletal and rotting corpses, fighting on his behalf. The man really was a warlock, it seemed. "I stood poised to defeat them all, to reign as the only king. But still, it was not enough. I had been insulted. My ego would not be quieted. But my desire for total power was not my greatest mistake."

The image of Aon upon the ceiling whirled and thrust his hand into the heart of the great winged snake. "What I was willing to do to achieve it, was…" The feathered snake screamed in silent agony, and she watched as it dissolved into ash.

The colors began to fade from the painting once more, and the area of the ceiling that contained the winged snake began to chip and crumble. Slowly, the picture took on its former appearance, and the moment was gone. "To commit murder is the greatest sin in Under. And I murdered King Qta. Without his power to draw from, all the others in the House of Dreams died. With him, I condemned our world to oblivion."

She was agog, processing all that she had seen and learned for a long time in silence, before she sat up from where she was lying on the floor. Aon's hands were folded on his chest, fingers clasped once more as if unfazed by his story. "What do you mean, oblivion?"

"My world is dying, my dear Lydia. It shrinks and fades with every passing day. Perhaps we have a hundred years left before it is gone. Our world is a shell of what it once was. The House of Dreams could summon monsters from the depths of their minds. With them, we did not need to feed on our beast-kin like cannibals. With the death of Qta went the nightmares and dreams that made our world a shifting tapestry of creatures of legend. Most importantly, without them, our world is quite literally dissolving."

She didn't know what to say to that.

He finally shifted and stood, gracefully getting to his feet in a few swift movements. He held his ungloved hand down to her. "Come. Let me show you."

Without any idea of what else to do, she slipped her hand into his. He lifted her to her feet, and in a blink, they were gone. She almost lost her footing as they reappeared, and he caught her, chuckling. "You will adjust to that in time."

"I don't know about that." She groaned. When she could stand on her own two feet, she looked up. And promptly wished she hadn't.

She had gone scuba diving once on a family trip. They'd been pretty far out in the ocean, and she had looked down off the edge of the continental shelf and had seen nothingness. A tremendous, empty, deep blue sea of *nothing*.

It had set off an instinctual fear in her at the time and a case of vertigo. To be able to see so far, and yet see absolutely zero along the way.

She thought that had been what empty space looked like, and she was wrong. *This* was.

This was the void.

They stood on a city street. It looked for all accounts like some warped and twisted version of Victorian London. It had uneven cobblestones, and the storefronts and buildings nearby were abandoned and empty. The moons overhead shone off the stones of the buildings and mixed with the amber light of the archaic-looking street lamps.

It would have been beautiful if it weren't *half gone*.

It was as though it was being pulled into a pit. Part of a building was missing, dissolved into the darkness that looked as though it were only at arm's reach.

It was terrifying to look into that nothingness and see only darkness. It felt like it was an illusion and that somehow it was right on top of her. Disoriented, she began backing away from the emptiness reflexively. It was so utterly *nothing at all* that she couldn't tell if it was one or a hundred feet away.

But Aon's arm was suddenly at her back, keeping her from backing away too far, and she found herself now less afraid of him than she was of the oblivion in front of her.

"This is what my arrogance wrought." He gestured into the darkness. "In my egotism, I have doomed us all." He turned her to face him, and his hand rested against her cheek, forcing her gaze away from the darkness that loomed maybe twenty feet from where they stood. It was so hard to tell.

His touch didn't help much to calm her heartrate; it just changed why it was racing.

"All that you have met here are souls that were once human. Such was not always the case. The humans who were taken here were only a small part of the tapestry of this world." His words were quiet, but there was a hollow kind of pain to them as he continued his story. "When I murdered Qta, all the creatures and monsters born of this place, original to our world, evaporated into dust. We would take humans from Earth to add their dreams and nightmares to our own. Now, we take them to survive. Our world is stagnant. It is emaciated. It is *dying.*"

He pulled her a step closer, and she was too swept up in his words to fight it.

"When I realized what I had done, I surrendered. I ceased my bloody war. And ever since that day, my dear, darling Lydia, all I have done has been an attempt to repair the damage I have caused." His hand stroked her hair back, and his skin was warm against hers as it settled down at the back of her neck. He tilted his head down and rested his metal forehead against hers.

His nearness made her head spin, and that, mixed with his story, was leaving her dumbfounded.

"The other kings and queens crawled into their crypts, accepting the fate of this world. They remain asleep to embrace the void. They have no desire to help me in my work. Edu remains awake merely to spite me. His hatred is the only reason he does not join them. He cares not for the destruction of our world. He thinks I am still after my original goal."

She felt, somehow, like she was a raft and he was a man lost at sea. The way he held onto her wasn't just his usual flirting. There was a *need* to it. His voice was soft, whispering, and... vulnerable. If he was lying to her, he was the best actor she had ever met.

"All my work. All of it, Lydia, all the pain and torment that I bring to others—even little Evelyn—is to bring them back. All I desire in this world is to restore the House of Dreams. To bring new life to my dying world. But I am failing at every turn. I do not seek the ability to stitch marks upon another for selfish gain. I seek to gift to another the lost power of the nightmares that fueled our world. Above all, I am a king. I cannot let my world die." He paused, and when he spoke, his voice nearly cracked. "After more than five thousand years of life, I still do not wish to die."

When she lifted her hand to touch him, to lay her palm on his metal cheek, he ripped away from her and hissed a sharp breath in through his nose. He took a few steps away from the darkness that loomed at the edges and turned his back to her.

He dug his hands into his hair and let out a low, agonized moan. His shoulders were hunched, and he looked like he was about to cave in on himself.

She could only watch as Aon took in a slow, deep breath and dropped his hands from his hair. The ends of his claws were tipped in blood. His fists clenched, then relaxed as if he accepted some great burden. He lifted his shoulders, but not his head. "Forgive me. These are not your woes."

What he had done to Evie was wrong. The methods he was using to try to save his world were ghastly and horrible. Maybe there was no other way, or maybe... he was going about it in the only way he knew how.

There was no forgiving him for his crimes, nor did it seem like he was really looking to be absolved of it.

He just wanted to fix his broken world.

She had a whole speech in her head. An entire rant was ready to go, detailing exactly how he was an unmitigated asshole, and how his story was just proof of that fact. About how this whole stupid world of demons and monsters of his could just fade out and die, for all she cared.

It was an impressive speech. But it wouldn't come out of her mouth.

No matter how hard she tried, it just wouldn't come. Instead, there was something worse holding it back. Something far more dangerous than an epic diatribe against the man.

Sympathy.

Empathy.

She cared. Not just about Under... but about *him.*

The realization didn't sit well with the other half of her that clung to normalcy. Let him rot! Let him suffer. After what he did to Evie? And God knew how many people were still going through that same hell. He had toyed and played games with Lydia as recently as last night. She listed his offenses, listed every reason she had to throw a rock at his head and run into the gaping black pit of oblivion that stretched on behind her.

But she couldn't help it.

Seeing him there, in such agony, broke her heart. *God, I'm so stupid,* she reminded herself again.

He had opened a part of himself to her that she didn't expect he showed many others. His shoulders were heaving as though he was struggling to keep his breath even.

She walked up to him slowly, like someone might a wounded tiger. Reaching out her hand, she placed her palm gently on his back. It wouldn't have been unsurprising for him to whirl around and grab her wrist or to laugh at her sympathy and yell "gotcha" and cackle like a movie villain.

Instead... he sank to his knees. His head lowered, his dark hair curtained off his masked face. She moved to stand in front of him and let instinct rule. For once, she tried not to overthink what she was doing. The man was in obvious agony, hidden face or not. She put her hand on his shoulder gently. She should hate him, but damn her, she just couldn't.

Maybe he'd slap her away. Throw her to the ground and scream at her for touching him. For overstepping her bounds.

He reached his hands out to her as if begging for her to come closer. Sheepishly and unsure, she did. His hands twisted in the knit fabric of her long sweater.

Reaching up her hand, she ran her hand through his hair. Maybe she had wanted to erase more of his suffering. Maybe she was curious what it felt like. Either way, she couldn't deny she touched him now simply because... she *wanted* to.

He pulled in a wavering gasp, and his breath left him in the same unsteady manner. Pulling her closer, he rested his head against her stomach.

Wrapping an arm around him, she continued to gently stroke his hair.

They stayed like that for what might have been minutes as she felt the heaving in his shoulders slowly resolve.

When he was breathing normally once more, he pushed himself back up to standing but did not step away from her. The smell of old books and leather washed over her.

In a blink, they were gone from this edge of oblivion, both the one in Under and maybe also in Aon's mind. They reappeared inside her room. She winced. "I hate that."

The rumble she felt was proof of a nearly silent chuckle on his part. "I know." After a pause, he stepped away from her slowly, seeming reluctant to go. He took two paces back, bowed, and disappeared without another word.

It left her standing there—alone and surprised.

He had just poofed into thin air without warning or any mention of what had just happened.

Wrapping her arms around herself, she sank down onto the edge of her bed and tried to sort out what had just transpired.

Twice, in one day, Aon had left her reeling.

If for two very different reasons.

* * *

Something strange woke her up.

After a few hours, emotional exhaustion had finally pushed her over the edge into sleep. It was a fitful sleep, but it was something. Now, she came out of her uneasy slumber with a strange sensation around her.

There was the heavy comforter that helped keep out the chill night air, but something else now literally weighed on her.

There was an arm draped over her.

Blinking her eyes open, she was too sleepy and too confused to do anything at first. Maybe it was just a lingering part of her dream. Maybe she was imagining things.

Her eyes focused on the hand that was resting atop hers where it lay, curled on the surface of the comforter. It was connected to an arm that was slung over her side. Moonlight from outside faintly glinted on black metal. The hand that rested on hers wasn't flesh and bone.

Nope. She very much wasn't making this up.

She was in bed, just as she had been, curled up on her right side. But now someone was there with her. Judging by the metal-clawed prosthetic of a left hand, attached to the arm of whoever was behind her, it was Aon. His right arm was under the pillow beneath her head, and she felt his other hand next to hers.

He was lying with her head tucked under his chin, and his knees behind hers. If she held perfectly still, she could feel the rise and fall of his chest against her back, slow and steady. He was asleep, or at least he was very good at faking it.

The warlock—the King of Shadows—was holding her like a stuffed animal. Or a lover. Neither of which she was, at least last she checked.

What the hell should she do?

She could scream, jump out of bed, slap him, yell at him—but she couldn't find the will to do any of those things. Something about the moment felt... brief. Fragile, almost.

He wasn't wearing a long shirt for the first time she had seen him. There was skin visible where his arm was draped over her, running to where the prosthetic of his hand attached. Lydia wondered if he was wearing a shirt at all, and the thought made her mouth go dry once more.

He was pale, which wasn't a surprise. Lithe, but muscular. The skin of his arm had lines and lines of markings. Row after row of small, thin black ink. It covered at least half of what she could see in twisting shapes and spirals, filled with lettering or circled in geometric shapes. It was beautiful, like a work of art. She found herself marveling at them and wished she could look at them more closely.

Shifting, she tested if he was actually asleep or not. As she did, his hand slipped from where it draped across hers to wrap his arm tighter around her. He pulled her back against him with a quiet and whiney *"nnnh"* in his throat.

Yeah, he was out cold. No one who took himself as seriously as he did would ever make a sound like that on purpose.

It almost made her laugh, but she bit it back before it escaped. The way she had seen him last—broken and distraught —it was clear he came here to seek comfort. He wasn't groping her, and he wasn't harassing her. He simply wanted someone to hold in the darkness and the dead of the night.

Could she really blame him? No. Not at all.

Nor could she find the desire to refuse him. In her sleep-addled mind, she let herself admit this... felt nice. She also desperately needed some comfort after all that had happened to her. After all she'd been through—even though a bunch of it was because of the man in question—this was something she didn't realize she had been needing.

This was something they both needed. For as short as it would last.

Letting out a slow exhale, she shut her eyes, and sleep claimed her again.

TWELVE

That morning, everything felt as normal as it could, given the situation. Humans were remarkably adaptable, she figured—especially when there wasn't much she could do about the situation.

She woke up, bathed, got dressed, had breakfast, wandered until lunch.

The staff were slowly starting to get more used to her, even if they still wouldn't make eye contact or talk to her much. But she was starting to convince the kitchen staff at least that she was still studiously avoiding meat products. Although halfway through a grilled cheese sandwich, she realized she had never asked where the cheese came from.

The servants had been very concerned for her, over her sudden nausea and insistence that she was going to throw up, until she explained why monster-cheese was *not okay*. Especially when those monsters used to be *people*. They had only laughed and helpfully recommended she become entirely vegan. Yes. That was starting to sound like a great plan.

After she had managed not to throw up, she struck out wandering in extended, lazy circles around Aon's estate. The continuous walking helped keep her mind off the man in question. If he really was in her bed last night, he had been gone when she woke up. She wasn't sure if she was relieved or disappointed. Somehow, she felt both emotions at the same time. It didn't help the fact that she was torn in half over what to do.

She couldn't very well ask him if he was there or not. If the answer was yes, she would be embarrassed for not kicking him out. If the answer was no, she had dreamed of him being there. Either way, it didn't help her turmoil.

The memory of how he felt when he touched her, how he felt pressed up against her last night, made her heart lodge in her throat. She wanted him. She could admit that now. But giving in felt... wrong. But she honestly couldn't put a pin into why. Dignity? Pride?

She sighed. Walking wasn't helping her keep her mind off him anymore.

It was halfway through the afternoon that a servant came up to her, bowed, and told her she had a visitor. That was odd. The man led her outside to the large fountain in the garden. It seems it had gained another statue—this one tall, thin, and all in white, his hands folded behind his back.

Smiling, she lifted her hand in greeting. "Oh, hi, Lyon."

The man turned and faintly returned her smile and bowed his head. "Ms. Lydia. I hope you do not mind the intrusion."

"Not at all. It's a nice distraction from debating the pointlessness of my existence." Shaking her head, she sighed. "Sorry. That came off a lot worse than I meant it."

"I understand. I came to see how you fare. I take it... not well?" He gestured for her to sit on the edge of the fountain.

"I'm all right." She sat down with him. "I just don't know what to do with myself. I'm wandering around in circles. Thinking in circles."

"It is understandable. Is there anything I can do to help you?"

"Unless you can bring me home, no."

"Sadly, there is no way to travel between the worlds unless they are aligned."

"I know, I know. I wasn't serious." Reaching out, she lightly pushed him in the arm, trying to cheer him up. The man looked so horribly morose all the time. The silly gesture of hers made him smile, if barely. She'd take that as a victory. "I'm all right. I promise. I just need to adjust to... whatever this new life of mine is."

"Is there anything else troubling you, besides your presence in Under?" His brow furrowed just the barest amount. "Is Master Aon being unkind to you?"

"No. Honestly? He's been all right. Besides what he did at the gala, with that mind control stunt he pulled, he's been... okay. In his own way, respectful." At least Aon took no for an answer. She was certain many people in Under would not. "He's trying his best, I think. The worst he's been is... incredibly intense."

"An apt description of the man." He reached out and put his hand on her shoulder. "He has not harmed you, though."

"No. Still safe. He's confusing me more than anything else."

"What do you mean by that? What has he been doing?"

"He isn't what I expected, is all. He treats me like a person, as much as I think he's able to. For example, he shows me his research. Told me the story of the missing House and about the Great War. Last night he took me to see the void and explained why he's stitching people's marks back on after sucking them out with that freaky machine of his." Letting out a breath, she shrugged. "I doubt he's normally that chatty with people."

The hand on her shoulder tightened as he turned her sharply to face him. His ice-blue eyes were wide. "What did you say?"

She blinked, unsure as to why that was such a big deal. Uh oh. Was she not supposed to have said that? "I mean... it made a lot more sense. It's still awful, but at least it's not for his own shits and giggles."

"Yes, but the marks, he told you why he is attempting to rearrange the marks of others in such a grotesque fashion?" In an instant, he was holding on to both of her upper arms, twisting her to face him. He wasn't hurting her, but something about what she was saying was far more critical than she thought it was.

Suddenly, it made sense.

Nobody knew why Aon was doing this.

"It's nothing. He was lying to me. I'm sure he was. Just feeding me a stupid line to make him look more sympathetic."

"What did he tell you, Lydia? Please. A lie or not, I must know."

Pulling out of his grasp, she leaned a little away from him. "It's not that I don't trust you, but this could get me into serious trouble."

"I understand. But the potential cost of withholding this information—it could cost the lives of many more."

"So, I should risk my life to save the lives of immortal monsters who mostly just want to murder me. Or fuck me. In whatever order?" She arched an eyebrow.

"I—" The Priest paused. His expression fell, if it was at all possible, to something sadder. "I do not blame you. I cannot ask this of you."

Shutting her eyes, she rubbed her hands over her face. Letting out a groan of dismay, she gave up. "I'm guaranteed to be dead, anyway. Whatever. Sure. Fuck it. What's a little torture between now and then? He said he was trying to restore the House of Dreams. That he was trying to save this world from dying."

He stood, faster than she had seen him move before. The look on his face was an unreadable mess of emotions. Confusion, fear, and surprise, all warred for supremacy. The Priest obviously didn't show extreme emotions, let alone so many at once. "Forgive me. I must go."

"Wait, I—" But she was too late.

He exploded in a swarm of white bats that flooded the air around her.

Shrieking, she threw her arms up over her face to protect herself as they soared into the night sky above her.

Bats. Freaking *bats*.

Right. Lyon was one of the creatures that started the stories of vampires.

"Screw this place sometimes, seriously." Putting her head in her hands, she let out a disgruntled sigh. Lyon was off to tell everyone why Aon was stitching the marks onto people. Now, it was just a matter of time before Aon killed her for spilling the beans.

Swinging her legs up onto the side of the fountain, she sat sideways and leaned back against the pillar of one of the statues that ringed the circle. She looked up at the moonlight glinting off the statue's stone carvings. Tired and overwhelmed, she shut her eyes.

"Boo."

Lydia screamed.

The word had been muttered into her ear from only a half inch away. Flailing, she fell off the railing of the fountain and straight into the water.

Freezing cold liquid met her like a slap as she wound up face-down in the foot and a half of water in the base's pool. She pushed herself up onto her hands and knees, getting her face out. Her blonde hair hung in soaking strands, and it was not the only thing about her that was drenched. It'd be easier to figure out what wasn't.

Lydia knelt, flicked her hair out of her face, and wiped the water out of her eyes. Something other than the cold water caught her attention—the sound of laughter. Looking over, she wasn't the least bit surprised that it was Aon who had appeared standing next to the fountain and had startled her into the water.

He was laughing. Not his usual laugh. Not his typically lofty, amused-if-dark Vincent Price-esque laugh. Nothing that was sinister or cruel. This was a real laugh that seemed to consume every part of him. He was leaning on the statue with one hand, his other hand on his stomach, doubled over in his hysterical cackling.

"Yeah, yeah…" she muttered angrily and got to her feet, still up to her mid-calves in the water. Everything was soaked. Her pants, sweater, the coat, shoes, socks, everything.

When he sounded as though he might stop, he took one look at Lydia with a lift of his black metal masked face and then cracked up laughing again. He had to sit on the edge of the fountain, and he slumped onto it, still snickering, if not the full-on belly laugh he had been sporting a moment prior.

"You're such a douchebag." Stepping up onto the edge of the fountain and off the other side, she looked down at herself. Water was quickly puddling around her feet. The coat she had worn was useless now and just making matters worse. Peeling it off, she dropped it to the ground with a wet *plap*.

Her sweater followed suit, leaving her in a tank top. Instantly, she was shivering as the cold wind touched her bare arms.

"Oh, your glum expression is not helping the humor of the situation." He started laughing again at how miserable she must look soaking wet and freezing.

"Whatever. Can you stop laughing?" Wringing out the edge of her tank top, she quickly realized it was pointless and stopped.

"I fear I cannot." The warlock was still snickering and seemed as though he might pitch back into laughter at any time. "That was… terribly fun."

"For *you*." Her indignation was ruined by chattering teeth.

"Yes, precisely." He stood and moved toward her, arms outstretched. "Oh, do not be so angry with me. It was all in good fun."

She stayed where she was and let him settle his hands onto her shoulders. He was so damn tall, looking like a black ink blot against the marble of the fountain behind him. "I'd have dragged you in there with me, but something tells me I wouldn't have been able to budge you."

"Hmh, yes, you likely would have failed." He curled the pointer finger of his metal prosthetic under her chin. "Although the thought is very much appreciated." A shudder ran up her spine, and she wasn't sure if it was because of his touch or the cold.

"Appreciated?" She narrowed her eyes at him. "I just want you soaked and freezing, like I am. See how you like it." She wrapped her arms around herself, trying to keep what little warmth she had.

"Yes, precisely. You wish to have me join you." He stepped toward her, and her face rushed warm at his sudden shift in tone.

Damn her face, damn her blushing, damn him being so... whatever it was she thought he was. Alluring. Dark. Dangerous. *Damn him to hell.*

When she took a step back, he tilted his head to one side in an inquisitive reaction to her retreat.

"I'm going to drip on your nice clothes." It was a lie. She wasn't sure why she felt the need to make excuses. Especially such a lame excuse. "I should go change and have a hot bath before my weak human self gets a cold. Maverick's gonna start charging you if I get sick." She turned to leave, but his hand caught her wrist.

In one movement, he turned her back around to face him, wrapped his arm around her waist, and pulled her into him. "I would rather you drip on my nice clothes than my nice carpets. One is more straightforward to dry than the other."

"I have to go inside either way—" Then she realized what he planned on doing. Not another teleport. "Oh, *no*."

"Oh, shush." With that, they were gone.

The world whipped around her, and she gripped onto his shirt with both hands, trying to keep her head from reeling and her stomach where it belonged. When she could open her eyes again, she realized the room was dark, hot, and the air was wet. The change in temperature from the cold night air to the steam made her feel strange and lightheaded.

There was the sound of rushing water like the fountain, but deeper. Turning to figure out where she was, she blinked, astonished. It was a small underground pool, maybe thirty feet in diameter. The liquid was nearly black, only shining purple in the light of the torches that burned on hooks along the walls.

The room was rough stone, hewn out of solid rock with minimal carvings. Only a few features were added in, etchings of creatures dotting the edges of the walls. The ceiling arched up out of sight, too far away to be seen in the dim light. The black water was coming from some source inside the wall, pouring down a dozen feet into the water. The side of the pool was circular, carved into rough steps, leading in.

"Well?"

His question brought her back to reality out of her stunned observation of where he had brought them. "Huh? Well, what?"

"I would hate to inconvenience the Elder of Words. Strip and get in, before you catch your death of cold."

The noises that came out of her mouth were not even identifiable as parts of words. She coughed, took a breath, and tried again. "Excuse me?"

Hands on her shoulders turned her to fully face him. He held her still and caught her chin in his gloved hand to ensure she didn't look away. When he spoke, he took the tone of talking to a child. "You are soaked and freezing. This is my private hot spring. Remove your soaked clothing and get in."

"Oh, hell no." She took a step back and laughed. "Just no."

"You seem to enjoy taking baths. What is the problem?" He seemed honestly confused.

"You're here."

"And?"

"Seriously, you don't understand?"

"Fah, I have already seen you naked." He waved his hand dismissively.

"Not willingly."

"I know your kind is prudish, but truly, you are unreasonable. Get in, or else I will throw you in."

"Then leave."

"This is my hot spring." He folded his arms across his chest. "And besides, do you forget that I am a king here?"

Lydia growled and then sighed. There was no way she was going to win a fight with him. She should be glad he wasn't demanding worse. "Then at least turn around."

His laugh had returned to one of lofty amusement, and shook his head. He obediently turned his back and threw his hands up in annoyance. "There."

"You'd better stay that way until I tell you."

"Threatening me now, hm?" He sounded anything but annoyed.

"Yeah. Fear the scary mortal." She began removing the freezing, soaked clothing. There was very little worse in this world—or any other—than wet jeans. She struggled to peel them off. They were uncomfortable and cold.

"Are you quite done yet?"

"No, I'm not."

"Whatever is taking so long?" He complained with the air of a man who was winning a game of chess.

"Wet jeans stick." She let out a grunt as she finally managed to get them off.

"I could help you." His words were a dark purr.

"Don't you *dare*."

He raised his hands in a show of harmlessness and laughed. "You are an audacious thing, you truly are."

Underwear went last. Retreating to the edge of the water, she didn't want to turn her back on him. She dipped her foot in the water, and holy hell, the water was hot. She gave herself a second to adjust before stepping farther in.

The water was opaque, and it made the going slow. Lydia didn't know where the ground was or wasn't. And she had no way of finding out except the hard way, edging her feet along carefully. The water felt amazing, even if it was creepy and a deep black, like an inverse of those photos of neon-blue hot springs from Iceland.

The water smelled like minerals, and the steam washed over her face in waves. She found a spot that allowed the water to edge up over her waist, and she sank down up to her shoulders. "Okay, fine."

Turning, the warlock laughed at the sight of her hiding her nudity, hunkered down under the hot water. "How is it someone can be so headstrong and defiant, and yet so immensely bashful at the same time?"

"Sorry I have a sense of dignity."

"Mmhm. Well. I will take your soaked clothes away and fetch a dry set for you. Enjoy your bath." He scooped up her wet clothes from where she had piled them, bowed, and disappeared in a blink.

She waited—a little confused that he had stood there while she'd undressed and then just vanished. Maybe she had rebuked him one too many times. Wait, no, she had admonished him exactly the right number of times. *Stupid girl, get those thoughts out of your head,* she scolded herself. Standing, she began to wade deeper into the water. The waterfall was calling her name. That was one thing this place didn't seem to be equipped with —a shower.

The deepest part of the pond reached just above her navel. She cupped her hands in the black water and lifted them from the surface, looking down at the inky substance in her hands. It was a mineral suspended in the water that gave it the black appearance. She could see little particles of it floating about in the liquid like teensy flecks of charcoal. Huh.

Moving to stand under the water, she let her eyes shut as the heat poured over her head. It felt amazing. It felt like everything could get washed away in that stream of hot liquid. She tilted her head back and let it cascade through her hair and down her back.

The sensation of it pouring onto her shoulders felt like it might get some of the tension out that had made its home there. She didn't realize how locked up she was every second she had spent in Under and how afraid of every shadow, every flickering light, she really was.

Every breath could mean her death. Even here, there was no telling if there was something lurking in the water, ready to kill her. She tried not to care. She really did. But the thought still lingered.

Finally, she took a step out of the stream and wiped the water from her eyes. Opening them, she squeaked.

She wasn't alone anymore.

Aon had come back.

Three thoughts hit her mind all at the same time. They rammed into each other at the door jamb, and not a single one could get through. It left her standing there stunned as she tried to consider all three thoughts at once.

The first was that he had snuck up on her while she was naked, and that was cheap.

The second was that he had a lot of marks.

The third... was that he was gorgeous.

Thought three and a half was that he was suddenly also nude.

The water reached where his abdominal muscles joined beneath his navel, hinting at what lay below the level of the water. He was cut like a swimmer or a track runner. Muscular, but lean. He was not overly broad, even if he was tall. His skin was pale, and it was offset keenly by lines of black writing.

A third of his body was covered in the writing and symbols, circles and arcs, stars and strange archaic and esoteric markings of power. They were arranged artfully as if someone had placed them there on purpose.

Even here, though, he was intimidating. He was like a panther with the way he moved in the water toward her. The liquid ran around him in small ripples as he walked, slowly, as if not to startle her like a frightened deer. His long dark hair was loose and hung around his shoulders in silken tendrils, only distinct from his back mask in the way it caught the light.

After the shock wore off, she covered her breasts with one arm.

He chuckled at the pointless gesture. Too little, too late.

She should yell at him to get out. She should get up to leave. But, God, she wanted to touch him. She wanted to find out if his flirtatious attraction to her was all a lie and a game or if he might really want her.

Two urges hit her at once. One to step into his chest and trace the markings with her tongue, and the other to kick him where it might actually hurt him. They wound up canceling each other out. It left her with a third route, which she took—indignity. "Doesn't it get humid in that mask?" It was a pointless angry question, but there was no way to communicate how she was feeling. She didn't even understand it herself.

"Perhaps sometimes." Aon stepped closer. When she flinched away, he let out a thoughtful *hmm* and tilted his head to look at her. "Why do you avoid me so? You show your fascination plainly on your face." He raised his hand, and his touch was bare against her skin as he ran his fingertips along her shoulder. Even in the hot air of the room, she shivered. "Do you share such disdain for me, as others do? Do you loathe me as a demon amongst monsters?" His tone was cold, detached, even as his fingers wandered along up to her neck and laced into her wet hair. His touch was somehow warmer even than the water of the spring.

"What?" That was not where she was expecting him to take the conversation.

"You are intrigued by me, even as you are disgusted by me."

Wait, disgusted? "No, I'm not—"

"Do not lie to me. I see your curiosity. You wish to touch me. You wish, more importantly, for me to touch you. Yet you deny us both. Why?" He stepped closer, even as his temper flared.

"I meant I don't find you disgusting."

He huffed a cruel laugh. His clawed hand was on Lydia's side, a strange sensation, bare against her skin. The sharp edges of his claws were tracing along her ribs, and she gasped and was reminded exactly how dangerous he was. "Truly. The king of warlocks? The torturer. The sadist, the tormenter, the fiend—" He repeated her words to him from the night of the gala.

"Stop." She put her free hand on his chest, and she instantly regretted it. He pulled in a hiss at her touch, and his head tilted back slightly. His skin was like marble, with just the barest sensation of softness at the surface. Oh, that was almost the end of all her protesting, right then and there. When she could find her words again, they were quiet. "I was angry when I said those things. It'd be easy to think that's all you are."

"Oh? And what do *you* think, then?"

"I think it's more complex. Truth is, I..." She paused. "I honestly don't know what to make of you."

Seemingly satisfied with her answer, he changed gears in a snap. "I know what I would like to make of you, my sweet." His voice was a low growl in his throat, and the hand that had lingered in her hair slid to cup her jaw. His clawed hand was wandering again, the points of his nails dragging lightly across the skin of her stomach. His metal hand gently grasped the wrist of the arm she was using to cover herself, and he carefully pulled it down to her side.

She let him. Her shyness was pointless, he was right.

"You did not answer me in full. Why do you yet avoid me so? Even now, you blush and look away." He ran the pad of his thumb along her cheek. "Do you not find me a suitable partner?"

"It's not that."

His prosthetic hand threatened to slide north from where it lingered at her hip.

Catching his hand, she laced her fingers between his gauntleted, metal ones and pulled it away. If she let him continue—if she let him press those daggers into her any harder —that would be it. She'd be his.

"Then what is it?" His voice was husky and thick as he opted to slide his hand from her jaw to her lower back and pull her toward him. She gasped as she was suddenly flush against him and felt the wall of strength that he was. Any proof she might need that he was attracted to her was now pressed against her stomach and sandwiched between them, skin to skin.

Shit.

He moaned low in his throat, and he leaned his head in down, his clawed hand squeezing hers. His muscles rippled in a wave against her as he seemed briefly overtaken by the sensation of her body against his as well. She hadn't expected him to be so expressive. That more than anything else now questioned her resolve.

That was almost it. Right there. That could have been game

over. She shut her eyes and thought about what it would be like, let her mind wander into what kind of things he might do to her.

It was right then that she understood why she hadn't said yes already. What it was that was keeping her from giving in. It wasn't pride. It wasn't dignity.

It was the fear that once he had her, he'd get bored.

He'd chuck her aside as he did to all his other lovers.

With a horrible moment of clarity, she realized she was enjoying his company. This strange game. Their time in the library, his peculiar fascination with her, and she, in turn, with him. The idea of letting that go... *hurt*.

She couldn't say that to him. She couldn't tell him that the reason she was avoiding this was that the idea that he would get what he wanted and abandon her was scaring her. She'd only just come to that conclusion herself.

A light bulb went off in her head. It was a dangerous stall tactic, but it might be enough to buy herself some time to sort her head out.

"I'll tell you what." She leaned her head in close to his to whisper to him. "I'll give you everything you want..."

"A dangerous promise." He pulled her tighter against him. "Be wary of what you say."

She swallowed thickly. But it didn't matter. He would never make good on her deal. "I promise to do *everything* you want." She reiterated her vow and let her breath pool against his ear. He groaned quietly. She had expected him to be stony and impervious to touch. She found him exactly the opposite. "If..."

"Say it." He sounded like a starving man. That plus the feeling of him against her was almost too much. "Before I become impatient."

Somewhere, she found the nerve to stick to her guns. "If just once... you kiss me."

He would have to take off his mask to do that. And she

knew he *never* would. He was a king. He was *Aon.* She was a worthless human.

It was the perfect stalemate of a dare, and it would at least buy her a minute before he thought of a way around it. She expected a witty retort, or for him to slide his hands in any direction and easily call her bluff. Anything but the silence she received.

He straightened and stepped back. He took two more steps back and was silent as he watched her. His body language was like a coiled spring. Ready to snap, but in what direction, she couldn't tell.

Oh God, she'd done it. Clearly, her dare had utterly offended him. But before she could call after him, say to wait and tell him she was teasing, he disappeared and was gone.

This time, she knew he wasn't coming back.

THIRTEEN

Edu reached out his hand and gently placed it atop the mass of red curls that tumbled down from the girl's head. Evelyn—or Evie, as she preferred to be called—was on the path to a quick recovery.

The result of the torture was slowly mending. Evie had color in her skin and life to her bright yellow eyes. She was inhaling a bowl of soup, happily tearing off chunks of bread and dipping them into the stew. She was talking to him in between bites, even though she knew he could not answer. Ylena was not present. But it seemed not to deter her in the slightest.

"Did you have a nice day?" Evie's cheery tone was unflinching.

Edu nodded. Yes, he did, insomuch as he was able. Insomuch as he was preoccupied with thoughts of the bastard warlock and his schemes. He ended his nod with a slight shrug, and she giggled.

"I know, I know. You're a king, you probably don't have nice days. Just a matter of degrees, huh?" The girl was a quick study of his silent mannerisms, reading his small motions and his gestures better than many who had spent years in his presence.

He wished he could say he was having a beautiful day now. Now that he was back in his home. With her.

Edu loved to play with her fiery red curls. He twirled some around his finger and watched them bounce back. She did not seem to mind in the slightest. Indeed, her features bloomed in a cozy and excited smile each time he did, so he felt no need to stop.

His home was titled the House of Flames, and yet it had not seen fit to collect someone with a persona like hers. How she Fell to the House of Words was a crime against the nature of this world. Maverick could not see the value in someone with an un-killable heart like hers.

Edu's gaze traveled to the girl's arm. It had healed. The sight of Aon's torture turned his stomach in disgust. As if draining Evie's power from her body via machine was not enough—to then stitch the girl's marks back on? Twisting her power to his own whim and grant it to her anew, in his own making? *Disgusting.* And to what end?

Edu had never seen anything like it. He had never been awake during Aon's reign, not once in the past fifteen hundred years. Since the day the Great War ended, when Aon surrendered after realizing what he had done and doomed the world.

Now in Aon's hunger to save it, he seemed just as blind to —or worse, just as joyful in—the suffering he would paint to see it done.

Worst yet, Aon's machine that Evie had described to him had *worked.* The marks on her arm remained, in their dull purple color, as Aon had placed them there. He had managed to drain the girl of her gifts and restore them to her in his own design.

It was a crime against nature. A crime against Under. That was not a power Aon had any right to wield.

That was for the Ancients alone.

"Are you all right?" Evie placed her small hand on his, and it broke Edu out of his rage. He snapped out of his train of thought and looked down at her. He must have tensed up without realizing it.

Edu shook his head idly, telling her it was not her fault, and it was no matter for her to concern herself over.

Somehow, the bright child understood, and Evie smiled cheekily at him. "For a boy who can't talk, you're an awful liar." She poked him in the arm.

She called him "boy" quite frequently. Edu had not been called that in thousands of years. Not in a way that was not an insult upon the battlefield. Not by a woman who was smiling at him as though he may be anyone else in the world. Evie was bashful around him for about ten minutes after he had brought her here. After that she seemed incapable of referring to him as "king" or "lord" or "master." Such was not her way.

She referred to him as "straight six," or "boy," or any other stream of seemingly endless nicknames. Never once did she defer to him.

Edu *adored* it.

On a whim, he scooped Evie up out of her chair and put her down into his lap.

She squealed and laughed and wrapped her arms around behind his neck. "Well! All right, then." Her smile was bright and beaming.

He had taken her to his bed as soon as she was strong enough to endure his attention. And Evie had not left it since.

If there was but one reason Edu might ever be glad Aon awoke early—if there was ever but one reason he would wish such torment upon another as he had inflicted upon this poor girl—it had given Evie the opportunity to be free and at his side.

She had told him of what had happened, the night Aon pardoned her of all crimes and sent her to the edge of the encroaching oblivion. Said that Lydia had bargained away a favor and an admission of her own fate to Aon in exchange for her freedom.

A favor from a girl with no right to exist in this world... it made no sense. Aon did not give anything up lightly. The warlock was a covetous, greedy, possessive tyrant. It was out of character for him to do something without a known value in exchange.

There was only one option—the girl was not as useless as she seemed. Aon must have discovered her purpose. And if he had, Lydia was a significant danger to this world and everyone in it.

Edu's thoughts of the end of his world and encroaching war were shoved aside as Evie's tongue began to trace a line along one of the scars on his neck. He let out a small sigh of contentment and leaned his head back to allow her more room. He had cracked the door of an invitation, and Evie had kicked it in. Her hands were already roaming his body, erasing any thoughts of the warlock and his fetid nature.

Let the thoughts of doom cease for now. Let each have their own method of coping with the eternity, or worse, the coming end to it. Aon fought for power and control. Edu fought for pleasure and distraction.

And Evie... was quite a distraction to be had.

* * *

It had been a week.

Seven days. Seven days had gone by since Lydia had dared Aon to kiss her and forced him to beat a hasty retreat. Seven days without a sign from him or a word he even still existed. More importantly, without any indication that she might still exist to him.

In his absence, she had taken up wandering the estate,

trying new doors, finding new corridors. On the first day, she was nervous and afraid Aon might take his wrath out on her as he did in the dreams where they had first met. That he might try to cut his pound of flesh differently than he had intended at first.

But even her dreams were quiet.

Day two had been spent in a *fine-be-that-way* kind of false indifference. If Aon was so upset with her as to never speak to her again, then whatever. In her wanderings, she had found a second, much smaller and less grand library, although she suspected it was just a sitting room that had books in it. That was her new place to hang out during the day, as it was off the beaten path, and most people didn't come through.

And, even better, it had some books that were entirely in English, so she had spent days three and four flopped onto the sofa, drinking coffee and reading. Some were books from home, Earth books by Earth people. But one she found was written by someone from Under. It was a book on the myths and lore of Under, and she fell headlong into it. It was one of those books she'd look up from and realize hours had passed, and she hadn't even noticed. Finally, some real answers!

The book was old. Hundreds of years, by the look of it. The date in the beginning made no sense to her. They tracked years differently here, naturally. The writing was a little dense, but the subject was engrossing enough that she didn't care. One chapter was all about the Pool of the Ancients, and how it was made.

* * *

The primordial Ancients could be compared to the prehistoric gods in many Earthen religions. The pattern repeats itself across nearly every Earthen culture, by my research. Zeus, Hades, and Neptune had the elder Titans. Ra, Osirus, and Set had their

Ogdoad. Even Thor, Odin, and Balder had the giants. The examples abound.

And so do the kings and queens of Under have their Ancients. The Ancients are not gods in a human sense, but far more ancient, far more powerful creatures than even the royals of Under may claim. The royals of Under were taken by the Ancients from Earth in bygone times as a means of amusement.

In speaking to King Rxa of the House of Blood, whose communion with the Ancients is unmatched, Under was a desolate world of dust and storms and a hell by any standard. The primordial creatures cared only to satiate their deep and terrible hunger, and oft treated those now known as royalty as a fox upon the fields, to be chased down and devoured by dogs.

It is for this reason we believe we cannot die while a soulmark is upon us. For the amusement of the Ancients. It was that cruelty that drove the royals to rise and do battle against them, in days immemorial.

Aon, in his boundless cruelty that would rival even theirs, tricked the Ancients into visiting a new shrine that he, Rxa, and the others had built to their glory. It was a grand and empty canyon in the ground, a deep and fathomless well. They did not expect to be betrayed, for the royals were their children.

The natural state of the Ancients is that of an incorporeal form, drawn to their altars of worship. In an ensuing battle, the Warlock forced the Ancients into physical shape, and once doing so, Rxa, their High Priest, could chain them into their prison.

When it was done, their new altar—the Pool of the Ancients —filled to the surface with their throbbing lifeblood. Even though the Ancients lay crippled and enslaved, broken and beaten, they are yet the source of all life that springs forth in this world, remade and corrupted as it may be.

Through the lake of blood, their influence is still felt. It is by their boundless power and their own Great Will that we are made. For even though they were cast down by the royalty, imprisoned and conquered, it is still their beating hearts that hold the fabric of our world together. Would they die, so would we all. Yet if they were ever to be free, our world would end. Such things are inevitable, and so will our world return to the cycle in time.

* * *

Reaching the end of the chapter, she shut the book and let out a quiet "huh." It was sad, really, to think that the ancient, primal gods were prisoners. But the description in the book painted them to be the worst kind of monsters, and this place was maybe the source of all the myths of a terrible underworld that Earth wound up owning.

Who influenced who? Did Under come first, or did Earth?

Deciding nobody would miss it, she opted to keep the book and bring it back to her room with her. It had answered a lot of questions, ones she hadn't even known to ask. There were chapters on Aon and the others, and she was itching to read them.

Day five was when she began to worry. Usually, Aon summoned her to his library at one point or another. Rarely could she go six or eight hours without him interjecting in on her, and it had been days. It was starting to claw at her mind.

Had she really offended him? Had she really pushed him too far and driven him away? Was her stupid dare really that awful?

There was an excellent chance she didn't understand the significance of what she had said to Aon. That the dare was a mortifying threat against his very nature and so on. She knew the masks were important. She knew he'd likely rather lose his whole arm than let anyone see his face.

But damn it all, she'd just been messing around and stalling for time. She was just trying to get some space between them so she could have ten seconds to sort out how she felt.

A matter she hadn't, truthfully, figured out in the past five days. So maybe ten seconds wouldn't have done it, after all.

For that matter, why did she care that Aon was ignoring her? Why did it bother her that she had pissed him off? Why was it deeply troubling to her that he had stopped pestering her? Wasn't that a good thing?

Day seven, and it was time to do some hard soul-searching. He must have grown bored or sick of their game and had tossed her aside. And, God help her, it gave her a painful heartache to think about it. She needed to sort out why that was.

Fetching a glass of alcohol, she took it out to the fountain. It was tempting fate by going back to where the warlock had startled her into the water, but that was the point.

Aon was a monster. But everyone here was, in one way or another. Lyon was maybe the only benign one here, and God only knew what he had done in his days. It was sad when the nice guy in town was a vampire.

Yet Aon had made a piss-poor bargain in taking a favor in exchange for Evie's freedom. Lydia knew it was a useless favor. What the hell could she do for him that could interest him except maybe something sexual? He seemed unwilling to call in the bargain for that reason and paint their experience as having been the result of coercion. Lydia was grateful for that.

She was grateful for a lot of Aon's kinder tendencies toward her. He was patient, forgiving, and damn it all, *playful* with her. The way he touched her drew her in and left her wanting more. That was what the blush meant each time, and he knew it. He could see through her bullshit, even when she couldn't.

The warlock had said as much at his hot spring a week prior. He knew what she couldn't admit, that despite his monstrous behavior to the world, despite his sadism, she wanted him. She was attracted to him. She loved his attention and desired to feel him draw her further into that dark web of his.

Which is why it hurt so much to think of losing it.

The only reason she was of any interest to the warlock was because she was coy, she was sure of it. It was only because she was holding out on him. The moment she gave that up, he'd get bored with her and toss her aside. And besides, she was probably a lousy lover, considering his over five thousand years of practice.

Looking down at her empty drink, she sighed. She wasn't much closer to a conclusion.

One thing she did realize was that she was sorry. Sorry that she had unintentionally driven Aon away. So at least she could apologize to the man. She stood from the fountain and walked back inside and made her trek to his library. She hadn't gone near it in the past seven days, not wanting to intrude on him if she wasn't welcome.

Rapping her knuckles on the door, there was no response. Turning the handle, she found the door unlocked. The room was quiet, and the lights were off. Aon wasn't here.

"He hasn't been in," a servant said from behind her. It was an old man who smiled at her when she would pass him, and she would do the same in turn. "I expect he's been in his workshop below."

"Workshop?"

"You haven't seen it, then? Bully for you." The man shifted the basket of laundry he was carrying. "It isn't anywhere anyone wants to be."

Ah. That was where Evie had been. His workshop beneath the ground. She nodded weakly, showing she understood.

"Master Aon does this. He might spend months down there, engrossed in his work, never coming back up." The man resumed his trek down the hallway. "I wouldn't take it personally."

Yet here she was, taking it very personally.

"Thanks," she said to the man as he walked away, and he let out a *mmhmm* of acknowledgment.

Stepping into the library, she shut the door behind her. It was dark and cold. The fire had not been burning in here all week. She walked to the chair Aon usually sat in and found a piece of paper and his quill pen.

It was stupid. But it felt right. Simply writing "I'm sorry" on the piece of paper in her much-worse-than-his-in-comparison handwriting, she folded it and put it on the seat of his chair. Having done what she had set out to do, she decided to head back to her room. Maybe she could score another stiff drink along the way.

God help her, not only did she understand that she wanted Aon... even worse, she *missed* him.

* * *

Lyon materialized in a swarm of white bats in the clearing in the woods. Four of their moons were bright overhead, illuminating the forest in various shades of pale jewel tones.

Kamira approached him and wove an arm around his waist, and he caught sight of several other shifters hovering in the shadows at the edges of the forest. But it was not for them that he had come.

Lord Edu stood in the center of the clearing, Ylena at his side. He was not surprised to see the king, as Lyon had called him here to avoid suspicion.

Aon would wonder why Lyon visited the mortal girl so frequently and would likely have his spies keeping an eye on Edu's keep. But no one would suspect Lyon visiting his wife.

"Master Edu received your message. You have news to tell us?" Ylena broke the silence from the side of her king.

He did not often feel nervous. At his age, very little made him uneasy. Yet he knew Edu's wrath and had seen it keenly played out upon this world and its inhabitants many times. Rarely did anything trigger the King of Flames' temper quite so vehemently as when Aon and the issue of the dreamers came to the surface.

That was, after all, how this whole mess began.

When last Aon had attempted to exert his control over the fabric of the world, the warlock still had a left hand, and Edu a tongue. Few but Lyon and some of the elders were present for that great and terrible war, and they were dark times that fewer wished to remember.

It was for that reason that he had summoned Edu. For if there was any action he could do to prevent another such catastrophe, he had to take it. Shutting his eyes, he braced himself for the chaos he was about to unleash. He begged silently for Lydia's forgiveness, for he knew the young mortal would be caught betwixt forces of nature she could not control. "Aon seeks to rekindle the House of Dreams. His experiments are to such an end. He seeks to control the marks so that he may restore the dead House."

Edu hissed in a breath through his nose. "Are you certain? How do you know this?" Ylena snapped. When Edu became too passionate, her sense of individuality became greatly diminished.

"Aon has spoken to Lydia of this. He may have lied to her, but I do not believe so. I think he viewed his admission as harmless, as she is not truly one of us."

"Hey! Is Lydia okay?" someone asked from the edge of the forest.

Lyon turned his head and saw the boy, Nicholas. He was adjusting quickly, by the looks of it. Although he did not care enough for Edu's temper to hold his tongue.

"Lydia is well. Aon has not harmed her in any way. She is confused and distraught, little more." Lyon did his best to console the boy.

"Can Aon do it? Can he raise the House of Dreams from the dead?" Ylena pulled the focus back to her and Edu.

Lyon could only shake his head, for he did not know. It had never been done before, as a House had never fallen to ruin in all the time Under had been in existence. If one had never died, who was to say that one could never be raised? It seemed impossible. Then again, so did much in this dark and dismal world.

Like a girl, cast into the Ancients but rejected.

It seemed Edu was wondering the same, as Ylena spoke up again. "And the girl? What part does she play in all this?"

"None that I can possibly discern. She is innocent in all this. I insist he has not harmed her in any way, save what may be considered remarkably benign antics on his part. I cannot sense any power in her. I do not think there is anything that dwells beneath, and I plead with you to look upon her with mercy."

"Aon does not keep useless pets." Ylena's fury was not her own. "He has a purpose in keeping her alive. If it is not a hidden strength, then what is it?"

Lyon shut his eyes. He knew the words he was choosing would bear significant weight on the events to come. There was little more in this world he despised more than the feeling of the world rushing away from him like a ball rolling downhill. No matter how he chased it, how he tried to catch it and stop the tumultuous decent, there was no scrambling or scraping he could do to cease the disaster in action.

"Priest, speak your mind."

Edu had stepped toward him, and even though Lyon could not see the man's face, his body language spoke plenty. He was rigid, locked in a singular desire to bring pain to something or someone nearby. Lyon knew if he did not answer quickly, it would be him.

"I have not known Aon to pay much attention to anyone. Not even potential lovers," Lyon admitted. "For that reason, either he has come to harbor a true fondness for the girl..."

Edu snorted. "Or?"

"Or..." Lyon paused. His heart hitched. He hated to even vocalize his concern. "While I believe she is ignorant to whatever may be happening... I wonder if Aon has not found some way to connect her to his goals."

"What would you have Master Edu do?" Edu tilted his head to the side slightly as Ylena spoke on his behalf. "He knows his choice. He wonders yours."

Lyon knew Edu's choice plainly; he would wish to kill the girl. Such had been his intention, ever since Aon began to wake from his slumber. Kill the girl to spare what Aon might do with her. Lyon let out a weary sigh and tightened his arm around Kamira gently. The shifter had remained remarkably quiet, even for her, sensing the seriousness of the affair. "I believe we must ask the advice of all the others if we are to commit treason and murder."

"Will you stand beside Edu in this matter?"

Lyon felt the muscle in his jaw twitch. "I will stand beside this world."

"Speak plainly, Priest."

"If Aon plans to resurrect Qta or the dreamers, I do not know as he could resist the temptation to control them as he sought to do once before." Lyon paused. "I do not know if Ms. Lydia has anything to do with these matters. I am hesitant to commit the girl to death without proof."

"Proof enough lies in his desire to keep her breathing." Edu's fist clenched, the leather creaking.

"Perhaps." Lyon held on to a fleeting prayer that perhaps Aon did hold some strange attraction to Lydia. "Perhaps I am a sentimental, hopeful old fool."

"That was never in question."

"I will not advise mutiny without the opinions of the others."

"Very well. We shall have them." Ylena was held fast in

Edu's rage. It was rare the girl became so impassioned in her speech. Edu must be quite beside himself. "But know this, Priest. If the others vote to take her life, he will not linger this time. Master Edu will claim her life *personally*."

"No!" Nicholas shouted and tried to break into the circle. The boy—her friend—had not taken kindly to the decision. "No, this is wrong!"

Two other shifters subdued him quickly and dragged him away. Kamira, shooting a weary glance up at Lyon, went to follow them.

Lyon bowed his head low in subservience to his king and felt the weight of the world press upon him. How he wished that Master Aon's interests in the girl were not bent toward his dark desires. That he was not scheming to give life to the fallen House, and therefore save their world, merely to clinch it in his metal fist.

Yet he could not fathom a world where that was not true.

"Yes, my king."

* * *

Something strange woke her up.

It wasn't as oddly comforting as when Lydia had woken up with Aon in her bed. No, this was like a slap. More correctly, it felt like somebody had smacked a tennis racket off her face. It hurt, sure, but it was more jarring than painful.

Sitting up abruptly, she put her hands to her face. But everything seemed to be where she left it. No wounds, no bruises.

She pulled her hands from her face and blinked. It was dark. But not the *usual* type of dark. It was that all-encompassing, utterly lightless kind of darkness that came along with a cave. The kind that made your vision do funny tricks, as your mind tried to process seeing absolutely nothing at all.

Weird. Blinking a few times, she rubbed her eyes. It didn't help, and her vision didn't adjust. Her room had some antique style electric lights, and one of them was on her bed stand. She reached out and fumbled for it, finally finding it and flipping the switch on.

Nothing happened.

No light.

She flicked it off, on, off, on, then off and on, one last time. Nothing.

Carefully climbing out of bed, she held her hands out in front of her to keep from walking into anything. After a moment or two, she finally found the wall and felt her way along it to the large window. She pulled open the shutters.

Nothing. There were always lights burning outside. Even when there were no moons in the sky, she could see the outline of the trees against the darkness. Or the lights that always glowed from the gardens or the property.

Slowly, with a sinking pit of horror forming in her chest, she realized what was happening. It wasn't that there was no light to be seen... she couldn't see it.

She was blind.

Her breath started to come fast and shallow, hitching in her chest. She pressed her back against the wall, palms flat against the textured wallpaper. She focused on breathing and on not panicking.

How? Why? She had gone to bed fine, and woke up *blind*.

Poison, maybe? One of the servants? Or a jealous some-body-or-other, slipping something into her drink? Maybe the alcohol she'd been drinking was poisonous to humans.

Tears stung her eyes as the fear tried valiantly to take over, and it was winning. Resting her head against the wall, she focused on breathing. In and out. In and out. In... and out. Good. Progress. The world didn't seem so wobbly anymore.

Okay. Options. Next steps. Come up with a list of next

steps. She needed to get help. But who? The servants would be useless. She had no way of contacting Maverick or Lyon. No, there was only one person who could do anything to help her.

If Aon was even listening. If he was still paying any attention. She didn't even know if this line of telepathic communication went both ways. He had only ever responded to her words when he had spoken into her mind.

And, to boot, Aon had clearly given up on her. He'd left her to her own ends.

But there was no harm in trying. It was try or... be blind. And who knew if it would get worse and lead to her death.

Taking a breath, she felt like a fool. It was hopeless. But now wasn't the time to cling to dignity. "Aon, I don't know if you can hear me, but help me. Please." Her voice broke as the fear surged to the surface again, and she wiped her hand across her eyes as if she might remove a film from them, but only found tears.

Hands caught hers, and Lydia let out a startled cry. She pressed harder back against the wall, trying to escape from whatever had just grabbed her. But whatever—whoever—was standing near her now, and there was nowhere for her to go. She could feel them, hovering near her. One hand was normal, the other metal. The smell of old books.

A sharp, low voice like a knife wrapped in velvet was suddenly close to her. "You needn't call for me, my sweet. I am right here."

"I—I can't see."

"I know." His voice was a whisper. She felt his breath brush against her cheek as he spoke. "Do not worry."

He released her wrists, and she shifted her hands to rest her palms against his chest. She felt the silk fabric of his shirt underneath her fingers, and she let herself clasp onto him as if he were the only thing keeping her above water in a driving ocean.

Aon's flesh-and-blood hand gently stroked her hair back away from her face soothingly.

His voice was soft, and she could feel it rumble in his chest. "All will be well in the morning…"

Wait.

Anger suddenly rushed to meet her fear, and she gripped the fabric of his shirt harder.

Hold on.

"*You* did this?" She was trembling now, as the adrenaline coursing through her body was split equally between terror and rage.

"Of course."

"You—but why? Why did you—"

She never got the chance to finish her sentence, as Aon silenced it with a press of his lips against hers.

FOURTEEN

The feeling of Aon's lips against hers stunned her to immobility. It was a tender gesture, meant to silence her. And it worked. She was struck.

He pulled away from her, and she let her hand roam to his face, resting her palm against his cheek in disbelief.

Her touch drew a small noise out of him. It was a strange, choked sound as she felt his skin, not metal, under her hand. Smooth and warm. His mask was gone. Nobody took their masks off around anyone else, not unless they trusted the other person with their lives.

Or if they couldn't see.

The warlock had taken her sight to kiss her, to make good on her dare.

"Okay." She sighed. "Clever."

"Not terribly. Kings and queens have often taken the sight of their partners." He was clearly amused.

She felt his face move as he spoke, and she found herself running her fingers along his cheek, curiously trying to picture what he looked like. "Please tell me you can reverse it."

"Of course." His expression bloomed into a smirk under

her hand. It was the first hint she had of anything like that from him. Honestly, it was the first proof she had that he even had a face. "Taking your sight would have been easy. Ensuring I had the proper method to restore it proved difficult. I doubt you would have wished to sit about, blind, while I sorted out the matter. What do you think took me so long?"

"I thought..."

"I know. I received your note. How wonderful, you thought you hurt my feelings." He chuckled.

She turned her head away shyly. "I didn't know what to think."

He turned her face back toward his with the press of metal fingers against her cheek. "Tell me... did you miss me?" He leaned in closer again, and she felt the warmth of his breath. She had never felt his breath before, not with him wearing a mask. His teeth grazed her skin, and she nearly lost the use of her legs.

Lying to him at this moment seemed entirely outside her faculties with him nipping at her earlobe. "Yeah... I did."

It was clear he didn't expect that response. He stopped tormenting her ear to speak. "You lie to flatter me, now? How terribly unlike you."

"I wish. I—I don't think I'm lying."

His voice was breathless when he spoke. "Oh, I do not deserve you." A metal hand tipped her head up to meet him, and he kissed her once more. He let out a low moan in his throat, and she felt him grasp at her tightly with his other hand, which had settled on her hip. His clawed prosthetic slipped from her chin and into her hair as he worked his lips over hers with more need than before.

Her stomach nearly turned over itself at his touch, and she sank against the wall at the feeling of his lips against hers. *Oh, holy hell.*

It had been a very, very long time since he had been kissed. And never had been anything like this. Leaning into his embrace, she roamed her hands over him, savoring in the sensation.

He let out a small sound of surprise at her impassioned response.

Settling a hand against his cheek, she stroked his skin, trying to learn what he might look like. But it wasn't like she had any experience being blind.

He had to break the kiss to gasp as she touched him, and she felt him clutch her tighter as she did. All his motions froze as she ran her fingertips along his features, then stroked them back and through his hair before returning to trace his jawline. There was a low growl in his throat, which ended in a breathy sigh as she cradled his face in her hands, caressing his cheeks with her thumbs. It felt as though he would melt against her at the sensation.

"I do not think you can possibly understand how it feels to be touched like this... after so long." His words were thick.

"How long?"

He let out a single huff of a quiet, sardonic laugh. "I do not remember."

She felt him cringe at the words. Felt his face twist in a moment of pain as he tried to summon something from the depths of his mind. She hadn't forgotten that the man was insane. But to never remember being kissed? To... be touched?

She pulled his face to hers and pressed her lips to his for real this time. She threw her conflict and her shyness aside and embraced the man as he deserved. The way she had wanted to do for *weeks* now. Her fervor surprised them both. A choked noise left him as she ran her tongue along his lips, asking for entry. He granted it, and a beat later, his stunned moment ended in a snap.

He pressed her against the wall as his temperance seemed to break. The kiss turned hungry, desperate, like a drowning man seeking for water. It was powerful, it was demanding, controlling and possessive. It was much more of what she had expected out of him. His whole body shuddered against her, but still, he didn't relent.

After she thought the air might be stolen out of her lungs and send her to the floor, he finally parted his lips from hers. They were both in a sorry state for air, and while he was the winner of the fight, she could feel his chest heaving beneath her hand.

"That, in and of itself, made the week well spent." He let out a small, contented grunt. His hands were still grasping at her, though the hand at the back of her neck was now drawing small circles at the base. The sensation made her shiver. He chuckled at her reaction and kept going. "You do so much like to be touched, don't you?"

"Don't gloat. You seem to be in the same boat."

"I have been deprived." He shifted himself closer to her, leaning his thigh up against hers. She couldn't help but gasp at the feeling of him, and how much she clearly affected him, pressing up against her. "And I think I have earned a little gloating, don't you? I beat your little challenge, did I not?"

Right. Oh, shit. Her dare. How someone could be so warm and cold at the same time, she didn't know, but damn it if she wasn't trying to somehow both blush and go pale.

"My beautiful creature." He chuckled and leaned in, his breath hot against her skin. "While I have bested your challenge to me, I cannot in good conscience hold you to your promise that I may do whatever I wish to you. You know not what you say. Now, I challenge you instead. See how you react to my touch?" His ungloved hand gently tilted her head away from him so he might press his lips to the hollow of her throat just underneath her ear. "And deny me once more without a lie, if you can."

A soft moan left her lips as he kissed her throat. He ran his tongue in a slow circle against her skin, and she writhed in his grasp, her moan turning into a sharper cry. It felt like her skin was electric. No, she couldn't turn him away and not be lying about how badly she wanted him. He growled deep in his throat at her writhing and gripped her possessively.

"My dear." He was breathless in his own right. "I warn you that now we stand here upon a threshold. Refuse me now, or know that once I begin... once you take my hand in *this* dance... once you decide to take me as your lover, I will not stop. I do not think I could if I tried." He took a step away from her, remaining just in her reach, with her hand against his chest. "What say you?"

It felt like the top of a roller coaster. The moment just before the drop, where everything goes silent. Her stomach twisted with fear and excitement at his words. His message was clear. If she decided yes... then all bets were off.

Did she think he was going to hurt her? Maybe. Did she think he was going to kill or maim her? Shockingly, no. And worse still, the thought of what he was threatening to do to her started a fire in her she never knew she was capable of feeling. It tapped into something primal inside of her, and God help her, she wanted it. Wanted him. Wanted to feel his control.

She twisted her hand in his shirt and yanked him back to her roughly. The gesture caught him off guard, and he came along with it with a small noise of surprise. She found his lips again and kissed him, silently answering his question.

Hands on her hips, he picked her up, sliding her against the wallpaper, and wrapped her legs around his waist. Her night-shirt rode up her thighs as he did, and she felt both claws and skin alike as he ran his fingers up along her legs. Neither was terribly gentle, but one came with the dangerous scrape of claws.

He broke the kiss as he dug his metal nails against her. Letting out a gasp, she squeezed her eyes shut reflexively. It burned, the way he slowly dragged them against her. She squirmed and found that... yes, it hurt. But what it triggered in her was far more frightening than pain.

His voice was a husky growl as he held her, trapped against the wall. "Know that I eagerly watched your fear upon waking. I wanted to see your terror as you discovered you were blind. It filled my heart with joy. I did not tell you I was here, for I wished to drink in your horror and know I had done it to you. That is simply who I am. This is your last chance to refuse me, my darling Lydia."

The sensation of him, the press of his body against hers, the strength she felt in his grasp, was too much. The slight burn of the scratches on her thigh somehow only added to the excitement. His presence robbed her of breath.

"I will have you say the words. Tell me you wish for me to stay or bid me leave you. I will not let this linger in ambiguity." He kissed her again, violent, hungry, and needy, teeth bruising her lips. It was passionate; it was rough. It felt as though he was attempting to crush her under his will. Both her arms were now around him, one still tangled in his hair, the other holding him close to her. Half to hold onto him, half to hold on for dear life.

The feeling of his strength against her made her want to melt and crumble into nothing and fall at his mercy. She pulled him flush against her body, and he closed the distance between them happily, pressing his chest against hers. She felt his hands slide up her body now that she supported her own weight with her legs. His palms ran up her sides, up her nightgown, caressing her. He moaned against her lips, and once more she felt him shudder against her.

He wasn't what she had expected. She had thought he would be a cold, distant lover. Quiet, dignified, and unresponsive. Instead, he seemed to feel no need to dampen the expression of what he felt, and he was caught up in the moment.

If she wanted to turn him away, this was her last chance. Even as she felt him pressed against her and felt the passion and want that burned in him, she knew he'd simply put her down, walk away, and forget any of this ever happened if she asked him to. For a man who was a tyrant and a villain, he was giving her every chance to change her mind.

Fuck that.

She caught his face in her hands and ran her lips to his ear, this time biting down. He let out a low snarl that ended in a breathy groan. His clear enjoyment of the moment gave her a bravery that she might regret later. She kissed him—slowly, gently, at her speed this time. He tasted almost like herbs, tangy and strange. She wanted more of it.

When her kiss ended, she whispered to him and knew she was walking over that gateway and could not come back from it. "A dare's a dare. I plan to keep my half of the bargain."

He shuddered at her words, and he wrapped an arm around her, clutching her to him as if she might give him purchase against whatever just overcame him. He buried his head into the crook of her shoulder, and she felt him press a hot, slow kiss against the spot where her neck and shoulder met. "Oh, my darling. My sweet and wonderful creature. You must stop teasing me with such wonderful games."

She let out a startled cry as suddenly the world moved around her. He whirled around, pulled her down from the wall, and half threw her away from him without any warning. Without being able to see, there was little she could do but stagger and flail. Her hands found the corner posts of the bed, and she clung onto it to keep from hitting the ground.

Hands fell on her shoulders and whirled her around. He placed the corner post at her back and pressed her there. When she tried to grab hold of him to try and slow him down, he merely laughed. He grabbed her hands and roughly yanked them behind her back. He bent them up behind her, each wrist on the other elbow.

Something else joined the feeling of his hands, cinching

around her arms, tying them together. Sure enough, when he slid his hands up to her shoulders, she couldn't move them. She could barely even wriggle them with such little slack, tied wrists-to-forearms as she was. It didn't stop her from trying as she squirmed, trying to yank her hands free to no avail.

The point of a sharp claw was tracing down her neck, and it suddenly made struggling dangerous. She pressed back against the bedpost and froze.

He chuckled darkly at her squirming. "I do not think you can even begin to comprehend what it is you do to me. Do you know how you have lingered in my thoughts? How much sleep I have lost, dreaming of what I wished to do to you? How you might look as you writhed within my grasp?"

The sharp claw worked its way across her shoulder, leaving goosebumps in its wake. He slipped it under the strap of her nightgown, and yanked upward, slicing the fabric. "I fear you became a bit of an obsession of mine, my darling Lydia." He pulled in a shuddering breath as he traveled his claw slowly across her collarbone. "I see in your eyes a love for the darkness that I bring. You are afraid to follow me down that path, yet you cannot pull away. How I longed to feel you since the moment I saw you... how tempting it was to simply ravage you like a beast."

His claw worked its way under the other strap of her nightgown and sliced it free of her body. The thin shift pooled at her feet and the cool air against her quickly gave her goosebumps. "But I will never steal what could be given."

She could only whimper as he pushed her underwear off her hips and to the floor. His hands lingered for a moment before he took a step back and let out an appreciative hum in his throat. She could feel the weight of his gaze on her body, even without being able to see him. Her face felt hot, and she knew she was blushing.

"How I would adore to lash you to that post and torment

you for hours, but I fear you have utterly ruined my restraint." A single sharp talon pressed against one of her already hard nipples.

Gasping, she tried to curl in to move her tender flesh from his reach.

But he was not deterred. He stepped in closer, his other hand slipping around her throat. He pressed himself against her side, pressing his burgeoning hardness against her. "Do you know how difficult it was to sit through that dull meeting with this? You are an insufferable tease. You wicked creature, so ignorant to what you've done..."

His confession of his desire for her twisted in her stomach, and she could only moan low in her throat at the feel of him against her and the sharp claw still pressing against her flesh. The hand around her neck made her feel lightheaded and strange. He was too much. He used his gentle grasp at her throat to tilt her head backward, arching her back and pressing her chest harder against his hand.

"I have desired you since the moment I saw you in my dreams. I have kept myself from ruining you—but oh, how tempting it has been all this time."

"I—" Her words broke off in a sharp cry as he shifted his metal hand to instead pinch her nipple between two metal knuckles.

"There we are! I have missed that sound. What a wonderful symphony you played for me in your dreams when we first met. It is much more charming in person, I must admit..." he growled the words into her ear and placed a hot, sensual kiss against her jawline.

She felt like this was all a dream. A nightmare that she never wanted to leave.

The hand around her throat tightened, restricting her air just the slightest amount. She writhed, moaning again. Before she could even get a straight thought in her head, Aon threw her onto the bed on her side.

"What a sight." He groaned.

Rolling onto her back, she felt him climb onto the bed with her. When she tried to shuffle back away from him, his hand went around her throat, stopping her retreat. Not tightening—but promising to. "Now, now," he scolded her. "It's far too late for that."

She swallowed thickly in her throat as he pushed her legs apart, and she felt him kneel in between them. The skin that touched hers was bare, and warm. The thought of him naked there so close to her made her remember the sight of him in his hot spring.

His hands roamed her body, surveying her. Sliding over her stomach, her sides—raking his nails and claws against her to watch her squirm in response.

"This is as blissful as I had imagined it would be," he murmured to her. The touch of his claws stung, but it only fed the fire that was burning inside of her. "No. Perhaps more so."

When his hand found her core, she gasped. He wasted no time before his fingers suddenly delved into her without warning.

Crying out, she arched her back off the bed at the sudden invasion. Her hips bucked up off the bed, seeking more.

He laughed as he began to work his fingers inside of her slowly. "Such theatrics! Such false pretenses! And here I thought you did not find me attractive." He goaded her over her own obvious state of arousal.

"Shut up, you—" she growled at him and gasped as the point of a sharp metal talon touched her sensitive nub. He called her bluff, and she fell silent, biting back her words.

"Hm? What was that?"

She didn't answer and grit her teeth.

"No, no, do say it. I'm curious." He twisted his fingers inside of her and plunged them deeper, as far as they would go. Her cry ended in a moan as he tormented her, her words forgotten in the rush of pleasure that cut through her. "I thought as much."

Of course he had to *gloat* and *monologue.* Of course he did. This was Aon, after all.

Her annoyance fled as he plunged his fingers slowly into her, again and again, exploring her. His thumb ran circles around her apex, taking the place of his claw, and she let out a sharper cry of pleasure and tossed her head back against the sheets. He brought her right to the edge of release before suddenly stopping.

She felt him bend down over her. The touch of his long hair against her cheek was all the warning she received before his lips descended on hers languorously taking her at his leisure. He finished by letting his tongue slide slowly along her bottom lip. "I adore how you taste. If it were not for your clever stalling, I would not know it. For that, I thank you." He brought his teeth down in a bite along her lower lip—growing in pressure until she let out a noise, and then relenting before kissing away the pain.

His human hand slid to cup her breast, kneading it in between his fingers. It brought a moan out of her throat against his lips, and she couldn't help but shift underneath him. God, she felt like she was on fire.

His lips found her other breast, and he took over the torment of her body with his tongue and teeth instead of metal and claw. Each time he would bite or twist at her, she writhed underneath him, squirming against his body. He continued until a mewl or a cry would leave her throat—until she tossed her head in helplessness—and then would relent, kissing or licking at the maligned and tender skin gently.

She realized he was testing her limits. Learning when the pain was too much for her. Worse still, he was muddling the sensations of pain and pleasure together until they were starting to become indistinguishable.

To her surprise, both were affecting her about the same. Each time he dug his teeth into her, she felt her body light up in electricity just as much as his tenderness. She wanted him to not hold back. She wanted to know what dancing with him truly felt like. Well, there was something she never knew about herself. Yet, it seemed, *he* did.

When he shifted his head to switch sides, he changed hands, as well. That brought a new level of danger and a new kind of pain as he dragged his claws over the exposed skin of her chest. The note she hit went higher as he pulled a single metal nail along the line of her bust. By the burning, she knew he had scratched her hard enough to make her bleed. All she could do was let out an open-mouthed gasp as she tilted her head back against the bed.

Aon ran his tongue, hot and slow, over the cut. He moaned and shuddered against her. His human hand was suddenly underneath her back, pressing her to him as he began to lap at the wound in slow, repeated strokes of his tongue.

He shifted suddenly, and she let out a startled noise as he pushed himself up to kneeling again, and with a hand on her hip and the other on her shoulder, yanked her up to follow him. She tensed, startled, as she was now sitting on his thighs. An arm banded around her lower back and tugged her flush up against him.

She moaned at the feeling of his chest pressed against hers and at the sensation of his arousal, pressed between them, hard and throbbing against her abdomen. It didn't help her nervousness and she felt her muscles lock up reflexively. She'd had lovers in her life, but no one like him before—nothing like what she felt up against her.

His clawed hand was slowly sliding over her shoulders and wandering around her neck, brushing her hair back away from her face. He shushed her gently, clearly seeing the nervousness on her face, as his metal prosthetic tilted her head away to give him room to lean his head down to kiss her. Even sitting on his lap, he was taller than she was.

"It's all right, my darling," he whispered to her. "Relax. I will bring you no harm that you do not enjoy. This I promise..."

His words were true, she realized. Even when he drew the line across her chest that still stung, she had felt her stomach twist in knots in excitement as he had licked away the blood. She couldn't even feel the scratch anymore, but there was no way to deny the furnace that was raging away inside of her. That every time his clawed nails brushed against her skin, she shivered.

"Besides..." He slid his metal claws across her rump, and when he squeezed, the tips pressed against her sensitive skin, making her yelp and squirm. His words were painted in a deep moan of pleasure as she rubbed her body unwittingly against his and his trapped arousal between them. "I think you may just be loving this just as much as I am. Well." He let out a single, breathless huff of a laugh. "Perhaps not as much..."

She went to open her mouth to insult him, to bitterly complain about him teasing her like that, but his lips silenced her before she had the chance. She melted against the assault as he kissed her.

The slight release of tension in her body was all he needed as a sign to continue. His metal hand grasped her and lifted her, and he used the other to guide himself to her entrance. She felt him there against her, and she let out a "mmnh!" against him. She broke the kiss and let out a breathless "Wait!"

Aon laughed, quiet and cruel. "No."

No sound escaped her as he drove her down onto him with such force it robbed her of even a cry. He sunk the entirety of his length into her in one motion, plunging into her and ramming into her end in an unapologetic collision of their bodies. It felt as though he was going to split her in half.

But it wasn't pain that drove her mind blank and took all sound out of her throat—it was the unexpected wave of pure ecstasy that crashed over her like the tide. His invasion sent her over the cliff and pleasure wracked her and drove everything else out of her mind. Everything in her was alight, leaving her trembling, all her muscles locked tight.

Both of his arms were wrapped around her now, clutching her to him. His body was tensing and releasing in waves, and he was shuddering against her. He let out a tight and broken moan, muffled where he had buried his face into her hair. "Oh, how I have wanted to be inside you—how I have imagined this. Hah... nnh! Oh, my beautiful thing." He gasped, tilting his head away from her and moaned low. "You nearly ended our fun so soon, right then and there."

Arms tightened around her and pressed her downward and he lifted his hips up against her, driving him harder against her end. It almost sent her over the edge into ecstasy a second time. It ached. And it was *glorious.* He was driving himself so hard into her body she knew she would feel it in the morning. God damn it all, she needed more of it. Needed it never to end. She let out a moan and wished she could grab hold of him. Wanted to do anything—but she was helpless with her arms tied behind her back. "Fuck—" was all she managed to say.

He slid his tongue slowly up her cheek toward her ear before whispering to her. "There you are. I thought I had lost you."

She could barely think through the feeling of him buried inside of her. She could only whimper as he slowly eased off, only to repeat the pattern again. He wasn't even moving yet— just changing the pressure he applied against her as he held her. He was relenting only to press her down on him once more, again and again.

"Aon—" her words broke off. She was trembling in his arms, feeling breathless and reeling. Her body was still tingling in the aftershock of what he had done. Whatever she had dreamed it would be like to be with him, her imagination had fallen short.

"Yes... that's it..." he praised her quietly, kissing her shoulder. He lifted her from him, barely an inch, before pressing her back down to the hilt. He did it with an unflinching force that it brought the sensation of him driving against her end back tenfold. He moaned loudly, meeting her sharp cry at the sensation. "Nngh! Do you feel how wonderful we fit together? I am just barely too much for you... this is perfect. *You* are perfect. Tell me; do you feel it, as well? When I claim you like this? When I take you as *mine*?"

It felt so goddamn amazing it made her head spin. "Yes," she admitted in a breathless moan.

"Do you want me to stop?" He did it again, somehow harder than before. She forgot that he was inhumanly strong. He could probably snap her if he tried. His fingers dug into her hips as he ground himself into her core.

She let out a moan, resting her head against his shoulder. Her body was electric. Tight and tense and full of him. She had never felt anything like it before.

"Well? Shall I stop? Love you like a gentle Seelie prince instead?" He relented on the pressure only to repeat.

Oh God. No. Anything but that. She wouldn't be able to handle it now, knowing what he could really do to her. "No... Please don't... don't stop."

"You want me to ravage you? Take you? Mold your body to mine? Say it."

Her stomach felt like she had been thrown over a cliff. She shuddered in pleasure at his dark words, even as much as the feeling of him inside of her. She whimpered and bit her lip.

"Say it," he growled into her ear, his voice husky and thick with need. He could feel the effect his words were having on her as she clung to him, she was sure.

"Yes. Please, Aon..."

"Good." Another slight lift of her body and he pulled her back down onto him harder and with a bruising force.

A second impact, and her head was reeling. A third time and it was too much—she almost wailed, overwrought as another crashing wave of pleasure drove over her. Her head was spinning, and she breathlessly cried his name.

He was shuddering, nearly overcome as well. "Aah... ngh, how quick you are to ruin me."

With that, she was suddenly bent backward as he pressed her back to the bed without breaking where they were joined.

Pain and pleasure both racked her body. Together, mixed as one, they were indistinguishable. And she never wanted it to stop. Her noises of agony and pleasure drew a deep laugh from him, painted thick with heated desire.

"Does it hurt?" he asked, his voice a deep, breathy purr.

She nodded, unable to find the words.

"Do you want me to stop?" he asked again. Giving her another chance to ask him to let up. Another chance to confess how much she loved this.

She shook her head. No, anything but that.

"Do you enjoy this?"

She nodded.

"Good. Because we have only just begun, my sweet..."

One of his hands was then pinning her shoulder to the bed, the other gripping her hips as he withdrew from her nearly all the way before slamming back in with all his force. A choked cry left her mouth as he did—and each time after that.

He was relentless as he pistoned in and out of her with a crushing force. Each time, a low, guttural noise in him met her sharper, mewling cry.

Her mind was dissolving into white noise. The only thing

that existed was his intense and amazing presence. If it killed her, she'd die happily like this. She could barely hear his muted praise between his own moans of pleasure as he unleashed himself upon her.

It was visceral, brutal, euphoric, and threatened to wipe her mind away for good as he overwhelmed her body in sensation. How long it went on, she had no idea. Ecstasy rushed over like a crashing wave, again and again, as she arched and writhed underneath him in a silent cry—so overwrought with it that she couldn't even form a noise. If she hadn't been pinned by him, she would have twisted from his grasp. His attacks never slowed and kept her pouring over the cliff's edge.

When she thought she might pass out, when she was at her absolute limit, his thrusts suddenly became desperate. His hand pressed her hard into the sheets, holding her still and pliable as he took his fill from her. With a deep, animalistic growl, he rammed into her and kept himself there. She felt him arch away from her in his own broken cry, and she felt him spasm against her, as he too, met his end.

The noise in his throat ebbed into a moan, and a heady gasping for air, as he caged her in, his arms on either side of her. His body was hot like a space heater over and around her. He clutched her close to him as if afraid she might vanish into nothingness. He was shivering as he slumped down over her, lowering his head to her shoulder.

"By all the gods in all the worlds..." He seemed unable to finish his sentence for once. She could feel the sweat on his forehead as he laid it against her shoulder.

When she thought she could find the strength to speak, she took in a slow, wavering breath. "Aon..."

He sounded as worse for wear as she was, out of breath and shuddering. "Yes, my darling?"

"I can't feel my hands."

Aon burst out in a quiet, broken laugh. "Ah. Yes. That."

She felt the binds around her arms disappear as miraculously as they had arrived. She let out a groan as she moved her arms—feeling her shoulders angrily protest and holler about having been misused like that. The pins-and-needles sensations in her fingers began to reside.

He was still hovering over her, his long hair brushing against her cheek. His weight was on his elbows, and while they were no longer joined, he still was lying idly between her bent legs.

She wished she could see his face. It hit her with an odd pang, and she reached up to touch him, running her hand along his cheek. He turned his head to her palm and kissed it with surprising tenderness.

She let her hand run through his hair, tucking it behind his ear before settling her hand against his shoulder. His heart was pounding like a drum, same as hers. She pulled in a deep breath, held it, and slowly let it out—feeling much better the air.

He leaned down to kiss her, but paused, his lips hovering just a hair's breadth away from hers, hesitating.

She realized he must be curious if she would turn away from him. Wondering if she would reject everything that had just happened. Everything that she had just felt. Her body ached. Everything hurt. But one thing she couldn't deny—one lie she couldn't tell—was that she had loved it.

Immensely.

Silently, he was asking her if she regretted their evening. She leaned up to kiss him—zeroing the distance between them. It was a warm, gentle embrace, and a far cry from how he'd just been seconds prior. When they parted, he let out a small contented sigh and felt tension melt away from him.

"Did you think I was going to be upset?" She ran her hand through his hair again.

He paused before answering and sounded reluctant when he finally did. "Yes."

"Why?"

"Once the allure has died away and thoughts run clear once more, most regret their choice to lay with me."

She couldn't help but look up at him in disbelief, even if she couldn't see him. He had been violent and rough, sure, but she had never once asked him to stop or slow down. He hadn't really hurt her. Then again, she was just a fragile mortal, after all. Perhaps he had started "slow" with her.

"Do you wish for me to go, or stay?" He interrupted her thoughts, guarded and devoid of emotion one way or another.

She gently took his flesh-and-blood hand in hers and brought it to her lips, kissing the side of his fingers. She let her eyes slide shut and felt suddenly exceedingly tired as her body calmed down. "Do you want to stay or go?" She turned the question around on him.

He let out a low, aroused growl in his throat as she kissed his fingers. "If you continue on like that, you will have something else against your lips in short order, and the question will not matter."

She grinned, feeling fiendish, and let her teeth graze along his skin, and she felt him twitch slightly in her hand and pull in a breath. "Maybe I just want to make sure you don't ditch me for another week."

"I do not think that is a concern." He leaned down to kiss the corner of her mouth. "May I assume then, you wish for me to stay beside you tonight?"

"Yeah." She entwined her fingers with his. "I think I'd really like that."

His lips curled into a smile against her. "Yes... I, as well." He rolled onto his back with a contented grunt, and she felt him sprawl out on the bed beside her. The feeling of the cool air against her felt amazing. She stretched, winced as she felt the soreness in her limbs and knew she was going to be bruised in the morning.

The tug of a hand on her arm and Lydia chuckled at how

needy and impatient he was. She moved to curl up against him, tucking her head into the crook of his shoulder. For a moment, she was surprised to feel a blanket settle down on top of them before she remembered. Right. Magic.

He pulled her tight up against him, and the last thing she remembered before falling asleep was the press of lips against her forehead.

FIFTEEN

This time, when Lydia woke up with an arm draped over her, she smiled. She could feel Aon up against her back, his knees tucked against hers. She felt as if she had just run a marathon. Everything ached and felt wonderful all at the same time. Moonlight was streaming in through the shutters of her room, ruddy and unnatural. At least she could see again.

Her mind drifted over the memory of what had happened the night prior. She hadn't been sure what to expect, spending a night with a man with a reputation like his, or with someone that... ancient. Someone *inhuman*. But it sure as hell hadn't been disappointing—it had been utter bliss, even if everything was sore because of it.

"Good afternoon," he muttered quietly to her.

"Mmhmm," she replied sleepily and pulled his arm in tighter around her, letting her eyes drift back shut. He was warm and comfortable. The smell of old books and leather was luring her back into sleep. Her tug of his arm drew a nearly silent chuckle out of the man, and he shifted up closer against her.

He had stayed with her through the night. No small part of

her had expected to wake up alone. This was... nice. Feeling him there against her back felt cozy. Safe. It made her happy. He hugged her to him, and she sleepily smiled. She wanted him here.

"Tell me, is this the first or second time you have awoken like this?" His question was playful.

"Second."

"Ah, so you did wake up that night. I suspected as much. Tell me, why did you not say anything?"

"If I'd dreamed it, you never would have let me live it down." She laced her fingers in between his, lifting his hand to kiss it. "If it was real, and I didn't kick you out, you'd never let me live it down. Either way, you'd use it against me."

"An astute observation." After a long pause, he sighed and shifted. "I fear I must go. As much as I would love to stay here with you all day, I do have a world to run. Rest." He stroked her hair gently as he pulled himself free of her. "Will you join me in my library tonight?"

"Mmhmm."

He might have said something else, but she was already too asleep to really know what it was.

* * *

"Let me *go!*"

The voice was half man, half beast. Or, perhaps more accurately, both at once.

Lyon sighed, watching the poor boy Nicholas struggle. He was chained to a tree, bound by thick iron coils around his chest and arms.

Kamira had summoned Lyon to talk some sense into the boy, but Lyon did not know there was much he could do.

"You should have known he would not take kindly to death

threats against his friend." Lyon shook his head as he glanced at his wife.

Nicholas had been present for Edu's assertion that Lydia must be some great threat to their world, lest Aon would have no other reason to keep her nearby. Nicholas had heard Edu pledge to kill Lydia, war be damned, should they vote to do so.

Kamira sighed and folded her arms across her chest and watched her youngest addition to her pack struggle against the chains. "Nick, calm down. Matters are not yet decided. There will be a vote."

The last time they voted, they opted to spare Lydia's life. Edu saw fit to change his mind upon learning of Aon's interest in the girl. Now that it was clear to them that Aon held some strange fascination with Lydia, Lyon knew the vote would go differently this time. He opted not to voice his opinion.

It would simply make matters worse.

"Fuck your vote!" Nicholas's voice was still mixed with an inhuman roar. His eyes were glinting orange as he thrashed against the chains. "I have to warn Lyd. I have to! Let me go!"

Kamira pinched the bridge of her nose. "And then what? Aon goes after Edu for treason? Do you want Edu to come after you instead? Do you think he'll take that kind of thing lightly?"

"I don't *care*." Nicholas was cutting himself open in his attempts to free himself. "I don't care if Edu comes for me. Or for any of you. I need to warn Lydia!"

Lyon walked up to him. The boy's struggles ceased as he approached. "Your loyalty to your friend is admirable. I commend you. Lydia is a fine soul. It is unfortunate that she has found herself in our world in such a state. But if she is what we suspect—a threat to the very fabric of Under—how can we allow her to continue to exist in Aon's grasp?"

"You're talking about murdering an innocent woman. She has nothing to do with any of this! How can you call yourself a priest?"

"I am not a priest of your god, Nicholas." Lyon clasped his hands behind his back. "I have not been such in a very, very long time."

The boy snarled. "This is a bunch of bullshit. This world is dying, anyway! What do you care if Aon has her?"

"It was by the warlock's hand we are now doomed. I have seen, firsthand, what Aon is capable of. We are better off in the void than to be subject to what he may do if left unchecked." Lyon frowned. "I do not enjoy the idea of Lydia's death. But if Edu is set upon this course and cannot be convinced otherwise, there is little I can do but attempt to minimize the likelihood that the world is pitched into war once more."

"Then warn her. Warn Aon! Let me go and I'll do it, since you're too much of a chicken-shit pansy!" Nicholas struggled uselessly against the restraints. "You're just full of bullshit, you stupid priest. You say you don't want her to die, but you won't do anything to stop it. You're just scared of Aon, and you'll do anything you need to, to make sure he never gets his way. Even if it means Lydia dies! You're just as fucked up—"

Kamira reached out and snapped Nicholas's neck in one quick *crack*. The shifter pup slumped against the chains, eyes locked open in death. He would come back in a few hours. "I cannot abide his shrill ranting. It sends me up a wall."

Lyon shook his head and wound his arm around his wife, pulling her close. "He is not wrong. I dread what Aon might know about the girl's mystery. I fear what he may do with whatever power she holds. Yet I am too cowardly to stand in his way."

"You simply know a fight you are doomed to lose. He is merely not old enough to know the difference between cowardice and wisdom. Still, Lydia is spirited. I like her." Kamira leaned up against him. "We will be lacking for her absence. It is a shame, but if she means the return of a dreamer in Aon's control..."

Lyon kissed the top of her head. Yes. A shame. Yet guilt gnawed and chewed at his gut.

Was this Lydia's fate? To die?

Lyon could only pray he was not wrong.

And that it was, as the saying went, better to be safe than sorry.

* * *

Lydia went to Aon's library sometime after dinner, after a long debate of whether she had heard him ask her to join him or if she had dreamed it. She had been half-asleep when he left her bed. Well, if he wanted her to leave, he could always send her away.

The fire was burning, and the lights were turned on low. This time, it didn't take her long to locate the warlock. He stood in front of the hearth, clawed hand folded at his back, the other grasping the ornately carved wood of the mantel.

It was amazing how much body language could tell you. Even without seeing his face, clad in metal and curtained off by his long dark hair as it was, Lydia could see he was upset. His shoulders were raised and tense, and his head was lowered.

Slowly approaching him, she wondered if he even knew she was there, or if he was caught in another one of his moments. But she figured if he knew she was here, he would have said something. He always had something to say.

She wondered if she was in danger when he was detached from reality. If he would lash out at her without realizing it. It was possible. But the other option was to leave him like this, when he was clearly in pain. That felt wrong to her. She had been surprised that morning when she felt content at his presence beside her when she woke up. Now, she was surprised to find that she... honestly cared.

Cautiously, she placed a hand on his back.

He hissed in a breath, and his clawed hand at his lower back fell to his side. He did not move or speak, and for a moment he seemed frozen in time. He felt wounded, just like he had that night when he brought her to the edge of his shrinking world.

Rolling the dice and acting on instinct, shoving away all thoughts of right and wrong, she stepped in and hugged him. Wrapping her arms around his waist, she rested her cheek against his back. Keeping her voice quiet, she greeted him. "Hey."

His metal prosthetic rested on her hands where she clasped them around him. "I did not hear you enter." His voice was thin as if straining on the edge of the abyss. "I was not certain if you were going to join me." It was a statement of disbelief and quiet amazement as if he was afraid to draw attention to it for fear it might vanish, like an oasis in the desert.

Had he been standing in here, worrying?

"I wasn't sure if I was still welcome company." There was no point in trying to hide the truth anymore.

He paused for a long time, and his hand on hers tightened slightly. "Why?"

"I thought that, well..." She trailed off, unsure how to say it, ashamed and doubtful all at the same time. "After what Lyon said—"

The warlock sighed darkly. "What, pray tell, did that meddling idiot tell you?"

"That you, uh..."

"Tend to discard my lovers? You feared that now that I had made my conquest, I would have no use for you?"

She paused. "Yeah."

He turned around in her arms slowly and cupped her face gently in his hands. When he spoke, his voice was barely above a whisper. "It seems we both fear the other was about to walk away." The thumb of his flesh-and-blood hand traced a slow path across her cheek.

She smiled faintly and shut her eyes, leaning into his touch. "It's not like I'm going anywhere."

"But if now, in the coldness of the day, you were to decide you never wish to see this wretched metallic visage again? To never speak to nor hear from me again? I will grant it."

That drove her to look up at him, concerned and confused. "What?"

"If you decide to spurn me now, it is your right. I made a vow, my darling—you may always refuse me. Do not feel you are somehow obligated to remain in my presence merely because I seduced you."

She blinked. She'd assumed he was going to throw her aside, not the other way around. Letting out a breath like he'd punched her in the gut, she hugged him tight and rested her head against his chest. He was warm, and the smell of old books had become pleasant by now. He went stiff for a long moment, as if unsure what to do, before gently wrapping his arms around her in return.

It took a moment before she worked up the nerve to speak. "I turned you away in the hot spring that night, because I... I don't know who you are, Aon. I don't know what this is between us. I don't know what the hell is going to happen to me, or why the *fuck* I'm here. But the thought of you getting bored and tossing me aside... hurt. A lot. And that week you were gone? I meant what I said when I told you I missed you. It may not be right, but it wasn't a lie."

Her world shifted abruptly, and she squeaked as he scooped her up in his arms. He took two strides over to a large, asymmetrical wing-back chair by the fire, and sat down in it, plopping her down onto his lap sideways without any say from her.

At first, she went tense, locked tight in surprise. But seeing that he just seemed to want to wrap an arm around her and hold her, she relaxed and draped her legs over one of the arms of his chair.

He leaned his head back against the plush upholstery and let out a small, contented sigh. She smiled at how... oddly romantic the man was. He was a sadist, a warlock, and a monster. Yet right now he just wanted her here, in his lap, in front of a fire. It was as much of a response to her admission that he seemed to be able to muster, and it would do just fine.

Tucking her head up against his neck, she let herself enjoy this for what it was. He would always be a rabid tiger in the darkness—dangerous and unpredictable—but oddly enough, she was beginning to trust him.

"Tell me something, my dear." Aon broke the silence between them after what might have been minutes. "What could I do to make you happy?"

"What do you mean?"

"I have seen nearly every other emotion from you. But I have yet to see you *happy*. Even when you saw your friend Nicholas at the gala, it was relief I observed. Not enjoyment."

"You're collecting my emotions?"

"Well, when you say it like that, you make it sound as though I am a sociopath." He playfully poked one of his metal claws into her side, just enough to make her jump before withdrawing. "Come now, do not evade the question."

She took a moment to think it over. What would make her happy? To go home, really—but that wasn't possible, not even for him—so she wouldn't insult him by asking. After a long time of turning the question around in her head, she came up with an answer. "I think I'd like to see more of Under. All I saw as Edu's prisoner was how much you assholes like to kill and screw each other. If I'm going to live here, if I'm really stuck here, I want to see the world I have to call home."

"Ah! A wonderful idea. I warn you, my world is a paltry, skeletal shell of what it once was. Under was once an expanse, about that of your world, perhaps larger. Now it is the size of

one of your European countries. Still, it has its wonders to see."
He sounded honestly enthusiastic.

She hadn't realized the devastation of the encroaching void
was that bad... a whole world, shrunk down to a country. Well,
it'd been shrinking for fifteen hundred years. He'd said it only
had a hundred years more to go, if that. At least she'd be dead
by then. Poor Nick. Poor everyone, really.

"Tomorrow, I shall take you to the galleries in our capital
city. Perhaps we will take in the opera that night. Consider it
done." It was clear he was... excited by the idea. Maybe he never
got a chance to show anyone around.

"Thanks." She leaned in and placed a kiss against the cheek
of his metal mask. Chuckling, she wiped the smudge she left
with her sleeve.

He let out a small sound in his throat and turned his face to
look at her. "Was that real? Tell me... please."

"Was what real?" Furrowing her brow, she hoped he wasn't
having another lapse from reality.

"The affection I just saw in your eyes."

She stammered and tried to look away, but his clawed hand
shifted to hold her cheek, the sharp points keeping her from
retreating.

"Please," he insisted. He sounded on the edge of a knife
once more. There was an intense kind of desperation to him
that kept her frozen in place.

That intensity kept her from lying to him. She felt peeled
away and exposed as she confessed what she felt. "Yeah, I... I'm
sorry, I—"

The warlock shifted abruptly, and she couldn't help but
squeak in surprise as his clawed hand tangled in her hair to press
her up against him, clutching her to his chest. He held her as
though he was afraid some ethereal wind was going to tear her
away. "Shush..."

She fell silent, her hand playing with the edge of his lapel as he held her, head resting atop hers. Minutes dragged on with them in silence before the tension in his limbs seemed to slowly release. "Are you all right?"

"Yes... I am fine." He loosened his grasp on her and sighed wearily. "Forgive me. You should not have to bear the weight of my madness."

"I don't mind." She lifted her head to look at him and managed a small smirk. "It doesn't scare me *too* badly."

"It should send you running in fear. It should terrify you, as it does all others."

"Hun, I hate to break it to you, but it's the least fucked-up part about you." She snickered. "How about how you chased me as that weird shadow monster? Or that you can invade my dreams? Or teleport? Or use mind control? Or your torture machines? Or that you can apparently," she pointed up at the painting overhead, and the depiction of Aon surrounded by his undead legions, "do *that?*"

"Pah. You mortals and your misplaced sense of priorities." He waved a hand dismissively, but there was a smile in his voice.

She felt no small amount of triumphant pride over breaking him out of his mood. He saw the grin on her face and picked her up in his arms once more. When he set her down in front of the fire, something about his demeanor quickly shifted.

It was amazing how much body language could tell you.

Instantly, Lydia went tense, her heart beating faster as he circled her like a panther. She swallowed thickly in her throat as he stopped to stand behind her.

"Undress."

"What?" She went to turn, but hands on her shoulders kept her facing away from him. The claws of his hand trailed up her shoulder, along the skin of her neck, and then slipped up into her hair. She gasped as he fisted the strands and yanked her head back. It stung, but what left her mouth was a moan and not a cry.

"You heard me. Unless you prefer I shred your clothes from your body, in which case, understand I will not find the need to be gentle with what I find underneath." His mood shifted drastically and like someone had flipped a light switch. He released her as he repeated the demand. "Now… undress."

Somehow, the scrutiny of what he was demanding made her want to hide. How the hell did that make any sense, after what they had done the night before? Nervously, she took off the cardigan she was wearing and let it drop to the floor. After a pause, she continued. Shoes and socks followed. She pulled her tank top off over her head, and then undid her pants and stepped out of them, leaving her in just her underwear. Even in the warmth of the fire, she shivered, more from the weight of his gaze than the chill in the air.

"And now the rest."

She wanted to whimper with the husky, dark way he said it. She jolted and let out a startled noise as his claws slowly dragged along the skin of her lower back. It sent her into goosebumps instantly. He let out a small, low chuckle as he watched her shudder in response.

"Or I will do it for you…"

She reached behind herself and undid the clasp of her bra and let it slide to the floor. Steeling herself, she pushed off her underwear and let it fall around her ankles. She gasped as his hands found her hips and pulled her back against him.

"You ruined my restraint last night. So desperate I was to have you, I fear I did not get the chance to truly enjoy you." He slid his hands slowly up her body. One metal and one skin—one warm and one cold. He took his time, carefully exploring her as if memorizing every curve.

His flesh-and-blood hand slid up to her temple, and she winced as she felt something snap over her. Just like that, her vision was gone. "*Ow!*" Once more he had taken her sight so he could remove his mask. "Shit—warn me next time."

He chuckled at her complaint, and she felt his breath against her cheek as he turned her head to kiss him. He gave as much as he took from her, forceful and yet teasing, making her chase his lips as she eagerly sought out more.

"Tell me." His voice was breathy when he broke the kiss. "Do you fear me? Do you dread what someone with my reputation might do to you? You are helpless if I wished to force upon you anything I desired."

"I know." She bit back a moan as his hands slid back down her body. Not rough, not forceful, but teasing her. Tempting her. She knew she was powerless to stop him if he decided to do... well, anything. He was basically a demigod. She was a mortal.

"Well? Do you fear I might string you up from the rafters? That I might pillage and ravage you, leaving you a broken, tormented thing?"

"No." Her heart was thudding in her ears at his words. There was a horrible kind of fear and excitement that twisted together into one confusing mess.

"Why?"

"If I told you to stop—if you went too far, and I said no—would you?"

"So many assumptions. One, that I am trustworthy. Two, that you were able to speak at the time?" His words were a dark whisper as he trailed his lips along her ear. She tilted her head to the side to give him more room. "That I had not found something more entertaining to do with that sharp tongue of yours and had not put it to good use?"

Her knees went weak at his words, and if he had not slung an arm around her, pressing her against his chest, she might have fallen over. He chuckled at her reaction, more of a rumble she felt at her back than anything else. Finally, he answered her. "Yes. If you objected, I would stop."

"That's why I'm not afraid." No, honestly, Lydia was more afraid she might enjoy the things he was threatening to do.

"I am a manipulator. I am a cheat and a demon amongst monsters. What if I am lying to you?"

"You've yet to lie to me." Why did that feel like an admission? It was true, he hadn't. He had played games with her and messed around with her. But never once had he ever *lied*. "If you were going to hurt me, you would have done it already and not waited for me to say yes. I don't think you're as bad as everyone says."

His hand trailed to her cheek, and she leaned in to kiss his palm. He let out a quiet grunt at the gesture. She slipped her hand against the back of his and began kissing the side of his fingers, one by one.

"Oh, my beautiful creature..." he said quietly, resting his head against hers. It was a tender gesture, even as his metal gauntlet tightened against her hip and pulled her harder against him. As the points of his claws dug into her side, she gasped and arched against him. She felt him grin against her cheek, and his breath was hot against her as he whispered into her ear. "Let us see if I can break you of such a charming notion... hmm?"

SIXTEEN

Lydia gasped as Aon's clawed hand returned, sliding up the back of her thigh and grasping at the flesh of her rump. Hard enough to sting. "Now go to the table... and lean over it."

When she went to whirl around, his other hand caught her hair in his fist and kept her from turning. "Ah-ah." He wound her hair around his fingers, once, twice, until he had a firm grasp. She could only cry out as he dragged her forcefully over to the table and tossed her forward.

She landed on her hands, and before she could react or even protest, he pressed down between her shoulder blades, pushing her chest down to the table. It left her bent over the hardwood surface. Exposed and vulnerable.

"Stay." It was an order.

Shocked and unsure of what else to do, she found her stomach had twisted into a knot and her body felt like it was on fire as if he had dropped a lit match into a bucket of gasoline. There was no way she could deny it. She was enjoying this immensely. She enjoyed *him* immensely. His command had been so direct, she didn't know how to react.

So she just quietly obeyed.

"You are so *shy*. Look at you blush, even now." He let out an appreciative hum as he let his hands roam along her backside, squeezing and fondling her. "You somehow manage to find the ability to be coy, despite how very clearly you love my manner of affection."

"It's news to me." She laid her head on the table on her cheek. He had taken her sight, otherwise she would be desperately watching to see what he was doing. As it was, she was helpless.

"Tell me you jest." He chuckled darkly as he ran his hands over her body slowly as if memorizing every inch, every nerve. "Tell me you have not just discovered this sinful part of your soul in *my* care?" At her embarrassed silence, he pulled in a wavering breath and let it out in a pleasured sigh. "Oh, my poor darling... you are a miracle."

When his fingers wandered to her core, he found proof of just how much she was "loving his manner of affection." She moaned as he delved inside of her.

When his clawed hand twisted in her hair once more and pulled her head sharply off the table, he let out a low groan in his throat as she writhed beneath him. "You quiver when you are in my hands. How I will delight in teaching you the joys of what I have to offer. But you must be honest with yourself, and with me, about what you want."

She could only whimper as he went back to wandering his claws down her back in a slow drag of sharp nails. She arched her back and cried out. Oh, hell. The way that mixed with what his fingers were doing to her body almost drove her mad. It nearly pushed her over the edge in seconds. It left her hungering for more.

"Yes, just like that." When his fingers left her, she couldn't help but whine in dismay. He only chuckled, as he replaced his fingers with something else of his now pressing against her entrance but going no further.

He was going to make her lose her mind. God, how her body cried out for him. She was squirming, on the verge of begging. He pressed against her and then relented, not slipping inside as she so very much wanted him to.

His lips descend on her jaw, licking along her skin until he took her earlobe in his mouth and bit down on it. She could only moan, digging her nails into the wood table. He chuckled as she continued to wriggle underneath him, and he released her earlobe only to whisper to her. "Say it."

She was trembling. "Say... what?"

"Say you want me. Say you want what I can do to you." Once more he put pressure against her entrance but did nothing else. Threatened but didn't fulfill.

She bit her lip as he traveled his lips to her shoulder, kissing and nipping at her skin. "I—"

"Say it, or I stop. Right here, right now." It was a threat she was afraid he'd make good on.

It sounded far, far more tortuous than anything he was about to do to her. "Please," she whispered.

"Please what?" He grinned against her shoulder as he kissed her, licking and teasing at her tender flesh. He pressed against her once more, right at the cusp, promising bliss before withdrawing. "Be specific."

"Please... don't stop."

"Say that you want me, my beautiful, wondrous creature. Say it, and you shall have me," he growled against her.

She couldn't take it anymore. "Please, I need you, Aon, I—ah!" Her words broke off in a loud cry as he suddenly and unapologetically answered her request. He let out a deep snarl as he filled her, hard and uncaring.

She arched her back against him. He straightened, pushing himself up with one hand and catching her throat with the other, pressing her up against his chest. Restricting, but still allowing her some air. It made her head spin, and she found she wanted more.

Lips met hers, passionate and driving. When he broke the kiss, his breath was hot against her. "Just like that..." He squeezed her throat, cutting off her air just a bit more, and she moaned against him. "Do you feel how you tighten around me when I do this? Do you feel how much you love it? What a wonderful thing to explore. But I think I have other plans for you tonight."

He let go of her, laying her back down until her cheek touched the wood as he straightened up. His hands drifted down her shoulders and her back. Slowly, meanderingly, taking his time, he grasped her hips in his hands, and slowly pulled himself all the way out of her, until he was pressed up against her entrance again.

Slowly, agonizingly, he pushed himself back in, bit by bit, inch by inch. She whimpered as she felt him split her body again as he filled her. Damn it, it felt incredible. But it wasn't enough. And she suspected he very much knew it.

As he reached her end, he pulled her against him harder—forcing the last bit of him that didn't quite fit inside of her. The ache was painful, but she moaned all the same.

"They call me a sadist. They are correct." He let up on the pressure and began to slowly withdraw. He removed himself from her entirely before he began to slip back into her. His pace was meticulous. It was maddening! "I delight in the agony of others. I derive pleasure from their suffering. But know this, my darling... torment comes in many forms."

"Aon," she whimpered as he repeated his action. Taking her inch by inch, pressing hard into her end until there was none of him left, and then withdrawing all the way. It was patient, was methodical, and it was *cruel*.

"Hm? Yes?" he asked as though he had no idea what he was doing.

Her body was throbbing, aching, begging for more. For him. What he was doing now kept her body pulled tight like a bowstring. Unable to find release, unable to reach real pleasure. This was more than simple teasing. He was right, it was torture. "Please..."

"Last night, I had intended to tie you to the posts and make you beg for me. Or, lay you out spread eagle upon my dinner table, and torment you until you cried in need. I wished to make you plead for release. I suppose this will have to do instead."

She groaned and squeezed her eyes shut, as he pressed hard into her end to accentuate his words. But still, he didn't pick up the pace.

He chuckled at her dismay and pulled himself all the way out once more, before repeating his action. "Know this, darling... I can—and will happily—do this for *hours*. Especially if it means that look of hungry suffering never left your stunning features."

She nearly wept and dug her nails into the lacquer of the wood table. "Damn you."

He repeated his action of slowly filling her, pressing painfully into her body, and then withdrawing. "Many people would say I already am quite damned."

She rested her forehead against the table and tried to keep her composure. Tried to keep from squirming in his grasp. Tried to stop the noises that left her throat, each time he filled her.

It went on for what felt like hours. He kept her body strung tight, unable to relax or let go. She couldn't stop focusing on the sensation of his length filling her, stretching her, promising more, before abandoning her once more. And still so *agonizingly slowly*.

Finally, she couldn't take it anymore. "Aon, please... I can't—"

"You can't what?" he asked, his voice thick with lust and false innocence.

"I can't take this anymore."

"Do you want me to stop?"

"No!"

"If you are going to ask me to deny myself such pleasure as watching you in such pure and utter suffering as you are experiencing right now... you will have to tell me specifically *why*."

She felt her face grow warm as she growled at him in frustration. Her angry glare over her shoulder made him laugh. His flesh-and-blood hand came down her ass cheek in a stiff slap, and she shrieked in surprise more than she did in pain.

"You are the one asking for favors. Mind your manners." His tone was so obnoxiously playful. Still, he didn't relent. Still, he pushed in and out of her like a machine, slow and unwavering.

She growled and almost sobbed. "Aon, please!" He was being so goddamn frustrating!

"Please what?"

When she wailed and thunked her forehead on the table, he cackled in laughter. He pushed himself into her to the hilt so that he could lean over her, his lips running low, sultry kisses up her shoulder and to her ear. "You make this too easy... and too much fun. How is it that your tongue is so sharp, and yet so shy? Tell me what you want me to do. I am at your command. I am your servant. Order me to do your bidding. Tell me your desires as law and I will grant them."

He turned her head to face him and kissed her. The kiss was everything she wished he would do to her—harsh and passionate, bruisingly strong and unforgiving. She moaned against his lips and wound her hand into his hair, holding onto the embrace and matching it as best she could. But the man was a rising tide, and she always lost the fight.

When he finally broke the kiss, she was breathless, and her

condition was worse than before. "Please, Aon... Stop teasing me... I need more."

"More of what?" She felt his lips curl into a smile where they hovered, a hair's breadth away from her cheek.

"Of you." She chased his lips with her own, kissing him once more.

He let out an appreciative moan and his hand fetched hers from his hair, twining his fingers between hers and pressing it back down to the table by her side. Slowly he parted from her again and ran his tongue slowly against her lips. "Very well. But you really must be more specific, you know." He grinned wickedly against her and straightened back up.

Now, he began to move within her. But it was like she was some wilting wallflower on her wedding night—tender and loving. He was being *gentle*. It was a farce. An utter and total farce. He was doing it to goad her she knew, as he rocked himself within her with all the care of a man handling delicate glassware.

"Damn it all, Aon!" She tried to pull her hand from his where he kept it pinned by her side, but he grasped her hand harder and only laughed at her dismay. Still, he was loving her like a goddamn storybook fairy prince, and it was going to drive her insane! She slammed her fist against the table.

"What?" He feigned innocence once more. "This is answering your request, is it not? Hardly my style I must admit, but, to each their own. I will cope. I am your lowly slave this night, after all. If you wish for something else, then simply say the word."

Growling, she tried to fight her desire—tried to keep her composure and call his bluff. It dragged on for minutes more, her body on the edge of having what it wanted so very badly but being denied. She tried to beat him at his game. Thought that with each stroke he might snap his resolve before she broke hers. But he showed no signs of weakening, and she felt like she was going to cry at this point. Her body was screaming for him and for what she knew he could do to her. For what he had done to her last night.

"You win!" She pushed herself up onto one elbow, her other hand still trapped in his. "I give up. I give up, you win."

He laughed, dark and horrible. And with that, he used her position over the edge of the table to ram himself into her so hard that her thighs hurt—bottoming out into her violently and pinning himself there, pressing painfully against her end. Something rattled on the table with the force of the blow.

She cried out sharply, and it ended in a moan as she lowered her head, her eyes shutting, feeling pleasure shoot through her like a crack of lightning. That's what she wanted. That's what her body *needed*.

Aon leaned his head over toward her, and she felt his breath hot against her ear. "Do you know how badly I have wished to see you like this? How many times I have played this scene over in my head—you, lying here on my table, at my mercy, crying for the release I could grant you? Since the first time you stepped into this room, I wished to tear your clothes from your body and have you *beg for me*. And now, my dreams have been made reality."

She could only whimper at his words and at what they did to her. They seemed to coil in her stomach, and she felt her body tighten around him.

He groaned at the sensation, and she felt his clawed hand slip up from her hip to tangle in her hair. "Oh, how I wanted to have you. Make you mine since the day I saw you. From the first glimpses in our dreams, I have wanted to hear you cry out in pleasure, in pain, in desire. I wanted to mold your body to mine. Admit you love this as much as I do. That this agony brings you pleasure."

She moaned and nodded. If she could, she would have

pushed herself back against him, trying to feel more of him within her. But he had her too well pinned.

"Say the words to me. Tell me you want me to ravage you... to take you... to make you mine. Say you want the kind of pleasure that I can bring you. *That only I can bring you.*"

"Yes, please, Aon—" She gasped as he dug his teeth into her shoulder. Hard enough to hurt, but not breaking the skin.

"Say it. I want to hear you utter the words," His voice was deep, dark and husky—overtaken with his own lust and pleasure. He was begging her in his own right, even if she was the one suffering.

"I want what you can do to me. Please—I can't take this anymore. I need you, Aon. All of you. And everything that comes with it. I surrender."

"Say it. Tell me what you wish, in the way only your filthy modern mouth can devise."

All shame was gone. It was freeing in its own way. "I need you to fuck me, Aon. Fuck me, as hard as you goddamn can."

"You are better than I could have ever dreamed..." He shuddered at her words as he placed a sultry kiss against her throat. "Well. If you want me, then you shall have me."

He made good on his word. She could barely think through what followed—the white-hot pleasure and pain as he unleashed himself on her. She had never experienced anything like him in her life. It was easy to forget how strong he was, how inhuman. He had promised to push her limits, and his skill in doing so left her feeling like she was wrapped around his fingers and utterly at his mercy.

She loved it.

He had tuned her up like an instrument and played her just the same. Ecstasy crashed over her like a wave, and she cried out his name. He was once more a machine, but this time he was pistoning in her with a force that was going to leave bruises on her thighs where she was pressed up against the lip of the table.

Suddenly, he turned her onto her back, pushing her up so she was laying on her back on the edge. He hooked one of his arms underneath her knee and leaned over her as he filled her again ruthlessly. The change in angle made her cry out again, but this time his lips swallowed up the sound as he kissed her hungrily. As if he was going to consume her whole. His tongue slipped into her mouth, claiming the space as his own without a pause. He was going to take all of her. And she wanted him to.

She held onto him for dear life, grasping the lapel of his vest with one hand, the other tangling into his hair at the base of his neck. Wave after wave of ecstasy crashed over her as he continued his assault. And it was an assault. He wasn't just filling her, he was destroying her.

And all she wanted was more.

Just when she began to grow lightheaded and she worried she might pass out, he let out a low moan in his throat. He clutched to her, pinning her down. The moan ended in a growl as his thrusts became erratic for a moment before he doubled over her. She felt him spasm against her, throbbing deep inside of her as he, too, met his end.

She wrapped her arms around him, holding him, feeling his heaving breath. She turned her head to kiss his cheek by his ear, and she could feel his pounding heartbeat. All at once, he was vulnerable and indestructible. He had broken a sweat.

He let out a long, heavy and sated sigh, and let go of her leg, but did not stand up. He seemed quite happy where he was. That was fine, she didn't think she could walk.

When she regained the ability to speak, she let out a long, ragged breath. "That was incredible."

He only grunted quietly in his throat. He nuzzled his head in closer to her, tucking his forehead against her shoulder. It was unlike him to have nothing to say. She realized he was as destroyed as she was.

After a long moment, he straightened up slowly, and she

squeaked as he scooped her up in his arms. Lydia held onto him as there was a rush of motion around her and it felt as though she had been dropped through a pit. He had teleported them somewhere.

Silk met her back, and he placed her down on a bed, she assumed—she was still blind. It smelled different in here. Something was unfamiliar. "Where are we?"

She heard him shucking the remainder of his clothes. "My chambers." He still sounded out of breath. She felt the bed depress as he climbed in next to her. This time, he didn't bother to ask if she wanted to spend the night with him or vice versa.

He pulled her close to him, and she curled up against his chest. He was naked now, and she could feel his warmth against her. His heart was still pounding loudly from the exertion. She scooted up to lean on her elbow and ran her hand along his cheek gently, glad to find he was still without his mask.

God, she wished she could see his face.

Her touch drew a low hum out of him, and she smiled, leaning in to kiss his other cheek. She kept gently stroking his cheek, wishing desperately she could see his face. "You all right? I've never known you to be silent."

"You may be the death of me."

"Don't be melodramatic, you know you can't die." She smiled and snuggled into him, letting her hand drift down to rest on his chest. "And that was your fault, not mine."

"I cannot help what you compel me to do."

"Oh, so I'm to blame?"

"Entirely. I have been entrapped by a succubus."

She chuckled. "You started it."

"Hmf." He squeezed her close, and let out a tired sigh. But she felt the smirk on his face. She kissed him once more before she nuzzled her head into his chest. Sleep was calling both of their names.

She drifted off with the warmth of him against her and found herself... content.

No, she was *happy*.

* * *

"You really must stop bowing to me, old friend." Ziza greeted Lyon, her cold voice gentle even as it was distant. The Lady of Visions never raised her voice louder than a whisper, nor did she ever need to.

When Ziza spoke, all listened.

She was old, nearly as old as himself. They had Fallen here to Under within a few hundred years of each other and had become friends. Although in the past fifteen hundred years, their friendship had grown harder to maintain and eventually faded to a fond memory for them both.

Once she was chosen to carry the heavy mantle of sight, it became impossible for her to hold on to anything but her sanity.

For she could see the past, present, and future, all at once.

Everyone in the House of Fate was caught up in the tangled strings of visions, but it was the woman with the stark white hair who had been chosen by the Ancients to be their true Oracle.

The woman who stood before him in her long, dark blue dress, saw more than even Queen Ini when she was awake. Ini had once been fiercely protective of her Oracle. But now the Queen of Fate lay asleep in her crypt with no intention to wake before their world was swallowed into the void.

Because of that, there was no one to shield Ziza from the task of governing her House along with her duties as the Oracle. The poor woman was often left overwhelmed and had come to spend most of her time in solitude.

Not that any might discern such things from looking at her

—a stoic, icy, emotionless woman, seemingly forever detached from all that transpired around her. But he knew better and would always treat the statuesque woman with kindness, for that reason. Many of the others treated her with disdain or left her at arm's length at best.

All, perhaps, except Edu.

The tragic tale of Ziza and Edu was another reason he treated Ziza gently. While many may choose to forget what had transpired on the day the Great War ended, Lyon could not. Kamira frequently reminded him of his bleeding heart, and in this, she was correct.

"You are lady of a House." He straightened from his bow. "And you are a lady, regardless."

"Such as you see it. For that, I am ever grateful. But bowing is far too debasing for someone of your stature."

"Unless you mean it literally, you forget that I am but a servant now." He made a rare joke at his own expense and considerable height.

"Your role in this world has not changed, whether you wear a mask or no. It shall ever remain that you are the true high priest in the eyes of all. For else why would Edu send you to me with his message?" Of course, she would know why he had come.

He smiled to himself faintly, scolding himself for being a fool to think she would not see the reason behind his visit. "You could spare us much travel, you realize, if you informed us ahead of time that it was so terribly pointless."

"And miss the opportunity to see my old friend? Hardly." She walked up to him and circled her arms around him in an embrace. He returned it gently, knowing the deep depression and the hurt that ached inside her very soul. She had always been a morose creature, even before the Ancients had chosen her. Now, the oncoming doom of their world sealed it as an inescapable state of being.

"How fare you?" he asked, knowing the answer.

"I manage to get by." Her voice cracked if but for a second. "I will always manage until the Ancients deem fit to return me to them." She stepped back. "But this is not why you have come. You have come to inform me that Edu wishes to conspire against Aon. You have come to tell me the King in Red suspects the warlock of raising the dreamers."

Lyon stood there silently, not bothering to confirm what the Oracle already knew.

"I have already informed Edu, Kamira, and Maverick that they should join us here tomorrow morning." She paced away and stood underneath the grand orrery swirling overhead in the center of the great hall.

"Tomorrow morning? What for?"

"I do not know. I have not yet had the vision. But it shall come tonight, and I may relay its nature after the rise of the white moon."

Lyon furrowed his brow, curious. "You know a vision is coming? How so?"

"Does one not know a wave in the ocean before it overtakes you in the surf?"

"Then what has given you sight of this... wave?"

She pointed up at the whirling and immense creation of brass, copper, bronze, glass, and every manner of material one could picture. It floated overhead, suspended in the air by forces unseen. It was the great clock of their world and all the powers that lay influence upon it. The duty of the House of Fate was to interpret these movements and relay such information as they saw fit.

As he looked up, he saw the orbs that represented each House. Black, red, purple, blue, white, and green each on their own orbits on carefully arranged metal tracks. The track could shift and warp as needed, shrinking or expanding. All but the Houses of black and red lay dark and immobile, having remained such since their respective kings and queens retired permanently to their crypts. Turquoise had shattered and fallen from the array the moment Qta lost his life to Aon.

And yet...

There it was.

Floating on a copper track, hovering immobile, was a glass orb of turquoise and blue-green swirls. It sat lightless, sleeping, as dormant as all but those that represented Aon and Edu... but it was there.

Lyon could only sink to his knees, for he did not know what this might portend. He did not know by what means this was possible. He did not know what it would spell for their futures. Yet he knew that it could only foretell one thing...

The House of Dreams would return.

SEVENTEEN

The assumption that Under was only a shadowy reflection of Earth wasn't quite accurate, she decided. She was forced to amend her opinion as she wandered Under's major art gallery with Aon. Simply called The Galleries, it sat in the city of Yej, their capital.

The building and the art—indeed, the world as a whole—was dangerous, eerie, and unnerving. Yet it was so hauntingly beautiful, all the same. *Not unlike Aon,* she observed as she watched the man in all black look up at a painting, his hands clasped behind his back. That man never ceased to steal her attention, and she struggled to keep her focus on the artwork she was here to see.

The Galleries showcased a mix of contemporary and ancient pieces. With over five thousand years of history, they had a great deal to put on display. Lydia knew she could spend weeks wandering the building, learning about Under's complicated and sordid past.

The conversation between them flowed easy. It wasn't hard, with Aon wanting to explain everything she became interested in. He very much did love the sound of his own voice, and she was entirely ignorant of everything around her. It was a perfect match. They had been here for a few hours already.

She was struck in awe of a large carved statue in the center of one of the gallery halls. It looked like something from an Aztec ruin, but like all things, layered with a dark and twisted feel. It was of a snakehead, and it was missing large portions of it as though it had been chipped and removed from the side of a building.

"What's this?" She pointed.

"Ah." He sighed and wrapped his arms around her waist from behind. "It is all that remains of King Qta, the House over which he ruled, and his Temple of Dreams."

"The one you killed in the Great War."

"Yes."

"Why did killing him doom Under? Just because they dreamed up monsters?"

"Not quite. This world was once ruled over by seven creatures we refer to as the Ancients. Each was the figurehead to a part of our world. They were," Aon paused as he searched for the right words, "unfathomably cruel. I do not remember anything of my thousands of years in their 'care,' save the blinding sun and sheer agony. Yet, the Ancients are the wellspring of our lives and our very existence."

He gestured aimlessly at a depiction of what she assumed were the ancients by one wall. Twisted, grotesque creatures with vacant eyes and skull-like features. "When we kings and queens of Under rallied to imprison them and chained their power to the bottom of the lake of blood, we subsumed their role as those figureheads. We became the representation of their aspects. While we still draw our strength from them, we must exist for that power to flow forward. We are the limbs of a tree, of which they are the trunk."

That was a useful metaphor. "Where are the other kings and queens?"

"Asleep in their crypts. They did not wish to greet the void or help me fight it for their own reasons. Edu remains awake merely to foil me."

"Shitheads."

He laughed and squeezed her tighter against him. "Crass, but I agree with your sentiment."

"So, when you killed Qta, the branches went with the limb. Everyone else in the House of Dreams died with him."

"Yes. Precisely." He leaned his metal cheek against the top of her head. "I did not just simply killed Qta. I murdered over forty thousand souls in one gesture of wrath." There was a deep, dark loathing in those words, and she rested her hands on his where they clasped around her waist.

She stood there silently for a long time as the weight of the cost of the Great War began to sink in. "Why did you kill Qta?"

"I coveted his power."

"But... why? What for?"

"I wished to rule this world as its one and only king."

"No, I don't buy that." She turned in his arms to look up at him. "I don't buy that at all. That's a straight-up lie."

"Excuse me?" He pulled his head back in surprise.

"If you were a tyrant, you would have just raped me if you wanted to. You would have chained me up in a tower and left me there to rot, not asked me what would make me happy. Instead of just forcing me to join you in your library, you struck a deal and gave me something in exchange. That isn't a man who kills for power."

She shook her head and continued. "Besides, as far as I can tell, you have as much power and influence as you care to have. You could be out there now, rampaging over the countryside, but you... just tuck yourself away in your rooms, and let people talk shit about you. No. I don't buy that bullshit at all."

He looked down at her in silence for a long time. At first, she wondered if she pissed him off. But after a long pause, he rested his gloved palm against her cheek. His voice was quiet. "You really are a marvel, do you know that?"

"Then I'm right. It wasn't about total power." Lydia smirked. "Now you're the one dodging."

"Yes. I am. And I will continue to do so. Forgive me." He let his thumb rest on the hollow of her chin just below her lip. "I will explain someday soon, but I do not know if I can bear to tell you in this moment. Please allow me this mystery, and this moment, for just a little longer."

She watched him, stunned. He implied that if she pushed, he would tell her. He seemed so damn vulnerable sometimes, for all his strength. Stepping into him, she hugged him and leaned her head on his chest. "Tell me when you're ready."

They stood there in silence. It was that deafening lack of noise that finally broke her out of his grasp to look around curiously. It was then that she realized that this place was empty. There was no one else here.

"Where is everybody?" They had been here for hours, and she had yet to see anyone else wandering the halls.

"Ah. I closed the building to the public for the day so we may have it to ourselves." He shrugged idly as if it were nothing out of ordinary. He seemed glad for the change in subjects.

She laughed and poked him in the chest. "Why? Ashamed to be seen with your pet human?"

"Hardly. No. I enjoy my privacy. I did not wish—" He broke himself off suddenly. Seeing her questioning look, he sighed and continued reluctantly. "You will learn soon enough how I am seen by my subjects in this world. I enjoy your innocence in such matters. To see others cowering away from me in terror might give you the wrong impression."

"I've seen enough on my own to know you're a demon." She smirked up at him.

"Mmh. A demon you asked to give you a grand tour of Under. Whom you have invited to your bed twice now." He lowered his head to rest his forehead against hers. He liked to do that, and she found herself enjoying the gesture.

"I never said I was smart. Or a good person."

"That is how many will view you, I fear, for choosing me as your lover." He traced a claw down her cheek. It made her shiver, and she knew that was very much the point. "Do you believe it yourself?"

"You're torturing people, even if it's to save the world. To restore the House of Dreams, or whatever, but... it's still horrifying. I don't know what that makes me."

"I understand. But you must realize there are those in this world who would not need an excuse to do such deeds. You must remember you are no longer on Earth."

"I know, I know. I'll catch up eventually." She smiled faintly. "C'mon. I didn't come here to mope." She wound her fingers into his gloved ones and pulled him along down the hallway.

It was an odd thing to wrap her head around. To honestly understand. This place still seemed like an impossible dream to her and still so removed from reality. But the more she saw of it, the more it began to sink in.

He walked beside her but was now more interested in watching her than looking at the art around them. The scrutiny made her face go warm. "Penny for your thoughts?"

"I am wondering if you would fuss if I tied you to that statue and had my way with you," He chuckled at the shocked look on her face. "You asked."

"Teach me not to ask."

He laughed harder and slung an arm around her shoulder and pulled her into him. "So, it is a no, then?"

"It's a no!" She shoved him, sending him away from her by a step, but found herself laughing at how incorrigible the man was, how utterly playful. It was addictive.

He let out an overdramatic and wistful sigh. "Oh, for shame. And here I brought the straps for nothing."

"You are the worst."

He folded an arm across his stomach and bowed low to her as if introducing himself for the first time. "Guilty as charged."

* * *

Lyon leaned against the blue marble and granite columns of the Great Hall. He knew he shared a resemblance to the statues that posed alongside him. Many were keen to make the comparison, and he must admit they were not errant in their observation.

Slowly and silently, the great orrery twisted in the chamber above them. It glinted in the light, shining copper against the pale blue stone behind it. Amber candlelight shone off the glass orbs of all the colors of the Houses. *All of them.*

Ziza stood across from him, dressed in a regal sapphire and black gown. She was lighting a row of candles one by one with a long wooden match, her lack of normal sight not bothering her in the slightest.

"When will you tell us what you know?" Kamira asked impatiently from where she sat perched on the back of a statue, some ten feet above where Lyon stood. She always wanted to be above and away from everyone else, like a great cat sitting on a branch.

"When Master Edu arrives," Ziza reminded her. Again.

Kamira growled heavily and kicked her leg, barefoot, idly off the shoulder of the statue of a long-dead hero of Under. The shrine to some venerated soul whose name he admitted he could not remember was now the perch of the lady shapeshifter.

"Be patient, Kamira," Maverick scolded from where he sat on a carved wooden bench along one wall. "Do not race so quickly toward treason."

"I am impatient to have our vote and be done with it. Besides, there is another form of treason afoot. Yet I do not see you complaining about Otoi being absent," Kamira goaded the scholar.

Maverick and Kamira had a strange relationship. The Elder of Words found her begrudgingly amusing, and she, in turn, liked to spend her time teasing and provoking him. Although he was many, many centuries Kamira's younger, Maverick acted as though he were some manner of older sibling to the wild woman.

It was sweet.

"That alone is enough reason for me to agree to this traitorous quorum," Maverick responded in his typically dry sense of humor.

Kamira snorted in response.

Lyon shut his eyes, listening to the banter between the Lady of Moons and the Lord of Words. It was an attempt to avoid that which was setting them all on edge, that which they could all see, but none had mentioned.

The turquoise orb, sitting upon its copper track, suspended in the orrery with the rest. It was lifeless as those that matched the four dormant kings and queens, but it was there. That was enough to set his hair on end.

With Lydia's news of the true intentions behind Aon's cruel research, revealing that he wished to restore the House of Dreams, it seemed far too much a coincidence that the glass orb would return in such a miraculous way. The King of Shadows had a great deal to do with this, Lyon surmised. And if Ziza had seen fit to call them all here—save for the warlock who was their rightful ruler—then she must know it as well.

Even for all that Aon had cost her, Ziza was notoriously neutral. The Oracle always was. Those who served Fate did not answer to any, not even their own Queen Ini. Those who wore blue served Under and Under alone. So, it must be in the best interest of their world that they now were to meet to discuss her vision without Aon present.

Lyon tried not to delve too deeply into that line of thought. He had survived the Great War, and he did not desire to see another play out upon the souls who lived here, sinful and hungry as they may be.

The question remained, what did Lydia have to do with all this? Lyon could not imagine the girl was playing a willful part, if she had any at all. But the mystery of the girl's rejection from the Ancients and her continued presence at Aon's side were facts that keenly suggested she was somehow key to the return of the turquoise orb in its track.

The doors to the chamber swung open, and he did not need to turn his head or open his eyes to know to whom the heavy footfalls belonged. Edu was no lumbering beast. He was agile, for his size. But when he did not feel the need to quiet his steps, he made the most noise out of any of them. His layered leather clothing did not help, with its jangling buckles and straps.

While he could not hear the woman who walked beside him, he did not need to guess that Ylena was also here. Her voice, carrying through the great echoing and expansive chamber, confirmed it. "Master Edu apologizes for his tardiness."

"No, he does not," Kamira said with huff. "You are tailoring his words poorly again, Ylena."

Lyon found himself smiling, if faintly, at the remark. It was true. Edu would not have found any need to apologize for any of his behaviors. Ylena was often left to do her best to temper the great king's far more blunt tendencies.

He could remember Edu when he owned a tongue and could speak for himself. He was quick to fight and quicker to laugh. He had once been a boisterous, sympathetic creature who would not hesitate to empty your skull upon the pavement or protect those who needed it. Edu had always been, amongst all his other failings, an honest man.

"Master Edu declines a retort but wonders if you plan to climb off your scratching post for this discussion," Ylena replied with a thin air of amusement herself.

Kamira cackled, taking no offense at the comment. In fact, quite the opposite. She always enjoyed trading words, if not fists, with the far bigger warrior. "No, I do think I prefer it here, thank you. It gives me a better view of the bald spot growing on your head, old man."

From the slight shake of Edu's shoulders, it was clear he found the quip amusing. He had no bald spot, nor did he show any sign of aging. Yet Kamira was one of the few who dared call Edu by anything other than the proper titles. She was also one of the rarer few who did not then immediately have her teeth scattered about the floor for it.

It was not surprising that Edu and Kamira were good allies and friends. The warriors in Edu's House and the violent shifters were closer aligned in nature than most Houses.

While each House remained autonomous and alliances were heavily discouraged—hence his own need to discard his lordship to marry the shifter—it had always been the expected tradition that the Houses of Moons and Flames were always of a like mind.

Nor was it surprising that Edu and Kamira had called each other lovers for many long years and even still do from time to time. It bothered Lyon none, for he alone had the tigress's heart. Such was the way of Under, after all.

Indeed, the only other Houses who could otherwise come close to assuming friendship were the Houses of black, and of his own, the priests in white. It was for that reason also, not just his repugnant behavior, that Otoi was absent. It would be but a bare heartbeat before the oaf scampered to Aon to speak of what he knew.

Lyon had once called the King of Shadows his dear friend, but Lyon could not forgive the warlock for his actions during the Great War or for the pain and torment he paid to all upon this world. The thought he may do it again was enough to ensure Lyon's silence. Aon was troubled and dangerous, especially so in the past few centuries of his rule.

"Now that we are met..." Maverick brought them back to the matter at hand and stood. He tugged on the bottom of his dark gray vest to straighten it. He lifted a silver-headed cane from the bench beside him and stepped forward. The metal tip made a resounding noise upon the stone as he walked. "May we discuss that?" He pointed a finger at the orrery overhead.

Edu turned his head to follow his trail, and when he laid eyes upon the turquoise glass orb that hung suspended in the air, his hands clenched into hard fists at his sides. The silent man's body language shifted, and he was a heated, tense coil. Even with his layers of leather and animal pelts, it was clear how angry he had instantly become.

"Yes, you see correctly, Master Edu." Ziza headed Ylena off at the pass. For if there was one person who could predict in this world what the great King in Red was thinking even before his empath, it was Ziza. For more reasons than one. "Last night, the orb that represents the House of Dreams returned. As you can see, it remains dormant. But it has returned, and ergo may wake."

"How is this possible?" Maverick asked the question they were all thinking.

"All things in this world strive for balance. And perhaps now the Ancients have seen fit to allow this to occur," Ziza replied, her voice icy and empty of all emotion.

"But how?" Kamira reiterated. "How exactly is King Qta going to return from the dead?"

"He will not. King Qta has been rendered back to the blood from which he came. The Ancients will not see fit to raise him."

"Then... who will lead the House? And how are they to

spontaneously gain the gifts that have lain dead for so long?" Kamira asked.

Ziza sighed and did not respond.

"One question at a time, Kamira," Maverick reminded her. "Ziza, who shall rise to lead the House of Dreams?"

"I do not know. In the visions, that part is unclear."

"Master Edu wishes to know if this is Aon's doing," Ylena interjected.

"Yes. It will be by Aon's hand that the House of Dreams rises once more."

Edu snarled low in his throat, a rumble that carried easily in the echoing hall. The muscles in his neck were twitching in a sincere desire to cause significant harm to someone, but no one was available on which to vent such frustrations.

Ylena laid a gentle hand on his arm, and he let out a long, angry sigh and lowered his head, doing his best to calm down. The two could communicate silently, and some powerful exchange had passed between the two, to simmer his boiling fury. Edu lifted his head after a long pause. "Will he seek to control whoever rises to the House of Dreams?" Ylena asked Ziza.

"I do not know. Should this come to pass, Aon will have great influence over the dreamer, that much is apparent. But he will not control them directly." Ziza's pure white eyes had slid shut as she focused upon what she could see in her mind.

Edu took a step toward Ziza but pulled himself to a halt. Lyon could tell even with his full mask and his silence that Edu wished to reach out and touch the Oracle. Perhaps he wanted to remember a time long passed, or perhaps to take her by the arms and insist she spoke clearly.

The Lady of Fate spoke in riddles. Always answering very literally the question that was asked, and nothing more. For while the Oracle would never lie, they would only say unto the speaker that which they have very specifically requested. A careless question had brought down whole families. A careful one had reshaped the world. To do anything more would be to delve too deeply into the stormy waters of the past, present, and future, the rushing tide of all that the Oracle could see. Targeted questions and one at a time were all they had the aptitude to divine from the chaos.

"Does Aon seek to rise to ultimate power, as he had once before?" Kamira asked.

Ziza tilted her head slightly. "No."

Edu snarled, not accepting that answer. He shook his head. Ylena spoke for him. "While he may not seek to rise in the same fashion, his intentions are clearly the same. If he would exert influence over the dreamers, nothing more need be known of his motives."

Kamira shrugged. "Just a question," she replied, clearly feeling out of her realm of expertise with the matter at hand.

"Do you see exactly how the dreamers return?" Maverick asked.

"Yes," came the icy response.

"How, then?"

"By blood."

Maverick sighed. A useless response. He had been too vague, too broad in his question. He rubbed his hand over the part of his face that was visible around the purple mask.

Ylena spoke for Edu once more. "Does the girl Lydia have anything to do with this?"

"Yes."

"Does Aon make her queen of the House of Dreams?"

"No," Ziza responded with the barest tilt of her head. There was something else there—something confusing to the Oracle. Her brow knitted into a bare furrow before smoothing a moment later.

Lyon may have been the only one who caught it. Lyon stepped forward from the wall and spoke for the first time in the evening. "Ziza..." She turned her head toward him but did not open her eyes. "What did you just see?"

"Lydia lying upon cobblestones. Her life bleeding out upon the ground around her. Aon, holding her in his arms."

Kamira laughed. "Likely to simply scrape her up from where he put her."

Lyon was not so sure. The way Ziza had said it, there was the barest hint of sorrow. As though there was sadness in the vision she had seen. What could it mean, that she felt grief in this vision? Surely it was not her own. She did not feel any barest emotion save for what she gleaned from what she saw. So, therefore, the melancholy belonged to someone in the apparition. Aon?

No one else seemed to notice the brief flicker.

Edu crossed the hall to stand in front of Ziza. He did not reach out to touch her, though it was clear he desired it. "Edu implores you, Lady Ziza. Tell us. What must be done to save our world?"

Ziza bowed her head, her stark white hair falling along her pale skin. After a long pause, she spoke. Cold and empty, with neither with joy nor suffering.

"Lydia must die."

EIGHTEEN

"This isn't fair!" Lydia slapped her cards down onto the table and sighed in a huff. "You don't even know how to play. How the *hell* do you keep winning?"

"The rules are simple enough." Aon looked down at the two cards he laid out in front of him. A straight. The bastard had pulled a *straight.* He didn't even bother to reach for the chips in the center of the table, knowing they would have to either call the game over, or she'd have to gather them up to start over, anyway.

He'd taken her to a restaurant in a city on the far side of the world from his home. It felt like Earth, if it weren't for the monsters and the masks, of course. It reminded her so much of Jacob Wirth's in downtown Boston it made her homesick. The polished dark wood, the flags, the simplicity of it. She'd asked him to take her somewhere different from his home, and he had apparently decided that something vaguely referencing a German pub was the answer.

This city, named M'url, kind of reminded her of travel shows she had seen on Prague. The real question was, which city had influenced which? Which world had been the inspiration? Slowly, she was coming to realize it was a mix of both. Some of this world was what Earthlings had brought here with them, and the rest was what Under had paid to Earth in trade.

Soaring chapels and statues left her gaping in awe. Twisted and warped architecture that had such amazing detail it would have made the designer of the Sagrada Familia squint and ask if it was too much. They had spent the day wandering the streets, with her pulling him off in random directions and peppering him with questions on how his world worked and how this place functioned. What was she looking at? Where was this? Why was this?

Aon answered every question with patience and an even temper and seem to even find happiness in his stories and explanations. He did love to tell a tale or to grandstand and he took every opportunity he could to spout off some anecdote from his past.

Yet again he had humored her with a sort of tenderness she hadn't expected.

The city was beautiful with its uneven cobblestone streets and achingly eerie street lamps that seemed to glow from within with tiny, glowing orbs of light of some kind. They almost looked like they should be insects, but he had said no.

Not even insects remained on Under since the death of Qta. But she wasn't wrong. The glowing lights were intended to replicate the insects the lampposts had all once contained so long ago. So, they were supposed to look like bugs, apparently. Even if they weren't real.

When she had asked why they had gone through all the effort and not simply replaced them with electric lights, he'd sighed. "To stave off the fear of the inevitability of the end. It is easier to embrace a falsehood than the void."

They had gone through all the trouble of creating fake blinking insects to avoid having to accept that their world was dying. It was tragic. It was rather beautifully human.

Walking around the city until her feet were sore, they finally stopped for dinner. He had taken her to his favorite establishment in the city, which was odd, seeing as he had admitted to never sampling the food or drink. There was a story there that he seemed reluctant to tell, so she let it slide. He had been so forthcoming with her, so honest and direct with his answers, she let his attempt to dodge go by without a challenge.

And so, here they were. In a German-style restaurant in a German-style city populated by, well, German-style monsters.

This place even had bratwurst. Aon had goaded and teased her until she finally agreed to try some of the monster meat. It was... honestly, damn good. So were the drinks, so she could hardly complain. She tried to adopt a more when-in-Rome mindset to her new world.

He was obviously not eating or drinking, as he couldn't while wearing his mask. He promised it didn't bother him.

But, to give him something to do besides watching her, she had asked the terrified waiter for a deck of cards and a set of chips.

Aon commanded much more than respect; he commanded fear. To his credit, he'd warned her. Everyone in Under seemed afraid to even look at him, let alone talk to him. All day long, people had turned and run from him. Or cowered and shrank away if they couldn't beat a hasty retreat. No one would look at him directly, instead choosing to stare down at their feet. Only those wearing black masks could even find the strength to raise their head to make eye contact.

But here she was, teaching him Texas Hold 'Em, and getting her clock cleaned by a man who claimed to have no knowledge of poker.

"You're different with me than you are with everyone else." She took his chips and hers and began to set them back out into starting piles. "Why is that?"

"What do you mean?"

"You talk to me differently than you do everyone else. I haven't seen it until now, since taking me out on the town. Everyone who sees you either runs away or collapses to the ground in worship. They're afraid to even look at you. I mean, I know that mask is stupid, but..."

"Careful, my dear," he warned, but there was a playful tone in his voice.

"And you treat them differently. You barely speak to them. You loom or stare in silence. It's clear the last thing you want in the world is for anybody to talk to you. You might as well be wearing a sign that reads 'look at me and I'll claw your goddamn face off.'"

"You are rather bold tonight."

She smiled at him cheekily and raised her beer to him in a salute before sipping it. Under had, she had to admit, really good beer. "Your fault for letting me drink. The filter shuts down."

"Does it, now?"

"You have no idea. I'm having fun and drinking, which makes this even more dangerous for you." Leaning back in her seat, she played with the chips on the table, flipping one idly between her fingers. She might be a crap poker player, but she was dexterous. Call it her one skill in life; she was good with her hands. She walked the chip across the back of her fingers from pointer to pinky and back again.

She blinked as Aon reached forward and took the chip from her hand. He was wearing his black glove on his flesh-and-blood hand, and dressing in all black, it made him hard for her to see in the dim room. He held it between his thumb and forefinger, and closing his fist around it, reopened his hand to show that the chip had vanished. He had used sleight-of-hand to vanish the chip somewhere, and she couldn't tell where. But the graceful movement of his fingers was enough to show her that he had done it for real.

That didn't stop her from teasing him over his shameless showboating. "It's not impressive if I know you can do real magic." It made her smile, though, and maybe that had been the whole point.

He huffed a laugh through his nose and with the snap of his fingers, procured the chip again between his middle and pointer fingers, and held it back out to her. She took it from him and turned it over in her hand as she thought. "And you didn't answer my question."

"As far as I could tell, it was an observation, not a question." Shrugging, he leaned back against the leather seat. "I saw no reason to deny or confirm your suspicion."

"I asked you why."

"You said you are having fun. Are you truly?" He avoided her question once more.

"Of course."

"Expound. Why?"

She shifted and looked off into the restaurant. Tables of people laughing, eating, drinking, and enjoying themselves. Engrossed in conversations. It felt real. It felt normal. Even if they were beasts and monsters, it was still... just... people being people.

"Why am I having fun?" Maybe it was the beer and her comfortably fuzzy head that made her so honest. "I'm exploring somewhere special with someone special, that's why."

He said nothing.

Frantically retracing her steps, she tried to figure out what had caused his silence. Had she screwed up? "I'm sorry, that was dumb, I—"

A finger on her lips stunned her to silence. He turned her head toward him with the gentle press of his hand. He leaned in on the table to speak to her, quietly, his voice barely audible in the din of the restaurant. "Then you have answered your own question."

* * *

When Aon "blinked" them back to his home, Lydia felt her stomach lurch in motion even as everything else stilled. Before she could recover from the teleportation, he had pressed her up against the wall of the library and leaned his body into hers, pinning her against the surface with the length of his thigh.

"Can you even fathom—" He slipped his hand through her hair only to clench it in a fist and pull her head backward. "What I have wished to do to you all damn day?"

She shuddered at his grasp and knew her small whimper from him yanking her head back was anything but a deterrent to him. He seemed to know precisely how far to go before it would be too much. There was nothing he had done to her that she hadn't adored.

He was possessive. He was needy. He was controlling.

And she loved it.

"I think I would like to taste your lips once more." He reached his hand toward her temple, intending to switch off her vision.

Maybe it was the beer.

Yeah, blame it on the beer.

Lydia caught his hand in hers and stopped him. He tilted his head to her curiously as if wondering why she interrupted him. She folded his hand against her shoulder and let her own hands wander across him. "Not so fast."

Now that she had a chance to finally touch him, she let her hands run up his chest, lacing the fingers into his hair at the back of his neck, and pulled him closer. He let out a low, appreciative sound in his throat as he obeyed.

She wanted him. That dark power was as dangerous as it was exciting. There was still a fear of what he was—of what he could do—but it only seemed to add to her desire. His predatory nature fed a fire in her she hadn't known she owned. He was a shark in the ocean, a tiger in the jungle, awe-inspiring and deadly.

His prosthetic metal hand dug its claws into her hip. He was already trying to reclaim control and make her squirm underneath his grasp.

But she had other plans. She gave up the exploration of him by gripping his wrist and pulling it away from her. She pointed with her other hand to his odd, asymmetrical wing-back chair by the fire. "Sit."

Oh, man. She was gambling big time.

"Pardon me?" He withdrew an inch in surprise.

It had been a command. An order. From *her.* He straightened his shoulders in haughty indignation at her ballsy move.

Lifting her chin, she doubled down. "You heard me." She pointed at his chair again like she might at a dog. "Sit."

He laughed. For a moment, she wondered if he was going to stick his clawed fingers into her ribs like he did in her dream. But his laughter calmed, and he shook his head. He withdrew from her like the prowl of a jungle cat and walked to his chair, dramatically slumping into it. He held out his arms as if to say, "now what?"

Lydia followed him and felt her conviction waver for just a moment. Oh, hell, what the fuck was she doing? This wasn't some guy from the bar; this wasn't some second date. She bit back her trepidation and her questionable self-assuredness. *You started it. You finish it.*

Putting a hand on the back of the chair beside his head, she shifted to straddle his legs. Lydia sat down on his lap, kneeling over him. She leaned into his neck, and he tilted his head away, letting her kiss his throat—slowly, lingering—wanting to taste him. Wanting to memorize how he moved. He moaned as she did, and he shifted underneath her impatiently. How she wished it were his lips. How she wished she could kiss him and still see what she was doing. And she'd need to see to do what she planned.

His hand ran up her back slowly, starting at her waist, slipping underneath her shirt.

Well, now was time to take her second gamble. Roll the dice and see what happened. She broke the kiss, grinning against him, and took his hand in hers and captured the other without a fuss from him. She placed his hands on the arms of his wingback chair. "No touching. You touch, I stop."

He froze and sat there silently, locked tight. Seemingly unsure—even for him—of what to do.

She suddenly knew nobody had ever done this to him, nobody had ever tried to turn the tables. He was *always* in control. Always the master of the situation. Always the commander of what transpired around him.

She was seriously playing with fire.

But when she released his hands, he didn't move them. He merely shifted his grip on the arms of the chair and sat perfectly still. Rigid and locked solid like a statue. He was tense, uncertain, as if he were wary about what she might do.

What on Earth did he think she was up to, that he was so wound up? "Oh, chill." Letting out a breathy chuckle, she kissed his throat once more. She couldn't kiss his face, so that would have to do. "What the hell do you think I could even do to you, anyway?"

The beer was *definitely* to blame.

"I do not know what you are plotting, my darling, but I warn you to tread lightly." It was clear he meant his words, even as he turned his head further to make more room for her.

She grinned and leaned in and kissed his jawline slowly, letting herself trace touches of her lips meticulously up along the curved line up toward his ear. "Don't you trust me?"

"I do not surrender control. And certainly not in such matters." His voice was husky and dark from her kisses. Even through his threat, he squirmed underneath her. Yet again, his responsiveness surprised her. When she dug her teeth into his neck just barely, he arched his back and let out a moan.

She let herself linger at each spot she tormented as she wandered up his neck and let him feel the warmth of her breath and the heat of her tongue. Slowly, she made her way to his ear, captured the lobe in her mouth, and bit down. Not gently either.

He hissed a breath in through his teeth, clenched his flesh-and-blood fist and pounded it into the arm of the chair. The breath left him in a deep growl. She could hear the claws of his metal prosthetic digging into the wood armrest of the chair, digging trenches in surface. He was a taut bowstring beneath her, needing to move, yanking against his proverbial leash. "You little succubus..."

She started unbuttoning his vest and then undid his tie. Forcing herself to take her time, she continued with his black silk shirt. She forced herself to let it linger. Her hands were now at his waistline, and she undid the last button and pulled the fabric apart. He had not worn an undershirt, and for that, she was immensely grateful.

The marks on his chest were beautiful and haunting in their geometric gatherings and lines. She had seen them in the hot spring that night, but she hadn't really been able to appreciate them.

He had the power of a god, but... he was here. Now. With her.

Letting both her hands roam up over his chest, she marveled at how he felt. Hard like marble, yet it gave way under her fingers. He twitched at her touch as though he weren't expecting it—no—like he wasn't used to it. As her hands wandered, tracing the lines, soaking in what he felt like, he continued to shift and twitch at her touch. "Don't you let people touch you?"

"Rarely, if ever. Few offer—even fewer are allowed."

She leaned her head in close, letting her tongue run along the line of his ear, before nipping at his skin and whispering once more. "Selfish man, trying to deny me this." She began nipping at his jawline, just under the edge of his mask, her hands slipping along his sides. "Both times so far, it hasn't been fair. You haven't let me really touch you. Really enjoy you."

A low growl escaped him again, a sound thick with need and frustration. His hands left the armrests and reached for her.

Pulling back, she ticked a finger in front of his face. "Ah-ah."

Slowly, as if it was agony, he returned his hands to the armrests. This was a game—a game he was willingly entertaining—but he was already straining at the end of his leash.

"I'm going to take my sweet time with you. It's my turn. She let the finger she had taunted him with run along his chest, tracing the lines of black ink. Leaning down, she replaced her finger with her tongue. "One of these days, I think I'd like to lick every line of ink you own."

For a moment, Aon cracked. With a snarl, he went to grab at her hips to pull her down harder against the proof of her efforts.

Chuckling, she quickly slid off his lap. She moved to stand in front of him. "The rules are so simple," she echoed his comments about their poker game.

He gripped the arms of the chair hard enough that the wood creaked. But neither he, nor the wood, snapped. With a long, frustrated sigh, he leaned his head back once more. "Very well."

This time, she undressed because she wanted to, and she took her time. She wanted him to watch as if she didn't care. It was a task to keep her hands from shaking. When she was finally completely nude, she slipped back on top of his lap, straddling him as she had before.

What a beautiful creature was beneath her. She stroked his hair back from his face, combing her fingers through the black tendrils as she tilted his head back against the wing-back chair.

"Oh, yes, judging by that sultry expression of yours, you have only just now discovered your attraction to me," he complained through a heavy breath. "Clearly, I am some lascivious beast for wooing you in such a toward and unkind fashion."

"Do you always have to monologue?" Lydia laughed and rested her head against his shoulder briefly. "Shut up and let me do my thing."

"And what is your 'thing,' exactly?"

She put a finger over the spot on his mask under which his lips would be. "Shut up and find out."

Sliding her body closer to his, she let him feel the press of her breasts against his lithe and muscular chest and began to make good on her threat, kissing and licking along the line of ink on his throat. He moaned, splitting his legs apart beneath her. He was doing it to pull her body closer to his. It was cheating—bending the spirit of the rules, but not breaking them. He shifted his hips toward the edge of the chair to try and gain more exposure to her.

She let a hand slide down to palm his arousal through his clothing and at the same time, bit down against his throat. She was going to do her damnedest to leave a mark.

The noise that came out of him was amazing. It was the most fantastic thing she'd ever heard, and she wanted to hear another one. It was half a roar and half a moan—a hitched, broken sounding thing that ended in a low, angry growl. He tried to form words, but seemed unable to do so, settling instead to shift underneath her and dig his fingers harder into the arms of the chair.

She began stroking him through his clothing slowly—rubbing her thumb along the full of his length, but still taking her time. She began to suck on the skin of his neck through her teeth, in time with her slow, firm touches on his body.

The growl had now broken back off into a moan, and he was writhing beneath her again, unable to sit still against what she was doing. When she finally broke her clasp on his neck, she licked the result of her work. There was a mark. Good! Finally, he'd have something to show for it, instead of just her and her myriads of scratches and bruises. At least for about two seconds before it would start to heal, anyway. "Turnabout is fair play."

He couldn't respond except to make a breathy, angry growl at her. But he didn't break his grasp upon the chair's arms or shatter their game. He would not be beaten. Although his breath was coming in heavier pulls, and she knew he was straining at the edge of his control.

She resumed her task of trailing kisses down his chest. As she began to slip down off of his lap and instead between his knees, he let out a low moan in his throat as he realized her destination. The man was eager, moving his legs apart to make room for her. Smirking, she knelt on the floor, and only when her lips reached his navel, did she let her hand release her ministrations on his captured arousal.

Looking up at him, he was a thing of beauty. His dark hair was falling along the sides of his metal mask in black silk tendrils. It stood in a sharp contrast to his pale chest with its cryptic and occult markings. She watched as they rose and fell in quick succession as his breath was heavy and needy.

He was gorgeous. A dark god. *Her* dark god. And she was never so sure of what she wanted to do than looking at him like this. And he watched her in silence, playing *her* game.

She worked the clasp of his buckle and carefully freed himself from his confines. He let out a breath of relief as the air touched his skin. She tried not to feel nervous at what she saw— she knew what she was doing, but... fuck. This was the first time she had actually seen him—each other time, he had blinded her.

Too far to stop now. Slowly, she ran her hand along him now with no fabric between them. He was hot in her hand, burning and throbbing. He moaned and tilted his head back against the chair, shifting himself closer into her touch, trying to rut himself against her hand in a desperate need to feel her touch him. Still, his hands never left where she had placed them on the back of the chair. He was both at once her willful "prisoner" and the object of worship. He looked like some great demon, sitting there like that. And at least for tonight, he was hers. It was that thought that drove her forward.

She was dead set on sending him to the brink of losing his control. And if he thought she was going to let him off easy—after everything he'd done—he had another think coming. She leaned her head in, and instead of kissing his throbbing length, she let her tongue swirl a slow circle against his lower abdomen, below his navel, before digging her teeth into his skin and biting him. At the same time, she pressed the fingers of her other hand into his thigh, finding the taut muscles there.

He tightened and nearly spasmed against her—arching his back and trying desperately not to press his hips up against her. The broken, hitching growl was astonishing and just as good as the last one. He threw his head back in a deep moan. "Ah, *yes*, my sweet—nngh! Oh, you temptress... do not dare stop. I have destroyed entire cities for *far* less."

Snickering at his melodrama, she decided to give him just a little of what he wanted. She let her hand gently grasp his length. She marveled for a moment at just how far she had pushed him, before letting her tongue run up along him slowly. Starting at the very base, and letting it languorously travel up to the tip.

The moan that left him was all the encouragement she needed. She let her tongue swirl around him slowly once, twice, before wandering back down. The pattern repeated, never picking up the pace. Not yet. She rested her hand against the valley where his upper thigh met the rest of his body and felt the muscles tense and relax slowly as she let herself explore him —taste him—learn every part of him and where he felt what.

Her slow exploration of him served a few purposes. She was driving him crazy, she knew, with the way the muscles in his leg were twitching. The small, urgent sounds he was making each time her tongue reached his tip and swirled around it, lingering for a moment at the parts she learned were sensitive. She was learning what he liked and how he was wired. Also, to be crass... she needed him wet for what she planned to do.

She took him into her mouth after what she hoped had felt like an eternity and the noise that he made confirmed it. She let her eyes glide shut. It was better with that sense turned off. She gently held his base, as she pushed him into her mouth slowly and withdrew, letting her tongue roll around him before repeating. She took her sweet time, gently sucking on him every time she pushed him into her mouth. He moaned loudly each time she did that, and she knew he was expecting her to go no further than that. *Hah.*

She took in a breath, held it, and pressed him down into her throat. She pressed him all the way to the hilt until there was nothing left, and her nose touched his body.

He let out a loud cry—a deep sound of pleasure and agony both, and it ended in a growl and a moan that inspired her to hold him there as long as she could. He was pounding his fist into the arm of the chair, and she heard the wood of the other arm give way underneath his sharp metal talons. Several times he tried to form words, but each time they were taken away in a mindless sound of sheer pleasure.

He filled her—cut off her air—pushed the limits of what she could take. It was *heaven.* She tried to count seconds before she had to retreat, before she couldn't control the muscles in her throat and her air supply was running low. She pulled back off him and let him leave her mouth as she gasped for air. Her head was spinning. God... she loved it. She didn't know what about it turned her on so damn much, but it was undeniable.

He was half sprawled in his chair, his head rolled back and to the side. This time she watched as she let herself run her tongue up his length again and placed a kiss at the underside of the tip of him. Teasing him. Pointedly making him respond to her before she did it again.

That got his attention. He lifted his head to turn it down toward her. "If you do not continue, I swear by the Ancients themselves, I will find a way to *make* you." His voice was a deep, hideously dangerous growl as he threatened her even as he begged her. There was a desperate kind of fury in him. She saw his hands clench the chair as if that alone was keeping him from breaking her game.

It was both a ridiculous threat and entirely sincere at exactly the same time. Taking her time, she pulled him into her mouth once more, swirled her tongue around him, and released him. "You're so overdramatic."

He snarled at her again. "If you think I am above strapping you down and forcing my way down your throat, you—"

She cut off his words in another broken, hitching sound as she did as he asked. She tucked her hair behind her ear as she tilted her head to allow herself a better angle. She pressed him back down into her slowly, the feeling of him pushing into her making her moan against him.

This felt astonishing. She began to repeat her pattern of pulling him out of her until just the tip of him filled her mouth, catching her air, and then sliding him back down into her. She couldn't help moan against him each time he slid into her— each time she felt him fill her throat.

Finally, after several minutes, she couldn't take much

more. It was time for a change of tactics. She needed to breathe more than this was letting her, and her head was spinning.

When she began to pull herself off him, it was as though Aon knew her plans and she felt his hand suddenly at the back of her head. He grabbed roughly by her hair and yanked her head back. Lydia gasped—both for air, as she was already short of breath and in pain as he finally, clearly, had enough.

Well... enough of her teasing, anyway.

Her game was over. But it was clear he intended to start his own. The thumb of his other hand traced her parted lower lip. "Oh, my darling, sweet little creature..." He leaned over to loom closer to her. The nightmare had been freed. "You should not have shown me your talent. For I will most certainly now find the need to *abuse it!*"

And with that, he yanked her head down and rammed himself down her throat. She let out a "*hnk*" and a moan at the same time, as she felt him grasp her head and take the reins away from her. He pushed his hips up as she reached the end of him and pressed himself hard down into her throat. As if by sheer pressure, he could find himself further in. He let out a long, deep moan, and began to pull her back on him, only to press her back down. "You think I would allow you to stop? Do you think I am done with you so soon? I cannot remember anything feeling quite so astounding, and you think to take it from me *now?*"

Her hands were pressed against his thighs, trying to control some of the momenta, but it was pointless. Each time he reached the bottom of his stroke, he lifted his hips up to meet her, questioning her control of the muscles in her throat. She couldn't waste the air to make a sound, but he could. And it was clear just how very much he was enjoying this. He groaned and gasped with every movement, praising her even as he taunted her.

"Give in, my beautiful creature. Surrender. Do not fight me. You cannot win. And you do not want to."

He was right. She could barely catch her breath, let alone muster the desire to fight back. She held on to his thighs as best she could as he continued to piston himself roughly deep into her throat and back.

As she stopped resisting, he let out a loud moan. "*Ngh!*" He gasped, his voice raspy. "Yes, *yes...*"

While his motions were faster than she had allowed, he gave her a bare moment in between actions to catch what air she could. She could scream or fight. She could, at worst, bite down. But like the rest of what she'd discovered with him, she realized... she was enjoying this.

How long it went on, she didn't know. She lost track as he kept her at the edge of not enough air. He was moaning, coaxing her along, offering her praise as he filled what she had clearly left him wanting.

He bottomed himself out into her once more, pressing hard against her as if intending to never leave. Her eyes watered as she felt her lungs start to burn, and she squeezed her eyes shut tightly.

Clenching his fist in her hair, he let out a ragged moan, suddenly spasming underneath her. He was throbbing, pulsing as he spent himself deep down her throat. His grasp on her loosened, and he gently eased her from him.

She coughed and gasped for air, but her head quickly righted. He had pushed her to the brink—but not a step farther.

It was beautiful, the way Aon laid back in the aftermath of receding pleasure. His head was rolled back, and his palm was pressed against his masked face. He was desperately gasping for air. His body twitched and spasmed as aftershocks racked him occasionally. He was clearly spent and looked utterly over-wrought. That was all she needed to feel the triumph, and as he finally managed to fill his lungs without his breath hitching, she lifted her head from him. Only now was she able to feel like she was getting enough air herself.

She could only squeak as he stood up, lifted her to her feet, and they vanished in a blink. Already dizzy, the world whipped around her in a mad dash as she found herself sprawled out on his lavish silken bed.

She watched as he lazily stripped himself of clothing and fell down onto the bed next to her. His head crooked into her shoulder, and his arm wrapped around her protectively. "Is that what I am paid when I take you out into the world? If so... I shall plot a grand tour immediately."

She laughed quietly and wrapped her arm around his, hugging him to her. "I did it because I wanted to. That's all. I'm glad you aren't mad about the game."

"I will never be angry over games... they are my greatest diversion. Especially never ones that end like that. But I fear we are not yet finished..."

His flesh-and-blood hand trailed down her stomach, and she let out a gasp as his hand found her core. It was very clear how much she enjoyed what she had done to him. He let out an approving growl in his throat as he pressed himself closer to her, as his fingers delved inside of her. One at first, followed quickly by a second. "My, my..." he teased. "What a wanton little harlot you turn out to be..."

"Shut—" She couldn't get out the second word as she cried out, his thumb rubbing against her nub and sending her into her own fit of breathless pleasure. Already worked up from how much she enjoyed what she had done to him, it didn't take long for his skilled touch to bring her to a frenzy, and her small, mewling cries were helpless as she grasped onto his arm.

She nearly wailed as he slipped a third finger inside of her, and he chuckled at how she thrashed in his hands.

His metal hand was at her back, nails digging into her—the

pain accentuating the pleasure. Her eyes went wide in fear as she wondered if he was going to tear her open.

"Trust me…" His words were a whisper in her ear.

Instinctively, she relaxed, sinking into his grasp. It hurt a little, but he didn't cut into her or break the skin. It was like a bed of nails at her back.

"Yes, let go… That's it. Trust me." He buried his head in the crook of her neck. Still, he was effortlessly twisting her into a wild pleasure. "Do you? Tell me."

Did she? Did she trust him?

Oh God help her… she did.

"Yes," she gasped.

"Say you are mine. Say you belong to me, and *me alone*."

She repeated her breathless "yes."

Shuddering, he grasped her tighter to him. Curling his fingers deep inside of her, he sent a river of ecstasy flowing through her.

She cried out, her eyes sliding shut. Clinging to him, she trembled in the wake of the ecstasy and his touch.

But he didn't relent, driving her through another wave and another as her orgasm shook her to the core. When he finally let her come down from the cloud, she was trembling against him. She could only cling to him in desperation.

He turned her so that her back was to his chest. He held her to him, his head resting at the top of hers. "Are you happy?"

"Yeah." Sleep was coming for her fast—a combination of the beer and what had just happened. She didn't feel like she could open her eyes for the world at this point.

Fingers were running in slow circles along the back of her hand, and that was enough to seal the deal. As she was drifting off, she heard him say something to her—something that felt important—but missed what it was.

NINETEEN

"Let me *go!*"

"For the last time, no. And if you ask again, I will snap your neck. Again."

A low snarl, and the sound of someone slumping down onto the ground. "Fuck this. This sucks."

"There you are, using that word again."

Lyon leaned against the tree in the wooded clearing, listening to Kamira and Nicholas bicker once more. The boy had not been freed from where he was chained to the tree for several days. Now, at least the chain wrapped several times around his neck, allowing him some freedom to roam like a dog on a leash. Kamira was staying with the boy, partially to ensure he would not escape, but also to keep him company. He was part of her own pack, and Lyon could tell she felt guilty for keeping the pup restrained.

Kamira knew Nicholas would immediately go to Aon and Lydia to warn them of what was to come. Lyon wished he could do so. He wanted to snap the chains himself and let the shifter pup go save his friend. Dooming Lydia to the grave left an awful taste in his mouth, but Ziza had been clear.

To save Under, Lydia must die.

It left no small ache in his heart, regardless.

Arms wound around his waist as Kamira stepped up to him. "I dislike this as much as you. The girl does not deserve this fate. But life in Under has never been fair."

Lyon went to respond but was cut off as a roar of flame burst up from the ground in the center of the clearing. The swirl of fire cast stark shadows, and Lyon had to wince and turn his face away from the unexpected bright light.

Neither Kamira nor Lyon were alarmed. They knew what the fire heralded. Nicholas, however, did not. He jumped quickly back to his feet and recoiled both from the blaze and who appeared standing in the center of the swirl as the flame died down.

Edu, with Ylena at his side.

"To what do we owe the pleasure?" Kamira asked the big man sarcastically as she pushed away from Lyon.

"Master Edu has come to take the boy, Nicholas. He will serve as bait to lure Lydia away from Aon," Ylena responded.

The young man was pressed up against a tree, wide-eyed and terrified as he watched the scene unfold, helpless to decide his own fate.

Kamira snarled and moved to stand between Edu and Nicholas, protecting her pack member. "No. He is one of mine. You have no jurisdiction here. You are not the reigning king, lest you forget."

Edu sighed. "Master Edu finds your use of Aon's status suddenly very convenient. You had no complaints earlier today."

"You were not going to murder one of my own this afternoon!"

"Master Edu has no desire to kill the boy," Ylena retorted.

"But you know it will happen. Using him as bait? What do you think Aon will do?" Kamira hissed, baring her teeth in a show of primal anger. "No. Bad enough the girl shall die. You will not take him too."

Edu tilted his head thoughtfully and watched Kamira for a long moment in silence. "Then Master Edu has another way in which you can assist."

* * *

To say this marketplace was impressive would be an understatement. Lydia had never experienced anything like it.

There was so much to see, it was dizzying. So much detail, so much texture. Colors of fabric of every kind, baubles, weapons, tools, and more were stacked in piles and arranged so they might stand out to passing customers.

Tents were arranged and stacked on top of each other at angles that might make sense to someone, somewhere. And holy hell, the crowds were another thing entirely.

Monsters and people alike, servants and masked, added to the mad array of the marketplace. Maybe if it was empty, it would be less intimidating. But the movement made it even more confusing of a display.

The vendors were hawking their wares loudly, even yelling at each other when one of them would step on the other one's announcements of "best this" or "best that." Spices and the smell of cooking foods were rich in the air. Something on a stick was being fried in deep oil that might have been some manner of rodent at one point or another.

She stepped backward and out of the way of a cart rolling by, and straight into the chest of Aon. He chuckled, a sound she felt more than heard in the din of the market, and he placed his metal hand on her shoulder. "Everything quite all right?" He sounded genuinely amused.

"I just... wow." She shook her head, stunned. "I guess I

didn't realize—" She stopped, realizing it might be insulting to him.

"Realize what, darling?"

"That you all *lived* here."

"Of course, we do. What a silly statement."

"No, I mean that you really have lives, that, uh..." She paused, watching someone walk by with a gigantic, vulture-esque creature walking behind him. It was one of the beasts of Under. It walked on the apex of its wings as though they were arms and plodded behind a hooded figure in green. The creature had a skull for a head, its large, gaping eye sockets housing only a bright white pinprick of light within them.

Its body looked rotten and torn away, the ribs of its chest cavity exposed. When it looked at her and fluffed its feathers, its ribs expanded and moved along with them. She took a step back into Aon, who placed a hand reassuringly on her shoulder. Seeing who she was with, the vulture turned its head away and kept walking behind its friend.

Now she'd seen a giant nightmare vulture. Great.

"So, people can befriend beasts?"

"Of course."

"I thought you guys just went around killing each other all the time."

He laughed, this time audibly. "Violence defines us, yes. But we are far more than that. Look around you and see a world of souls building lives for themselves."

She tried not to be sheepish at his rebuke. He was right. She had thought everything on Under were just monsters living in holes, waiting for their next meals. Of course, there was more to them than that.

"You believed we were but strange creatures, haunting the halls of our abodes, with no manner of commerce or comings or goings? We eat. We love. We build families, even if we cannot have children. We seek to better ourselves. We practice our trades, such as any others may do. We are a people just like yours, in all ways save our inherent superiority."

It was a nice speech, except for that last bit. "Hah, very funny. I'm not touching that with a ten-foot pole."

"Better to concede the argument before it begins, I agree." There was still a deep amusement in his voice. He was poking her, and she wasn't going to take the bait. So instead, she did something much more mature—she stuck her tongue out at him.

He laughed again and shook his head. The metal hand on her shoulder squeezed reassuringly. "Come."

Even with the thickness of the crowds, everyone parted for Aon like the Red Sea, clearly afraid to come too close to the King of Shadows. It was hard to remember that he commanded so much fear until she saw it etched on the faces of the people around her as they cowered away from him at his passing.

He was different with Lydia. He humored her insolence. It was clear the way the others bowed or shrank away from him— or both, which was a difficult thing to manage—that wasn't a thing he was known for.

They walked for some time through the tents and stacks of items. Baskets of spices piled up like dust, fabrics draping in the wind in colorful and strange patterns, some with symbols blazoned upon them like flags, for each of the six living Houses. When she stopped to watch at a street performer, who was sitting and playing a percussion instrument she'd never seen before, she felt a hand rest on her lower back.

Aon had come to stand up beside her. The way he stood with his body just barely touching hers, it'd be clear to onlookers what it meant. "Careful," she said to him in an aside, not wanting to interrupt the performer, "people might think you're here consorting with an inferior human. Think of the scandal."

"It troubles not my reputation, I assure you. I have no reputation left to lose. This show of affection will impugn yours worse than mine."

"What reputation? To them, I'm nothing more than a ham sandwich. I don't really care what people think I am or I'm not."

"Good." Aon wrapped his hand around her waist. "Besides, better they know you are under my protection." His flesh-and-blood hand, wearing the black glove he always wore in public, tucked a strand of her blonde hair behind her ear.

When the performer finished, she applauded with the crowd. Aon didn't. They walked from the gathering and resumed wandering from row to row of tents and stalls. The fabric stretched over their wares were meant to protect their goods from... what, exactly? Moonlight? Rain?

Suddenly, she realized she had never seen a cloud in the sky. She looked up and saw nothing, just an empty black abyss. No stars, only the three moons that hovered in the sky this night. "Aon?"

"Yes, my dear?"

"Does it ever rain here?"

There was a long pause. When she looked at him, his shoulders were stiff. The question had triggered something in him.

Instantly, she regretted her question. "Never mind. Forget I asked."

"Merely another part of our world that has faded and died." His words were as dark as the void. "Along with the stars in the sky, went with it the rain, the storms... the snow. There are no oceans to move the wind. No mountains to gather the clouds."

She felt her heart ache at the deadness in Aon's voice and the emptiness there. Reaching out, she took his hand and laced her fingers with his, squeezing it. "I'm sorry."

"It is not your sin for which to apologize."

Lifting his hand to her lips, she placed a kiss against the back of his knuckles. "C'mon. Let's keep going."

Another row of booths over, there was a stall selling lanterns. The glass globes were filled with blinking false insects. They were the magical, replacement bugs she had seen in the lampposts in M'url. They came in all colors, even black, somehow. Lydia had never seen a literal black light, but sure enough, they managed to glow. More because they illuminated the things around them in a ghastly gray tone than they lit up in any way.

"My lady," the man inside the booth addressed Lydia.

It took her a moment to realize the man was talking to her. Nobody here even dared look at her, let alone *speak* to her. He wore thick glasses on the top of his head and no mask. Purple writing was etched down one side of his kind, craggy face. He had barely glanced up at her as he was bending a thin piece of silver wire into a careful filigree shape on his workbench.

She bet that if he had seen who she was—or more importantly, who was looming beside her like a black inkblot—he might not have decided to talk to her. "They're beautiful." She smiled warmly at the old man. "You do amazing work."

"I thank you! It is difficult magic to control. When they are happy, their shows are quite stunning."

"They're sentient?" She'd thought they were glorified plastic fake fish in a tank.

"In a manner. They are artificial, so they have no souls. But they have moods and personalities, even still." The man chuckled.

Aon scoffed quietly from beside her.

But she'd seen plenty of stranger things since she had come to Under, so fine, semi-sentient blinking magical orbs. Why not. "They're happy, locked up in there?"

"A cage to one is a home to another." The craftsman let out a gentle laugh. "They are little marvels, aren't they? I assure you, they do not mind their containers. Indeed, it is how they thrive. Out in the open air, they cannot survive."

That sounded familiar. "I can sympathize." She shot a playful grin at Aon.

It earned her a heavy sigh from the warlock. "Must you *always* find a reason to taunt me?"

"Call it a gift."

"Hmm?" The older man looked up finally and lowered his glasses over his eyes. Seeing her—and Aon—his eyes shot wide, and he nearly fell from his stool. "My lady! My king, forgive me! I did not know."

Aon remained silent, just staring at the poor older man. No wonder he gave everyone the creeps. The lantern-maker stammered helplessly, apologized again, and was very nearly on his knees, begging for mercy.

"It's fine, it's okay—I promise." She smiled reassuringly at the craftsman. She went so far as to elbow Aon in the ribs, and he turned his head to look at her. She shot him a glare, reminding him to play nice.

Aon moved his head in an exaggerated version of what she imagined to be an exasperated eyeroll. "You have committed no crime. Speaking to her is not against the law." He dropped his voice to mutter to her. "Although her speaking may soon be."

She resisted the urge to stick her tongue out at him again. "Sorry to disturb you," she said to the craftsman.

"No, no! You are not a disturbance." He stood and brushed himself off and bowed low at the waist. "I have never been in the presence of a king before. I am pleased to meet you both."

No, he probably wasn't. But she didn't blame him at all. "My name's Lydia." She extended her hand to shake his.

He reached out to take it but glanced to Aon and stammered. The merchant nervously lowered his hand.

She tried to redirect the suddenly incredibly awkward moment. "Really, they're beautiful."

"Oh! Well, if I may..." The craftsman turned to the back of his booth and began leafing through parts and pieces. He opened a drawer in what looked like a cabinet on wheels and was digging about for something or other. He was muttering to himself, and then let out an "Ah!" and turned back around.

The man held in his hands what looked like a chrysalis of a strange butterfly, cast in hand-blown glass and delicate silver details. It was on the end of a long, delicate chain. Inside it was a single blinking tiny orb, one of the odd black ones. It was tiny, much more so than the orbs in the other containers, and at least it seemed to have plenty of room.

"It doesn't get along with the others," the man said with a faint smile. "It prefers to be alone and is quite happy in here, I promise you. It did not glow once until it was by itself."

"This is nonsense. They are not *alive*," Aon muttered under his breath behind her, unheard by the merchant.

"If I may give it to the lady as a gift?" the older man asked Aon.

"If she would have it."

"I... I couldn't." She blinked, surprised. "It's too beautiful."

"I insist." The craftsman held it out farther, smiling.

Carefully, she took it gently from the man and held it in her palm. The little black spot of light was blinking steadily like a tiny firefly. It was beautiful. It almost brought her to tears, and when she looked up, the merchant's craggy face was creased in warmth. He knew how much it meant to her, just by her expression.

"May it give you some light in the darkness." He could tell by her lack of marks on her face who she was, she knew. It was a gesture of pure kindness.

She slipped the long silver chain around her neck and let the little blinking orb dangle in its glass chrysalis. "I can't thank you enough, really." Placing the glass container in the palm of her hand, she continued to marvel at the little thing.

"It is my honor. I am glad it has found a proper home."

Aon was apparently done with the sappy exchange. He

pulled her by the elbow. "Thank you for your gesture, merchant. We will be going now."

The man bowed low as they walked away.

She stammered out a half-attempted goodbye before shooting a half-hearted glare up at Aon. "That was rude."

"I was bored. At least now I might be able to find you in a dark room. To think he believes them to be *sentient*." Aon huffed.

"You don't?"

"They are the product of magic, nothing more. He is an old, lonely man anthropomorphizing an inanimate object." He suddenly seemed deeply invested in the conversation as though something had touched a nerve in him. "Magic cannot create a *soul*."

"You sound like you speak from experience."

He ignored her comment. "Truly, is that abomination going to blink incessantly?"

"I like it." She defended the little thing.

"You look like a boat out at sea."

"I do not." She tucked it down the front of her shirt. "There, better?"

"Much."

Suddenly, there was shouting and a ruckus from the center of the market. It wasn't the sound of panic or fear. It sounded more like the crowd at a boxing match.

As they approached, the center of the market was cleared into a large circular area. In the middle was a monster that looked as though a lizard and a spider had a strange nightmare baby. It was huge, probably twenty feet long and ten feet tall. It was howling and screeching, and it had great black insect wings that it fluttered with an angry and nearly deafening buzz. All right, a lizard, a spider, and a *fly* had a three-way nightmare baby.

"Whoa," was all she could muster.

Aon laughed and drew her closer to the edge of the circle. The crowds parted for him without a thought, although a few spared her a second glance. Right. She was the freak here, not the insect-lizard-spider monster in the center of the clearing.

Three men in full armor were standing down the monster. They were armed to the teeth with swords, shields, or one man had a spear. Judging by the way the crowd was cheering, this hadn't just broken out.

"What's happening?" She had to tilt her head toward him and shout over the crowd to be heard.

"A contest. Either the men will win, or it will kill them."

"For fun?"

"And food. The creature must be starving, after all." Aon moved to stand behind her and placed both of his arms around her, holding her against his chest. Lydia sank back against him, unafraid. Not so long ago, she'd have locked up and cowered. Now, she found real comfort in his embrace. More than that, she had found herself enjoying it.

The fight was brutal. The three men would edge closer, trying to catch the beast unawares or at a weak moment and trying to expose its flank or get it into a compromising situation. But the creature could fly, and it jumped up and over one of the men.

When it sent the other two sprawling with the flick of its long, whip-like tail, it crushed the third underneath its jagged foot. Jaws lowered, and the sound of snapping sinew and tearing flesh was nearly drowned out by the screams of excitement from the crowd.

The sick crunching of bone like twigs breaking underfoot made her whip her head away and try to turn away from the fight. "I don't want to watch this."

The creature was tearing the man apart. She could tell by his screams and the sound of meat being wrenched from the bone.

Aon was looking down at her, ignoring the fight. "This is

my world. Our world. He suffers and dies and will rise again on the morrow as though nothing had happened. This violence is as much a part of this place as the bauble you wear."

"I get it, I just don't have to *like* it."

"Watch."

Sighing, she did as he urged.

The monster's meal was interrupted as the other two men had rejoined the fray. The creature had been distracted with its kill, letting one of the other men dig a spear deep into its haunches. It was screeching in pain and thrashing violently at them. Some of the crowd had to leap back to avoid its tail as it shattered a stack of boxes in its agony.

But it was not done yet. The second man fell to the creature, similarly as the first. This time, the beast had learned not to worry about eating him, only to crush his ribs in its jaws and toss him aside. The man rolled like a ragdoll, limp and lifeless. His blood was pooling out on the cobblestones.

Her hand flew to cover her mouth, and she tried to pretend this was all just a show, a horror movie. None of this was real. The man's body was not twitching in death throes.

The last man put an end to the fight when he rolled underneath the monster, ripping his fallen compatriot's spear from its haunches and digging it up straight through the thing's skull, from under the jaw and up through the exoskeleton.

The noise was like if you had dropped a pumpkin from the roof of a building. Splintering and wet, all at the same time.

It made her stomach flip over, and she was glad she hadn't eaten lunch. She turned her head away and this time had to shut her eyes. The sound of the creature falling to the ground with a loud *thud* was once more nearly buried underneath the shouting of the crowd. They were cheering on the lone survivor, chanting his name. Tim.

Wait. Tim?

She looked back in time to see the man rip off his helmet.

Sure enough. The greaser, the one who served Edu. He was grinning, sweating, and oozing from a gash on his chest. But he looked otherwise not much worse for wear.

"I know that guy. He's one of Edu's."

"Is he, now?" Aon was bored again. "Charming." He turned them away from the scene and began to walk back through the crowd the way they had come.

It was astonishing how fast chaos happened.

One moment, they were walking away from the fight, and the next, Lydia was sitting on the ground. It took her a split second to realize Aon had stepped in front of her and pushed her. It took her a second longer to realize he had two arrows rammed all the way through his chest. The tips were dripping in crimson.

They had been meant for her.

The crowd screamed and ran, emptying from the market-place as quickly as they could, wanting nothing to do with whatever trouble was brewing.

Something rushed toward her face. She flinched and threw her arms up in reflex. When she looked, a third arrow hovered in midair. This one, Aon had managed to stop with a gesture of his hand. It burst into black flame and crumbled to the ground.

He grabbed the arrows in his chest, and they, too, burst into flames and were gone. Lydia pushed herself back up to standing, wide-eyed and confused. It wasn't until she saw the figure standing twenty feet away from them that she understood what was happening.

Edu.

He was wearing his full armor, standing like the nightmare she remembered when this whole ordeal began. He held his broadsword in one hand.

Aon turned to face the man in the armor. Lydia could see several people standing behind Edu, two with bows in their hands. The source of the attack. Aon was still bleeding from the chest and back, his crimson blood hard to see against black clothes as it ran down him.

Fear, like an old friend, came rushing back to her.

It was amazing how fast hundreds of people could just get the hell out of the way when they needed to. Everyone was gone. Merchants had abandoned their wares, deciding it was not worth also abandoning their lives, probably permanently.

"What is the meaning of this cowardice, Edu?" Aon's voice was thin with pain and anger. While two arrows apparently wouldn't kill him, it was still an injury. The feeling as though she were standing near a raging fire came over her, and looking down, his clawed hand was consumed in black flame. She took a step back further away from him, afraid she might get burned.

Edu pointed at her. He wanted her dead. The message was clear.

"Lydia... run." Aon took a step toward Edu. "Turn and run and do not stop. Hide. Do you understand?" His voice was calm and even. "He will not pass me. But you will be in great danger here. Go to the church, if you can—you will be safe there. Lyon would see to that."

"No, just—let's get out of here together. You can teleport us away, can't you?"

"I am too injured to make it far. I would then be too weak to protect you. I will stop him from pursuing you. Find somewhere to hide, and I will come for you. Now, be a dear, and do not argue with me for once."

She took a step back, unsure.

"*Go!*" Aon snarled at her as Edu stepped toward the warlock, lifting his sword from the ground, ready to attack.

And so, she did.

She turned and ran through the empty marketplace and through the twisting stalls and winding corridors of colors and strange objects. The sound of mayhem was behind her. Cracks of lighting and the sound of objects being blown to pieces. She didn't dare look. If Edu were smart, he'd know he couldn't kill Aon, so Edu would be coming after her. Aon only had to stop him until she could hide. Until she could get away.

Her job was to get as far away as possible, as fast as possible. To wedge herself somewhere Edu wouldn't find her until Aon could rescue her.

Adrenaline pushed her forward. Still the sounds of a fight raged on. She reached the edge of the market and was now in the streets of the city itself. Tearing through the streets, she stopped at an intersection and looked around. The buildings were warped and strange like the streets of an ancient city. Buildings were too close together and had settled in and away from each other at strange and bizarre angles. The lanterns were filled with the same blinking fake bugs, casting the streets in a flickering, odd light.

Leaning against the wall, she tried to catch her breath, and vowed to take up cardio if she survived this. She tried to think. The sound of the fight was still raging, and it didn't sound like it was much farther away than when she had started.

That settled it. Edu was coming for her. Already injured, Aon was only managing to slow him down. Time to run again.

Several streets later, she came across a small city square. A giant statue of a monster was in the center. Wings were twisted like strange tendrils around its body, looking partly like a cloak, or like a thousand octopus tentacles had replaced its feathers.

Someone was standing at the base of the statue. He was a massive, hulking figure clothed in leather and animal pelts. A red mask, shaped like a skull, covered his face. A woman, dressed in floor-length crimson, stood beside him, hands folded neatly in front of her.

The man moved into the light, and she skidded to a halt.

Edu.

This wasn't possible. Edu was fighting Aon!

"H... How...?" she stammered.

"Kamira the shapeshifter," Ylena provided. "She may take the form of more than just beasts. She will be enough to keep Aon busy for a few more moments. We needed a distraction. We needed a means to remove you from his side."

She turned to run the other way and smacked into someone who had come up behind her. A man in bloody armor. "Hey, toots," the man said down at her, grief in his voice. Tim. "I'm really sorry about this, kid."

She tried to run around him, but he grabbed her and yanked her back. Screaming, she tried to kick at him, to bite or claw or punch or *anything*. Tim's fist impacted her head, and she crumpled to the ground.

Dazed, she put her hand to her head and let out a groan.

"Like I said... sorry."

A hand twisted in her shirt and pulled her back up to standing. She was being pushed forward. Shoving Tim off her, she tried to run, but it was too late.

A massive hand closed around her upper arm. She knew that terror. She'd felt it once before. Edu.

"No, please—please. I haven't done anything!"

"This is not your fault," Ylena said gently from where she stood. "Please know he takes no pleasure in what must be done. But you are a threat to this world."

"No, I'm not! I'm just a stupid—I don't even belong here!" Tears were rolling down her cheeks, unchecked. She didn't care. "Please, I don't... I don't want to die."

"He promises he will make it quick. He prays your soul will rejoin your people. That you may find peace." Ylena's attempts to sound comforting didn't do any good.

Edu's other hand settled over her heart.

There was no point in struggling, but she couldn't help but try. She couldn't help but yank against the hand that had hold of her.

"Please, I don't understand!"

He shifted, wrapping his arm around her to keep her still. If Aon was inescapable, this man was a vise. "Master Edu is sorry. He hopes your soul will forgive him. But he does this for Under and for the people he serves."

"Wait!"

Power crackled between his fingers like lightning, crimson and dangerous arcs of electricity. It ran into her, and she felt as though she had been plugged into a wall socket. Her words gagged off in pain. No, it was more than the word *pain* could do justice. It hurt badly enough that she couldn't even scream. She would have collapsed if Edu hadn't been holding her.

Tick.

When it ended, when the electricity finally stopped, something else went away with the pain. Something else was missing, now that the agony had ceased. There was a deafening silence in her ears. The great absence of something she had always heard, every day of her life. In the lack of it, there was a gaping, empty hole.

Tock.

Edu had stopped her heart. She had to look down to make sure he hadn't torn it out... but no. Just five burned fingerprints. A second ticked on like agony, as she felt a cold sweat form on her body.

Tick.

She looked up at Edu, wide-eyed and breathless, begging for him to make it stop.

Tock.

Oh God, this was too much. This was simply... *wrong.* It hurt, it burned, it ached and froze her all at once.

Tick.

She shivered, and everything felt cold. Cold was what won over her mind. And it was going to send everything else into the depths of the Arctic with it. She could no longer stand, and Edu knelt on the cobblestones and laid her down upon them.

Tock.

She could taste blood on her lips. She coughed, and she felt the ooze clog her throat. She rolled onto her side, and her body heaved, trying to clear her lungs of what had no business being there. Coppery, bitter, and thick.

Oh God, please, please make it stop...

Tick.

The shock was starting to take over. Her eyes rolled back into her head, as nothingness thankfully came forward to claim her. This wasn't merely the darkness that had come before in the lake of blood. This was the hand outstretched. The voice calling her away to safer shores. This was death that came for her.

Tock.

TWENTY

At first, he thought it must be another hallucination.

At first, he swore it must be his ever-failing mind.

To have it be anything else would spell wrack and ruin for this cursed world. For if it were true, what lay on the stones before him, he would burn this wretched kingdom to the ground.

As the moments dragged on, the corpse upon the cobblestone street still did not vanish into the echoes of his psyche. The uneven stones of the road were shining a wet crimson in the blood that pooled from her lips. Her eyes, once bright and flashing, were dull and lifeless. They stared unseeing at the empty abyss of the skies above her.

Aon dared not move. Dared not even breathe. For what ran through his mind could not allow for anything else.

Traitors. Mutineers.

She was harmless. She had no power. No secret lying within her.

No gifts were hers that were not those earned by her own soul.

The only reason to bring her demise would be to hurt him. An act of spite, nothing more!

How could they know? He had not even spoken the truth of it to himself in the privacy of his own mind.

Would you have come to feel the same?

There is more at work here.

Aon lifted his daggered prosthetic to his chest and pressed the sharp blades through the fabric and into flesh. He hissed in pain, though he welcomed it. He dug deeper, feeling the needle-sharp talons cleave through skin like butter. He could feel the blood dampen his shirt. It joined the stains left by the arrows from the fray. He cared not.

His attempt to use pain to banish the illusionary corpse did not work.

When he pulled his claws out of his chest, the wounds had already begun to heal. He had been standing here for quite some time—hours, perhaps—frozen in this moment of weakness.

His encroaching illness had been so quiet as of late. Little did the girl realize what benefit she brought him in such regard. It had been centuries since he had felt so lucid in his thoughts. Now, the shattered mirror of his soul was left to fracture and split apart once again.

If this was no ghastly vision before him, what was it? Was she genuinely dead, his little mortal creature, here on the ground before him? How could it be? He had forced Edu into retreat.

But that was a lie. A farce. Aon knew it as clear as day, the moment the fight began. The thing that stood against him was not Edu. A good enough imitation to fool anyone, perhaps. Anyone, except he who welcomed the second stolen into this world like family, as Aon once had to Edu.

He, who had spent over five thousand years hating the King of Flames. He, who had stood against him time and time again upon the battlefield. It was Aon, then, who would know the warrior for all he was.

Each of the outcomes had already spun themselves out in his mind, following the silk thread like so many of Vjo's webs. Aon knew already what had transpired.

Traitors. Mutineers.

Kamira. Only one shifter knew the Red King's mannerisms well enough to play such a frighteningly dangerous game against him. Only one woman would dare oppose Aon so. Only one woman had the skill to take that form.

It meant the Priest was complicit. Lyon, his oldest friend in this world. Or at least he had once been in days gone by. The High Priest who had cast away his lordship to wed the shifter could never bring himself to forgive Aon his great impositions on justice and dignity of the heart.

Even Lyon would not have taken such rash action without the support of others. It meant, therefore, they were *all* complicit in this act. With Lyon, the House of Blood was represented well enough. It followed naturally that Maverick and Ziza had a hand to play in this as well.

She was harmless... She had no power. No secret lying within her.

But the great question remained. Why? Why destroy the girl? Why, if not to cause Aon pain? Was this finally recompense for what Aon had done to Ziza that had shattered Edu's heart, so many years past?

Edu had gone to great lengths to kill Lydia out from under Aon's protection. Ambushing him, injuring him so he could not save her. Aon cursed himself for his weakness. He had become beguiled by the girl's exploration of his cursed world and had allowed his guard to drop.

The blood on his metal prosthetic was already becoming thick with time. A perverse gradient of his plasma ran in reverse order from fresh to coagulated. He had been standing here for quite some time, indeed. He could heal with abnormal speed, but that would not have any effect upon that which he had already spilled.

His was not the only blood left drying. The flecks upon Lydia's lips were already a dark tone, set upon flesh that had been such an alluring tint like roses, already beset by an unnatural and unwelcome blue cast.

No gifts were hers that were not those earned by her own soul.
Oh, Lydia...

He finally stepped toward the girl.

The heels of his wingtip shoes were the only sound in the city square as he walked toward where she lay, placed there by he who killed her. The wounds upon her chest were clear enough markings of who had done the deed. Five burn marks, like fingertips, charred into the fabric of her shirt.

Edu would have been the one to perform the act. The "noble king" would have seen it as his burden to murder the innocent girl. Streaks of dark eyeliner were the only proof that she had cried before she fell. The only evidence that she might have fought her attacker.

Lydia would have fought. Her only power was in her strength of will.

The young human who had been rejected by the Ancients. The only one to enter the pool and to return a mortal. The indomitable soul who had attempted, nay, successfully escaped from Edu. She had taken to uncertainty and hardship with a strength that would leave many of those lords and ladies of this realm of nightmares wanting and embarrassed.

The only reason to bring her demise would be to hurt him. This was an act of spite, nothing more!

It was about their hatred for him, Aon knew. That was the only possible answer as to why they had done it. Lydia was merely a casualty in their long-standing and traitorous grudge against him. Could they not see that Aon wished to save this world? That he desired to set right what he had done?

Something felt wrong to him still. Was this merely about paying him insult? Was it their anger that he might find solace in the company of another that had led them to this?

No. Aon dismissed the idea that they might have taken her life because he had chosen to have Lydia for his own. That was far too petty and childish, even for a puerile simpleton like Edu.

Not unless Lydia's value to Aon was far more than that of a mere consort.

How could they know? He had not even spoken the truth of it to himself in the privacy of his own mind.

A deep sense of horror pooled in him. That moment of adrenaline of being caught in a lie. How could it be? No. No one in this world knew of what he felt for Lydia or of what she truly meant to him. He had not even entertained the idea in his own mind, let alone out loud. Lydia herself remained ignorant, let alone Edu.

Aon knelt beside her, dropping to one knee, and reached his gloved hand down to gently shut her unseeing eyes. He ran the pad of his thumb carefully across her lips, wiping from them the remains of dried blood.

He reached around her neck and carefully pulled from her the glass chrysalis she had been gifted by the idiot merchant in the market. The little false firefly inside blissfully blinked away, content and oblivious in its mindless existence to the tragedy to which it stood witness.

Aon slipped the chain around his own neck and took a moment to examine the tiny, runtish orb of magic. The merchant who made it insisted they had moods. Personalities. It was only content when it was alone, the merchant had claimed. Happy only when it was secluded and away from the others.

How lovely it would be to pretend the little ball of magic in the case had a soul or a mind. Even enough to pretend it was an insect. Aon knew better. He knew quite well the futility of such a belief. Even if he, too, wished nothing more than to pretend.

The false insect would be a fitting reminder of her death. A reminder of the futility of hope and that he would always be alone. He tucked the pendant beneath his shirt.

Reaching down his clawed gauntlet, he stroked the girl's hair away from her face gently. Lydia had been, and died as such, the only soul in this world who had not been a hapless toy of the Ancients.

Even Aon himself, in his hatred for them, served them. Knew their superiority without question and wielded their power as his own. The dreams of the burning and blistering sun haunted him. The feeling of sand stinging and biting into the fresh wounds upon his back still woke him from his dreams. With all of what they had brought him, the pain and suffering of what may have become tens of thousands of years as their so-called favorite son, he would always be theirs.

Lydia had not.

She had belonged to no one but herself.

Free of the confluence that swirled unseen within this dying world, she had seen and judged all as she would choose. She did not kneel before Aon as king because he was declared so. She did not bow to Edu's judgment of execution because the Ancients deemed him righteous.

Lydia lived and died her own. It was that clarity of vision that Aon had cherished so keenly. It was for that reason he found her like a lake of calm water in the raging inferno of his mind. For with her, no influence could be wrought. No strings of fate or silent compulsion led her along.

May the Ancients lay damned in their prison until this world ceased to be.

For Aon had loved her.

Love.

The unthinkable. The impossible.

Yet... so she had been.

When she stood from the ground after being tossed from

that horse in the woods, when she stood against all that had been levied upon her, he wanted her. When she offered him nothing but contempt, he adored her. When she feared him and desired him all the same, he hungered for her. When she held such compassion for him, he was transfixed.

But when he had first laid eyes upon her, in his dreams as she reached to touch his mask as he lay in his crypt, his heart had already been hers.

He had loved her then. And he knew he would love her until the world was swallowed whole.

Would you have come to feel the same?

Aon would never know. For now, she lay dead.

Such a waste. Such a shame that he would destroy every last one of those traitors for this meretricious act of barbarism.

He had loved Lydia. He was not the heartless, soulless monster that many believed. It was easier to think such things, and often he found shelter in their condemnations. Yes, he was a beast. He was a cretin, a gargoyle, a fiend. A worthless tyrant whose sins had damned this universe to a fate worse than death.

Was that why Edu had killed her? To take from him what Aon had stolen from the warrior so many years ago? How could Edu have known words he had not spoken to himself until this very moment? How could he have divined the truth that now twisted like a dagger inside his stomach?

There is more at work here.

Aon lifted the young girl into his arms. Lifeless and limp, she was nothing more than flesh and bone. He would take her back to the Ancients. For they saw fit to set her down this path, he would ensure they kept the proof of their work.

The secret to Edu's motives revolved around Lyon. Not perhaps for his involvement in engineering the scheme, but for his consent. If the bleeding-hearted Priest were to condemn this poor thing to death, it meant he felt it was for some great cause. Or at least the perception of one.

Was Edu truly so foolish as to think the girl had beating within her heart some great mystery that might unhinge this world? Could he not see her for what she was?

She had been harmless.

So *why?*

* * *

Lyon sensed the dark presence the moment before it arrived. He knew the great King of Shadows was now within the cathedral. He bowed his head in prayer where he knelt at the edge of the Pool of the Ancients, the great and glowing lake of blood that was their source of power and life. Lyon did not pray to their altar tonight. He wished to hope the Ancients would hear his prayers far louder, and joined them at their prison.

If Aon had come here, it meant the deed was done.

Forgive us, Lydia. My friend. He begged her soul, wherever it may be, for forgiveness. He hoped she had crossed the barrier to her own manner of an afterlife.

Footsteps behind him sent him up from his knees. As he turned, he froze. There stood Aon at the top of the landing to the platform. He was not alone. He carried in his arms the limp form of the young girl.

Hours had passed since Edu had gone to finish that which he had been set upon since Lydia had been rejected by the Ancients themselves. Now, Aon brought her here to bury her as though she were one of them.

"Leave us." Aon's voice was unreadable.

"My king..." Lyon bowed his head.

"Go and be with your wife. For come the morrow, this world will end."

Lyon looked up, eyes wide. "You cannot be serious, my lord."

Aon laughed cruelly and laid the young woman down on

the altar in the center of the platform. "Tell me, my *old friend,* chosen High Priest of the Ancients, what spurious vision did the Oracle have that sent you all upon this path to self-destruction?"

Lyon gritted his teeth. Of course, the warlock would come to such a correct conclusion. Aon's mind, while broken, was still faster and far more intelligent than any other he had ever known.

"What did Ziza tell you?" Aon repeated, stepping around the dais to face down the Priest. "Did she tell you I was bent on destroying this world?" His temper snapped. "Our world is already dying, you fool! I was merely seeking to save it!"

"Save it how, Master Aon? By rebuilding it in your image?"

Aon roared in rage, and Lyon found himself upon the ground. A metal fist had struck him there. His face bloomed in pain, but he ignored it.

"How *dare* you! At least I do not stand idle or sleep in my crypt until the end of days like the others. But that was not what I asked you." Aon pointed a claw at the body. "There upon that dais lies a soul whose heart did not deserve to be set ablaze in her chest. Lydia is dead. I demand you tell me *why!*"

"In a vision, Ziza saw her death. She said to save this world, her life must end."

"You killed her for you feared what secret she might hold? Lydia had no power! No gifts! Do you not think I would not have discovered them already?"

"We feared you had."

"Feared! You had no proof. Is this a human inquisition now? Looking for enemies where they do not exist. Not once did you idiots come to ask me!"

"If you had found in her some secret, you would have lied." Lyon pushed himself back to his feet.

"Is that what you think? When was the last time you have simply asked me a question, *Priest?* Do you know why I never told anyone the nature of my research? Not a single one of you inquired over it. All of you wish so desperately for me to play the villain. So be it. All of you stand idly by, waiting for death like bloated, empty corpses. I seek to save us, and you kill her out of *spite for me!*" Aon punched his fist into the altar, and Lyon heard the stone crack underneath his fist.

"Her death troubles you deeply. You come to bury her personally. Why? What has she become to you?"

Aon hung his head, his shoulders tense. Hands gripped the edge of the dais and clenched hard enough he heard the leather of his glove creak. "Begone."

"My lord, if we are all to be condemned to die for this act, I, too, would like to know why."

A hand twisting in his collar dragged him down to his knees. Lyon grunted in pain as the warlock had moved faster than even Lyon could perceive. His metal claw had gripped his shirt and held him there.

"It is in memory of the friendship we once shared that I will answer you thusly. I have decided after long efforts... this world is no longer worth saving. And if it is to be destroyed, then I shall not see it wither into indignancy. I shall see it burn."

Lyon was hurled to the ground once more, and he quickly stood back up. Fear pulled at him, for he knew the dread king meant every word.

Aon stalked toward him slowly, forcing Lyon to retreat. "For millennia I have had to listen to you all whimper and whine like simpering children over how I seek to destroy this world. Heed me now, Priest, and know that *you have not once seen me try.*"

Lyon disappeared into an explosion of white bats. He would no longer seek to temper the man in his rage, for it was a hopeless endeavor.

Aon was grieving deeply, such as Lyon had never seen, and it could only mean one thing. It was then that he knew whose sorrow Ziza had seen in her vision of Lydia, dead upon the stones. The agony had belonged to the warlock.

Aon had loved Lydia.

What have we done?

* * *

Once that insufferable man was gone, Aon let out a wavering breath. Off the vampire would scamper like a white rat to his allies and tell them of what he intended. It did not matter. They could not stop him from razing what was left of Under back to the dust and sand from which it came.

He returned to the dais and looked down at what remained of Lydia. In death, all were taken back to the Pool of the Ancients from which they were reborn. She was not of their kind, yet the Ancients were to blame for her all the same.

It seemed only right.

Reaching up, he grasped his metal mask with his hand and pulled it from his face. It felt more foreign without it than with. The slab of metal was his face now. He recognized it better than his own flesh and blood in the mirror.

He held it before him and contemplated it for the first time in centuries. To be so shrouded was a benefit. None could read his features for clues as to what might lurk inside his mind. Its design was his own creation. Aon had sculpted it himself to create a blank and empty visage for none to penetrate.

Kiss me once, and I will.

That had been Lydia's game for him, the wager to finally win her. Of course, his love would not be seduced by typical means. Of course, she would not give in to her desires without some tremendous and insurmountable circumstance.

Somewhere in his gaping hole of a heart, he wondered if Lydia had also merely wished to kiss him.

Fool, he chided himself. *Such sentiment is wasted now.*

Setting his metal mask down upon the altar, Aon heard it clink against the stone. He would answer her dare one last time. Her lips were cold, not warm and soft as he would choose to remember them.

When he retreated, there was dampness on her cheek. It took him a long moment to realize they were his own tears. Since when had he been crying? Since when had he been once more capable of such things?

One last time, he would go before the Ancients. He lifted her body into his arms and walked to the edge of the pool. The stairs that descended into the pit went down beneath the liquid into the chasm filled with blood. The stairs that he had carved with his own hands, so many thousands of years ago.

He could not remember much of his days as their mindless slave. Only the biting pain, the burning and blistering sun that sank beneath the horizon as they sank beneath the waves, both never to rise again. He could remember the cruelty that made his own pale in comparison. How the Ancients had delighted in his suffering. They would pay him kindness only to magnify his fall back into misery when it was taken away.

It seemed nothing had changed.

"Is that why you gave Lydia to me?" He glared up at the carved visages where they poured the red and glowing liquid into the lake. "One last time before this world ended, you wished for me to suffer? Very well. You shall have it."

He took a breath and realized he was still crying. It did not matter. The Ancients had seen him weep before. He was a child to them, after all. He took a step into the blood, not caring for his shoes or his clothing. Down and up to his thighs, he descended the stairs. "You took her from Earth for that reason alone, didn't you? Etching that mark upon her arm, you had her fetched here, knowing all this would occur. Your capacity for callousness is astonishing to me, even now. Even on the verge of the death of this world, you find time to have your revenge."

That was why they had given Ziza such a false vision that Lydia must die to save the world. It was a lie, nothing more. For the images of the future, of Fate, came from the Ancients themselves. She did not see anything they did not wish her to know. And they had demanded Lydia's life for one simple reason. To hurt him. They had known he would love her.

They would not allow him to have the one thing he had always desired.

For that day so long ago when he had taken Qta's life, he had demanded Qta make for him a bride. He had demanded the King of Dreams create someone who could love him.

Qta refused, and Aon murdered him in his rage.

In the desire to love, and more importantly, to *be* loved, he had destroyed the world.

He remembered Lydia's speech to him in the museum, claiming she did not believe his words about why he began the Great War. She was right. And that deep and horrible truth was what he did not dare speak to her. How could he confess such a deep and empty need to the woman who had unwittingly answered his hollow prayers?

Now, on the eve of their destruction, they taunted him with hope, only to dash it away upon the cobblestones. They chose to mock him with that he could never have.

Touché, he supposed.

"Take her now, for you would not have her then." He took a step deeper into the water, sank now up to his waist, and lowered Lydia into the pool. Her body was pulled from his grasp by unseen hands, their power dragging her down into the chasm.

Climbing from the liquid, he returned to the altar, putting the metal mask back on his face. There was comfort in it. He could bury his sorrow there. He could hide it all. He turned to look back at the pool for one last time.

"Know that I will be the death that will rain down upon all you have made."

* * *

"Will you live, or die?
For what will you wish?
You have suffered, Our Child. You have done well.
For that reason, your path will be your own.
We will always let you choose.
That is Our promise to you.
That is Our vow."

A LETTER FROM KATHRYN

Dear reader,

I want to say a huge thank you for choosing to read *King of Shadows* If you did enjoy it, and want to keep up to date with all my latest releases, just sign up at the following link. Your email address will never be shared and you can unsubscribe at any time.

www.secondskybooks.com/kathryn-ann-kingsley

I hope you loved *King of Shadows* and if you did I would be very grateful if you could write a review. I'd love to hear what you think, and it makes such a difference helping new readers to discover one of my books for the first time.

I love hearing from my readers – you can get in touch through social media or my website.

Thanks,

Kathryn Ann Kingsley

www.kathrynkingsley.com

 x.com/vodriel
 instagram.com/kathrynannkingsley

PUBLISHING TEAM

Turning a manuscript into a book requires the efforts of many people. The publishing team at Bookouture would like to acknowledge everyone who contributed to this publication.

Commercial
Lauren Morrissette
Hannah Richmond
Imogen Allport

Cover design
BRoseDesignz

Data and analysis
Mark Alder
Mohamed Bussuri

Editorial
Jack Renninson
Melissa Tran

Proofreader
Catherine Lenderi

Marketing
Alex Crow

Melanie Price
Occy Carr
Cíara Rosney
Martyna Młynarska

Operations and distribution
Marina Valles
Stephanie Straub

Production
Hannah Snetsinger
Mandy Kullar
Jen Shannon
Ria Clare

Publicity
Kim Nash
Noelle Holten
Jess Readett
Sarah Hardy

Rights and contracts
Peta Nightingale
Richard King
Saidah Graham

Printed in Great Britain
by Amazon